Wild Lords and Innocent Ladies

Lord Hunter, Lord Stanton and Lord Ravenscar

Three wild rakes whose seductive charms and aristocratic titles have the ladies of the *ton* swooning behind their fans. United by their charitable foundation to help those scarred by war, these lords are the firmest of friends.

But they guard their hardened hearts almost as closely as they do their riches...that is, until they encounter three very special women.

Could these innocent ladies be the ones to tame these wild lords once and for all?

Read Lord Hunter and Nell's story in

Lord Hunter's Cinderella Heiress

And look out for linked stories about Lord Stanton and Lord Ravenscar—coming soon!

Author Note

Lord Hunter's Cinderella Heiress is the first book in my Wild Lords and Innocent Ladies series about three friends who are infamous for their rakish past and supreme skill with horses. But though this is a romance, it touches on some serious and timeless topics—among them the impact of suicide on those left behind. The three friends are a product of their time in history, a generation shaped by a costly war and just as costly an aftermath. Many veterans of the Napoleonic wars returned to England wounded in body and mind, without an income or the ability to find employment. There were several hospitals dedicated to caring for soldiers "broken by age or war" (the most famous was the Royal Hospital Chelsea established by King Charles II in 1681), but they were a drop in the ocean after such prolonged, bloody and devastating wars that affected not just veterans but their families and led to many unreported cases of suicide (still a serious problem in most active armies today). My three wild lords share tragedies revolving around the wars and together they establish an institution, Hope House, to help veterans and their families rebuild their lives. In this first book my hero, Lord Hunter, is emotionally scarred by his brother's suicide after being captured and tortured in France, and his guilt at failing to protect his adored younger brother becomes a driving force in his life and very nearly prevents him from opening himself to the healing power of love. Luckily Nell, my horse-loving heroine (who has a few scars of her own), is not easily dissuaded...

LARA TEMPLE

—

Lord Hunter's Cinderella Heiress

ISBN-13: 978-0-373-29954-6

Lord Hunter's Cinderella Heiress

Copyright © 2017 by Ilana Treston

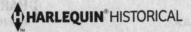

HARLEQUIN®HISTORICAL

Recycling programs
for this product may
not exist in your area.

ISBN-13: 978-0-373-29954-6

Lord Hunter's Cinderella Heiress

Copyright © 2017 by Ilana Treston

Printed in U.S.A.

www.Harlequin.com

Lara Temple was three years old when she begged her mother to take dictation of her first adventure story. Since then she has led a double life—by day an investment and high-tech professional who has lived and worked on three continents, but when darkness falls she loses herself in history and romance (at least on the page). Luckily her husband and two beautiful and very energetic children help weave it all together.

Books by Lara Temple

Harlequin Historical

Lord Crayle's Secret World
The Reluctant Viscount
The Duke's Unexpected Bride

Wild Lords and Innocent Ladies

Lord Hunter's Cinderella Heiress

Visit the Author Profile page at Harlequin.com.

To Myrna, Mark and Arik,
who miss David as much as I do.
He couldn't hold on but gave so much love
while he did.

Prologue

Leicestershire—1816

'**Y**ou're wanted, Miss Nell. The master has some viscount or other wanting to take Petra through her paces. Lord Hunter, I think his name was. Knowing fellow.'

'Another one? I hope she takes him head first through a hedge, Elkins,' Nell replied, her voice muffled as she bent to examine Pluck's fetlock.

'She'll have to go to someone and he seems a fair choice—no bluster about him.' The elderly groom smiled.

'I don't know why Father insists I escort his guests anyway. As head groom you are far more qualified than I.'

'It's simple, miss. You've got the best seat in the county and that gives them fellows the idea their wives or daughters might look the same if they took home one of these prime bits of blood. They won't, no how, but there's no harm in it. Your father's a hard man, I know, but he's right proud of the way you are with horses. You're like him there, see you.'

Nell wrinkled her nose—she didn't want to be like

the brutish sot in any way whatsoever. She secured the stall door, but Pluck shoved her arched neck over the side and shook her mane. Nell relented and came back for one more stroke.

'No, you can't go to your mama yet. And, yes, I will go and see if he is worthy of her and if he isn't I'll have her toss him into a pond. You like that idea, don't you, you little rogue? Father and Aunt Hester will skin me, but for Petra I just might find the nerve. Now I *must* go or I will be late and Father will be furious and then Aunt Hester will be furious, too.'

There was no way the filly could understand how serious that was, but Pluck's head ducked back into the stall.

Her father was already in the stable yard. He was hard to miss—even braced on his cane and his face lined with pain and puffy from years of hard drinking, his height and booming voice intimidated everyone around him. However, this time he was diminished by the man who stood by his side. Not in inches—they were probably of a height and the stranger certainly hadn't her father's massive and blustering look. In fact, the first thing that struck her was that he was very quiet.

They hadn't seen her yet and she watched as the stranger approached Petra. His movements were economical and smooth, and his hands, though they looked large and strong, were calm and travelled slowly over the mare as he examined her. It was just the right way to approach a high-spirited horse.

It was only when her father called her over that she looked at the man's face. He was probably close in age to Charles Welbeck, who had just turned twenty-five the week before she and her father had gone to Wilton, but he *seemed* older. There were creases of weariness about his eyes and a bruised look beneath them as if he had not slept well for a long time.

She couldn't imagine such an expression in Charles's cheerful blue eyes. But other than that she had to admit he was almost as handsome as Charles, though in a completely different manner. She wondered if he was perhaps part-foreigner and that might account for the dark chestnut hair and the warm earth tones of his skin and the sunken golden brown of his eyes. It wasn't a comforting face—its sharp sculpted lines didn't make her think of princes and dancing through the night at the village fête in Wilton; it was an arrogant face more suited to the weighty matters of a beleaguered king and she doubted a glance from his tired eyes would make her think of dancing.

Not that Charles had ever asked her to dance. He hardly even looked at her for more than a kind greeting. Except for just once, when she had been fourteen. Her father had been furious at her for cramming one of his horses at the Welbeck jumping course and she had stood, humiliated and wilting under his wrath until Charles put his arm around her and said something which made the men around them laugh, but the smile in his eyes as he glanced down at her told her it wasn't unkind. It had calmed her father and filled her with a peaceful warmth she had begun to forget existed. At that moment she had known there would never be anyone else for her but Charles.

She had no illusions her love would ever be reciprocated. Charles was perfect and she…she was a beanpole, almost as tall as he but painfully scrawny. The village boys would snigger and call her Master Neil behind her back and she was accustomed to the dismay in young men's eyes when she was partnered with them at the informal dances held at her best friend Anna's home in Keswick. It was only when she was on a horse that her height didn't bother her. In fact, very little bothered her when she was on a horse.

So as she watched Lord Hunter mount Petra she hadn't in the least thought about him as a man, or herself as an unattractive and overly tall seventeen-year-old. She was Miss Nell and she could ride a horse better than anyone—man, woman, boy or girl—in the county.

She tensed as Petra sidled at the man's unfamiliar hand and weight and was immediately checked, but so gently that the motion was almost invisible. She couldn't decide if his calm was innate or assumed, but she met Elkins's gaze and shrugged. He would do.

'Fells Pasture or Bridely field, then, Miss Nell?' Elkins asked.

'Fell's Pasture, I think,' she replied and turned to the man. He was watching them with a slight smile, clearly aware he was being weighed and judged. His eyes gleamed gold at the centre, or perhaps that was a trick of the sun, which was just catching at the edges of the trees behind her. She herself preferred light-haired men, like Charles, but Anna would probably think him very handsome.

'Is that good or bad?' he asked.

'It means we presume you can stop Petra from throwing you, Lord Hunter,' she replied, surprising herself. She was not usually so direct. 'But if you aren't comfortable with her yet, we can start with some easy riding. It's just that Fell's Pasture has a few miles of open runs and safe jumps. Alternately once you ride her I can show you her paces myself. She is probably our fastest mare and it would be a pity if you didn't see just how beautifully she gallops.'

He cocked his head to one side with a glimmering smile that turned the lines of tension she had noticed into laugh lines. She had probably been wrong about the signs of strain; his smile didn't allow for the presence of the darkness she had sensed.

'I don't think you meant any of that as an insult, did you?'

Nell stared at him, running through her words in her mind.

'Not at all, my lord. You appear to handle her well enough, but I just want to do justice to Petra. Father must have told you she can be a little resistant at first, but she knows me and will open up more easily with me in the saddle. I merely thought you would want to see her at her best.'

'We won't have time to switch to side saddle anyway, so let's just see how I manage, shall we?'

She shrugged and turned to Hilda, her mare, allowing Elkins to help her mount.

'We don't put a side saddle on Petra; she's trained for a man's saddle and weight. But as you said, we'll see how you do.'

This time she heard the condescension in her voice and almost smiled at it.

'I'm almost tempted to do an abysmal job of it just to see what you mean, Miss Tilney.'

He didn't, of course, and as she watched him gallop across the field she didn't know whether to be relieved that Petra was being delivered into the capable hands of a man who would treat her right, or disappointed that she hadn't been given the opportunity to show him her mettle. In this one corner of the universe where she was completely capable, she rarely wished to show off, but today she felt that urge. She watched as the man stopped just short of where she and Elkins waited. There *was* gold in his eyes, she realised, and the colour was heightened by the clear enjoyment on his face, making him look younger.

'Can you match that?' he demanded, bending forward to stroke Petra's damp neck.

Elkins chuckled and Nell didn't need further prodding. She tossed her reins to Elkins and slipped off Hilda.

Clearly Lord Hunter hadn't expected her to actually accept his dare because he looked disconcerted, but she just laid her hand on Petra's muzzle and raised her brows, waiting.

'Are you serious?' he asked. 'Now? But she's probably winded and you can't ride her in skirts...'

Nell unhooked the fastening that held the wide train of her skirt and hooked it over her arm.

'These skirts work as well on a regular saddle. I made them myself. And far from being winded, Petra is just warming up, so instead of sitting there while she cools down, you can dismount and I'll show you what she can do and then you will probably ask Father to buy Pluck, her filly, as well. Now, down you go.'

He dismounted meekly, still watching her with curious fascination as she placed her leg in the stirrup, swinging her other leg over, and with a practised flick cast her skirts over as well, the long folds of fabric covering her legs to her boots and obscuring the riding breeches she wore underneath. She plucked out the pin which held her riding hat and handed them to Elkins, and then she was off.

Petra didn't disappoint her. If ever a mare flew, the grey blood mare rose off the ground, as smooth and slick as water, her small head down and extended like an arrow. Nell didn't bother with proper lady's riding posture, but leaned low into the shape of the horse, laughing as Petra's mane stung at her face like a brace of tiny whips. Nell wanted that man to appreciate what he was getting, and if she managed to convince him to buy Pluck as well, it would be worth it. She hated when mare and filly or foal were separated too young.

She took Petra over the hedge at the far end of the pasture as if it wasn't even in the way and then led her back for the long jump over the stream. When she drew up she was bursting with the excitement of the run. She could even cope with the knowledge that she probably looked a fright. Her hair was too straight to stay confined by pins and she could feel it hanging down about her face.

'Well? Isn't she amazing?'

He took the reins she held out to him as she swung out of the saddle and she realised he really was very tall because she actually had to look up, an unusual feeling and one she didn't quite like since it reminded her too much of Father stalking at her. She hurried to mount Hilda, her exhilaration fading.

'Indeed she is,' Lord Hunter said as he stroked Petra's sweating neck. It was easier now that she was mounted and he had to look up at her. 'What is the name of her filly?'

'Pluck. Well, that's just my name for her, though Father prefers to call fillies and foals after their sires, so she's known as Argonaut's Filly, but that's a mouthful, so I just call her Pluck, because she is. Plucky, that is.'

'Like you.'

Her eyes widened.

'Hardly. I'm the least plucky thing that ever was.'

'Now that's not quite fair, Miss Nell,' Elkins interjected as they turned back towards Tilney Hall. 'There's none like you for throwing your heart over a fence.'

She shrugged, annoyed at herself and at them, though she didn't know why.

'That's different. I know what I'm doing when I'm on a horse. You can see Lord Hunter to the house, Elkins. Goodbye, Lord Hunter.' She rode off, feeling very young and foolish she had succumbed to showing off. He had been kind about it, but she still felt ridiculous.

She hoped her aunt didn't have one of her whims and insist she dine downstairs because then he would see how wrong he was about her pluck. She wasn't yet formally 'out' in society and she rarely dined with guests, which suited her just fine because those occasions when her aunt did demand her presence were sheer purgatory. Her father's temper was nothing next to Hester's vindictiveness.

Just when Nell thought the hour of danger had passed, Sue, the chambermaid, rushed into her room.

'Her majesty says you're to join the guests for supper, Miss Nell.'

Nell shook her head, desperately trying to think of some way to avoid this disaster, and Sue clucked her tongue.

'There ain't nothing for it but to go forward, chick. Hurry, now. Luckily I added a flounce to your sprigged muslin and it isn't quite so short now, but you'll have to keep the shawl over your shoulders because there's nothing we can do now about the fact it won't close right.'

'I can't… I won't!'

'You can and will. There isn't aught else to wear, chick. Really, your father should know better but men are fools. That's right—best heed me. Men are fools and you're better a mile away in any direction!'

Nell stood like a seamstress's dummy, rigid and useless as Sue busied about dressing her in her one decent muslin dress with its childish bodice and equally childish length. Though Mrs Barnes was an excellent cook, neither she nor Sue were capable seamstresses and the new flounce was clearly crooked and this would surely be the night the straining fabric would finally give way to her late-budding bustline. She would sit down and there would be a horrible rending sound and everyone would look at her and her aunt would sneer and oh so kindly suggest Nell go change and perhaps ask her why she had insisted on wearing that dreadful old dress and really she despaired of the girl because no matter how hard she tried to make her presentable there was only so much one could do with such a hopeless long meg… Nell would leave the room and of course not return because she had no other dress that was suitable for evening wear and because she couldn't face their contemptuous and condescending stares and sniggers, and tomorrow her father would rant at her for having humiliated him in front of his guests and for being as dull as dishwater and less useful.

'I can't do it. I can't. She is just doing it so she can make a fool of me again. I won't.'

Sue squeezed Nell's hand.

'I wouldn't put it past her but it will be worse if you don't go. Here, don't cry now, chick. Think—in two days you'll be on your way back to school.'

Nell pressed the heels of her hands to her eyes.

'I wish I could go tonight. I hate coming here. I wish I could stay with Mrs Petheridge always.'

'Well, Ma and I are glad you are here summers at least.'

Nell scrubbed her eyes and blew her nose.

'Oh, Sue, I didn't mean I don't love you and Mrs Barnes. You know I do.'

'Aye, you don't have to say a thing, chick—we know. I wish for you that you *could* stay there year-round. Lucky your aunt doesn't know how much you like that school or she'd have you out of there in a flash. Proper poison, she is, and no mistake. Now go stare down at your nose at the lot of them. Lord knows you're tall enough to do just that. Bend your knees so I can get this over your head, now. Goodness, what do they give you to eat in them Lakes? I swear you've grown a size since you had to wear this just a month back.'

Nell chuckled and slipped her arms into the sleeves, struggling against the constricting fabric. Thank goodness for Sue. She was right—Nell could survive two more days.

This optimistic conviction faded with each downward step on the stairs. Her aunt was already in the drawing room and the familiar cold scrape of nerves skittered under Nell's skin, almost painful in her palms and up her fingers, like sand being shoved into a glove. She kept her eyes on her pale slippers peeping out and hiding back under her flounce as she made her way to the sofa where she sat as meek and as stupid as a hen, praying that was the worst people thought of her.

The door opened again and out of the corner of her eye Nell saw two pink confections enter the room, followed by an older couple. She had learned to look without looking and she inspected the two pretty, giggling girls and their mother, who wore a purple turban so magnificently beaded with sparkling stones Nell couldn't help staring.

'Stop gawping, girl!' a voice hissed behind her. 'Keep your eyes down and your mouth shut or I'll send that slut of a maid of yours packing, cook's daughter or not! And pull that shawl closed. You look like the village tart with your bosom spilling out like that. Ah, Mr Poundridge, and Mrs Poundridge! So wonderful you could come for supper. So these are your lovely daughters! Do come and meet Sir Henry's daughter, Miss Helen. She is not yet out, but in such informal occasions she joins us downstairs so she can acquire a little town bronze. Sometimes I wonder what we pay such an exorbitant amount to that school for, but what can one do but keep trying? Perhaps your daughters could give her some hints on the correct mode of behaviour in company. Oh, what lovely dresses! Do come and meet our other guest tonight, Viscount Hunter...'

Nell kept her eyes on her clasped hands as her aunt sailed off, dragging the Poundridges in her wake, only daring to raise her head when she heard her aunt's voice mix with her father's. None of them was looking at her except Lord Hunter. He stood by her father, flanked by the old suits of armour Aunt Hester had salvaged from the cellars, and together they looked like Viking and Celtic warlords under armed escort. She hadn't seen him when she entered because she hadn't looked and her mortification deepened as she realised he must have seen everything.

Nell's eyes sank back to her hands. The gritty, tingling pain and the clammy feeling was still climbing, and though it hadn't happened quite so badly for a while, she knew there was nothing to be done but wait it out. If she was lucky it would peak before her legs began to shake. She tried to think of Mrs Petheridge and her friends at school, but it was hard. Her left leg was already quivering. She wanted to cry at how pathetic she was to let this woman win each time, but self-contempt didn't stop her right leg from beginning to quiver as well. Think of brushing down Petra. No, Father was there, glaring. Think of Mrs Barnes and her cinnamon bread... No, her mother had died with an uneaten loaf by her bed, so she could smell it. Of Charles's sweet smile as he helped her mount the first time they had come to the Wilton breeders' fair; of how he had put his arm around her when Father had raged. If he were here, she might be able to bear this...

Two days. Just today and tomorrow. Her right leg calmed and she pressed her palm to her still-shaking left leg. In two days she would see Anna and sit in Mrs Petheridge's cosy study with the chipped tea set and ginger biscuits, helping the girls who cried for home or who threw things, because she was good with them. She breathed in, her lungs finally big enough to let the air in, and the clamminess was only down her spine now and between her breasts under the scratchy shawl.

'Your father has agreed to sell me Pluck as well. Will you miss her?'

The sofa shifted and creaked as Lord Hunter sat and she looked at him in shock.

'What?' Her voice was gritty and cramped and his golden-brown eyes narrowed, but he just crossed his arms and leaned back comfortably.

'I went to look at her as you suggested and I have to admit she is a beauty. By the length of those legs she might even turn out to be half a hand taller than her mother, but time will tell. I'm hoping she will win me points with Petra. What do you think?'

Think. What did she think? That any minute now her aunt would come and sink her fangs into her for daring to talk with someone. What was he talking about? Petra and Pluck. He was taking Pluck, too. It had been her idea. Yes, yes, she would miss her, but she would be gone by then, just two days. Oh, thank goodness, just two days. Just two. Say something…

'I think…' Nothing came and her legs were starting to shake again.

'Do you know I live right next to Bascombe Hall? Were you ever there?'

Why was he insisting? She wished he would go away! Bascombe Hall…

'No. Mama and Grandmama didn't get along.' There, a whole sentence.

'No one got along with your grandmama. She was an ill-tempered shrew.'

She stared in surprise. How did he dare be so irreverent? If she had said something like that…

'That's better,' he said with approval, surprising her further. 'I understand you inherited the property from your grandfather, but that your father is trustee until you come of age. Since she never made any bones about telling everyone she had disapproved of her daughter's marriage to Sir Henry, I'm surprised she didn't find a way to keep you from inheriting.'

'She did try, but the best she could do was enter a stipulation that if I died before my majority at twenty-one, my cousin inherits. Once I'm twenty-one there is nothing she can do.'

'Well, with any luck she'll kick the bucket before that and save you the trouble of booting her out of the Hall.'

She pressed her hand to her mouth, choking back a laugh. Surely he hadn't said that! And she hadn't laughed... She rubbed her palms together as the tingling turned ticklish. That was a good sign; it was going away. Had he done that on purpose? He couldn't have known.

'I keep hoping she might actually want to meet me. Is she really so bad?'

His mouth quirked on one side.

'Worse. I know the term curmudgeon is most commonly applied to men, but your grandmama is just that. You're better off being ignored.'

Oh, she knew that.

'Had you ever met my grandfather?'

He nodded.

'He was a good man, very proper, but he was the second son and he only inherited it when your great-uncle died childless. Those were good years for us.'

'Why?' she asked, curious at this glimpse of the relations she had never met.

'Well, the Bascombes control the water rights in our area, which means all our crops are dependent on them for irrigation and canal transport, and for those few blissful years we had a very reasonable agreement. When he died your grandmother made everyone in the area suffer again. Thankfully your father is trustee now, which means he has the final say in any agreement.'

'But if I'm the heir, I can decide now, can't I?'

'Not until you're twenty-one and by then you will probably be married, so do try to choose someone reasonable, will you?'

A flush rose over her face and she clasped her hands again. Charles's smile shimmered in front of her, warm and teasing.

'I don't think I shall be married.'

'Well, you're still young, but eventually—'

'No,' she interrupted and he remained silent for a moment. He shifted as if about to speak, but she made the mistake of looking up and met her aunt's gaze. Pure poison, Sue had said. She pressed back against the sofa and drank in some air. The man next to her shifted again, half-rising, but then the door opened and the butler announced supper.

Hunter smiled at the pretty little brunette who was chirping something at him. She didn't require any real answers and he could cope with her flirtatious nonsense to her utter satisfaction with less than a tenth of his attention.

Tomorrow he would have to return to Hunter Hall. It had been cowardly to escape the day after Tim's funeral, but as he had watched his brother's grave being filled with earth, the thought that it was over, all of it, pain and love, hopelessness and hope, had choked him as surely as if it was he being smothered under the fertile soil. He had needed some distance and the negotiations with Sir Henry over the fees for access to the waterways controlled by the Bascombe estate had provided an excuse to disappear. At least in this Sir Henry appeared to be reasonable, unlike his dealings with his daughter, and it appeared they would not be required to pay exorbitant waterway fees to the Bascombe estate, at least until the girl inherited.

No wonder Sir Henry had let drop that he was concerned his daughter, who would come into the immense Bascombe estate in four years, would be easy prey for fortune hunters. After her performance that afternoon Hunter had assumed that was because Sir Henry wasn't confident he could keep such a mature little firebrand under control. But it was clear this girl would probably throw herself into the arms of the first plausible fortune-hunting scoundrel simply to escape this poisonous household.

He glanced down the table to Sir Henry's daughter. She was barely eating, which was a pity because she was as thin as a sapling. She definitely didn't look strong enough to have ridden Petra so magnificently that afternoon. In fact, if it hadn't been for the fact that he knew she was an only child, he could easily believe this girl was a pale twin. No wonder she had recoiled at being called plucky. When she had entered the dining hall that evening he had stared with disorientation at a completely different person from the pert and intrepid horsewoman. A prisoner on the way to the guillotine had more jump in their step than the pale effigy that had somehow made her way to the sofa in the corner. Her skin had been ashen under its sun-kissed warmth, almost green, and he wondered if she was going to be ill. Perhaps someone petite might have looked fragile, but she just looked awkward.

He had almost started moving towards her when her

aunt had reached her, and though he had only been able to make out part of her words, the vitriolic viciousness had been distressingly apparent and the coy comments to the Poundridges had almost been worse. She had humiliated the girl in public without compunction and Sir Henry had stood unmoved as a post.

It wasn't until he sat down by her that he had noticed she was shaking and immediately he was back with his brother. Tim's legs would leap like that at the onset of the attacks of terror; that was how he could tell it was starting. He hadn't even been able to hold his one remaining hand or touch him because of the constant pain. All he could do was sit there with him until it stopped. Not that it had helped in the end. To see that stare in the girl's face and the telltale quiver of her legs had been shocking. She had finally calmed, but he hadn't. He was still tight with the need to do damage to that vindictive witch. That poor girl needed to get away from this poisonous house.

He glanced at the girl again. She still wasn't eating, just sitting ramrod straight, staring down at her plate. But there was a stain of colour on her cheeks as the aunt leaned towards her. She was at her again, the hag, he thought angrily. Why doesn't her father do anything about this? If she had been his daughter he would have ripped this woman's head from her shoulders long ago.

Something the pink-festooned brunette said to him required his attention and he turned to her resolutely. This wasn't his affair and it wasn't as if he had been so successful helping the people who mattered to him. It had been his father's death that had partially released his mother from her humiliation, not any of his puny efforts to protect her. And Tim… He might have saved his brother's broken body from a French prison, but he had failed on every other level. This girl was just another of a multitude of cowed women, just like his mother, beaten down until they could no longer imagine standing up for themselves. There was nothing he could do to change the trajectory of her fate.

'Are you really fool enough to try and flirt with Lord Hunter? Do you really think someone like him will be interested in you?' Aunt Hester hissed under cover of the conversation. Her witch's smile was in full bloom, the one she used while spewing hate in company.

In a year this would be her life, Nell thought. She would be eighteen and for three long years until her majority she would have to suffer the whip of her aunt's tongue and her father's anger and indifference. No, she couldn't do that. She wouldn't.

'He doesn't need your money, so don't think you can snare someone like him just because you're an heiress. Like mother, like daughter. That's how your slut of a mother caught Henry, you know...'

Nell stood before her mind registered the movement.

'You will not speak about Mama. Not a word. Not ever.'

She hardly recognised her own voice. It was low, but the room fell into shocked silence. Her aunt's face was turning the colour of fury, but Nell was far away. Soon the walls would collapse on her, but for a moment time had stopped and she could walk through this frozen little world out into the night and keep walking until she reached Keswick.

Then she saw Lord Hunter's face. There was a smile in his honey-brown eyes and he raised his glass towards her and time moved again and she realised what she had done. Her aunt surged to her feet, which was a mistake, because she was much shorter than Nell.

'If you cannot behave in a ladylike fashion, you will beg everyone's pardon and retire, Helen.' The words were temperate but the message in her aunt's eyes wasn't. I'll deal with you later, they said.

Nell almost hung her head and complied, but looking down at the purply-red patches on her aunt's cheeks, the thick lips tinted with the pink colour she favoured, she felt a wave of disgust, not fear. She took a step back and turned and curtsied to the others.

'I apologise for not behaving in a ladylike fashion. I hope you enjoy the rest of your evening. Goodnight.' She turned back to her aunt. 'I will never listen to you again. Not ever. You have no voice.'

She heard her father bellow her name, but didn't stop. She would leave for Keswick in the morning and she would never return.

Chapter One

London—1820

'There's no one there, miss,' the driver of the post-chaise said impatiently as Nell stared at the empty house and the knocker-less door. How could this be? Her father's last letter had been sent just two days ago and from London. As far back as she remembered he always spent the week before the Wilton horse-breeders' fair in London, assessing the latest news and horses at Tattersall's.

'We can't leave the horses standing in this rain, miss; they've come a long way.'

Nell turned back to the post-chaise. The driver was right. The poor horses had made excellent time over the last stage and they must be exhausted. But where could she go?

'Do you happen to know where Lord Hunter resides?'

The words were out before she could consider and the driver cocked a knowing brow.

'Lord Hunter, miss? Aye, I do. Curzon Street. You quite certain that's where you'll be wanting to go? Not quite the place for a respectable young lady.'

Nell breathed in, trying to calm her annoyance and fear. Nell knew memories were often deceptive, but she had found it hard to reconcile her memory of the troubled and irreverent young man with Mrs Sturges's report of a noted Corinthian addicted to horse racing, pugilism and light women. Nevertheless, it was clear the driver shared Mrs Sturges's opinion of her alleged fiancé's reputation. Mrs Sturges might teach French and deportment, but she was also the school's resident expert on London gossip, and when Nell had received the shocking newspaper clipping sent by her father, she had immediately sought her advice. Mrs Sturges had been delighted to be consulted on such a promisingly scandalous topic as Lord Hunter.

'He is a relation of mine, so, yes, that is precisely where I'll be wanting to go,' Nell lied and leaned back into the chaise as it pulled forward. She, like the horses, was tired and hungry and just wanted to sleep for a week, but she was not going to back down now. She was twenty-one and financially and legally independent, and no one…no one!…was going to decide her fate any longer. She didn't know whether it was her father or Lord Hunter who was responsible for the gossip in the *Morning Post*, but she wasn't going to wait another moment to put a stop to it.

'This here's Hunter House, miss.'

Nell inspected the house as the postilion opened the chaise door. It looked like the other houses on the road— pale, patrician and dark except for faint lines of light sifting through the closed curtains in the room on the right. The hood of Nell's cloak started sliding back and little needles of rain settled on her hair. She tugged her hood into place, wondering how on earth she was going to do this. She turned to the driver.

'Will you wait a moment?'

The driver glanced at the sluggish drizzle and a little rivulet of water ran off the brim of his hat onto his caped greatcoat.

'We'll see if there's someone in, but then we'll have to get the horses to the Peacock Inn, miss. You can send for your trunk there.'

She almost told him to take her to the Peacock as well, but the thought of asking for a room in a London posting house without maid or companion was as daunting as bearding the lion in his den.

Not a lion, she mused, trying to recall what Lord Hunter had looked like. Too dark for a lion. Too tall and lean for one, too.

Whatever the case, he was unlikely to be happy about her appearing on his doorstep at nine in the evening. However, if he had a hand in this outrageous stratagem, he didn't deserve to be happy. She still found it hard to believe the handsome and wealthy rake described by Mrs Sturges really wanted to wed her at all, especially after her shocking behaviour four years ago, but it was equally hard to believe a columnist would dare fabricate such a libellous faradiddle.

She climbed the last step, gathering her resolution, when the door opened and golden light spilled out and was immediately obstructed by a large shadow. She stepped back involuntarily and her shoe slipped on the damp steps. She grabbed at the railing, missed and with a sense of fatality felt herself fall backwards. She instinctively relaxed as she would for a fall from a horse, adjusting her stance, and she managed to land in a crouch on the bottom step. She pushed to her feet and brushed her gloved hands, glad the dark hid her flush of embarrassment. The figure at the top of the steps had hurried towards her, but stopped as she stood up.

'That was impressive.' His deep voice was languid and faintly amused and she glanced up abruptly. Apparently she did remember some things about her betrothed.

'Lord Hunter...'

'Impressive, but not compelling. Whatever is on offer, sweetheart, I'm not interested. Run along, now.'

Nell almost did precisely that as she realised the driver had been true to his word and was disappearing down the street at a fast clip. She drew herself up, clinging to her dignity, and turned back to the man who was thoroughly confirming Mrs Sturges's indictment.

'That's precisely the issue, Lord Hunter. I am not interested either, and the fact that you don't even recognise the woman that according to the *Morning Post* you are engaged to only confirms it. Now, may we continue this inside? It's cold and I'm tired; it was a long drive from Keswick.'

At least that drew a response from him, if only to wipe the indolent amusement from his face. The light streaming past him from the house still cast him into a shadow, but she could make out some of the lines of his face. The dark uncompromising brows that drew together at her greeting, the deep-set eyes that she couldn't remember if they were brown or black, and the mouth that had flattened into a hard line—he looked older and much harsher than she had remembered.

'Miss Tilney,' he said at last, drawing out her name. 'This is a surprise, to say the least. Where is Sir Henry?'

'I don't know. May we talk inside? It is not quite...'

She paused, realising the irony of suggesting they enter his house to avoid being seen on his doorstep. His lips compressed further, but he stood back and she hurried into the hall, her heart thumping. Everything had been much clearer in her mind when she had been driven by frustration and anger and before she had made a fool of herself tumbling down the steps.

'This way.'

He opened a door and she glanced at him as she entered. She went towards the still-glowing fireplace, extending her hands to its heat and trying hard not to let her surprise show. How had she managed to forget such a definite face? Had she remembered him more clearly, she might have reconsidered confronting him alone. She had vaguely remembered his height and the bruised weariness about his eyes; even his irreverence and his tolerance of her skittishness. But she hadn't remembered that his brows were like sooty accusations above intense golden-brown eyes or the deep-cut lines that bracketed a tense mouth. If she had grown up he had grown hard. It was difficult to imagine this man being kind to a scared child.

'Lord Hunter,' she began. 'I—'

'How did you get here from Keswick?'

She blinked at the brusque interruption.

'I came post. What I wanted to say was—'

'In a post-chaise? With whom?'

'With a maid from the school. Lord Hunter, I—'

'Is she outside?'

'No, I left her with her family in Ealing on the way. Lord Hunter, I—'

He raised a hand, cutting her off again.

'Your father allowed you to travel from the Lake District to London and come to my house in the middle of the night, unattended?'

He spoke softly but the rising menace in his voice was unmistakable.

'My father knows nothing about it. Would you please stop interrupting me?'

'Not yet. What the…? What do you mean your father knows nothing about it?'

'My father sent me a letter on my birthday informing me I have apparently been betrothed for four years. I wrote back and told him I most certainly wasn't. His response was to send me this clipping from the *Morning Post*.' She fumbled inside her reticule for the much-abused slip of paper and shoved it at Lord Hunter. He took it, but didn't bother reading it.

'And rather than communicating your…distaste in a more traditional manner, you chose a melodramatic gesture like appearing on my doorstep in the middle of the night?'

Although his flat, cold voice shared nothing with her aunt's deceptively soft but vicious attacks, Nell felt the familiar stinging ache of dread and mortification rising like a wave of nausea. She gritted her teeth, repeating for the umpteenth time that Aunt Hester had no power over her and that she was no longer a child. She was twenty-one and very wealthy and she was done being treated like chattel.

'Do you find it more melodramatic than concocting this engagement behind my back and keeping it from me for four years? You have no one to blame but yourself!'

That might have been going too far, Nell told herself as his stern face lost some of its coldness, but she couldn't tell what the increasingly intent look on his face portended.

'Clearly,' he said, still maddeningly cool. 'Where are you staying in town?'

Some of her bravado faded at the thought of the disappearing post-chaise.

'Nowhere yet. I thought Father was in town, but the house is empty and the post-chaise is taking my trunk to the Peacock in Islington.'

The gloves jerked in his hands again.

'I see. And now that you have delivered your message in person, what do you propose to do?'

Nell had no idea. She was miserable and confused and hungry and she wanted nothing more than to sit down and cry.

He moved away from her and for a moment she thought he might just leave her there and her shoulders sagged, almost relieved. But he merely strode over to the bell-pull and gave it a tug. At least in this her memory had been accurate—he walked lightly, unusually so for someone of his size, but it just added to that sense of danger she had not associated with him at all from their meeting all those years ago.

'Sit down.'

He tossed his gloves on a table and took her arm, not quite forcing her, but it was hard not to step back and sink into the armchair. It was as comfortable as it looked and for a moment she contemplated unlacing her shoes and tucking her cold feet beneath her, leaning her head against the wings, closing her eyes... Perhaps this would all just go away.

He stood above her, even more imposing now that she was seated. Neither of them spoke until the door opened.

'Biggs, bring some…tea and something to eat, please.'

'*Tea?*'

Nell almost smiled at the shock in the butler's voice. Lord Hunter glanced at him with a glint of rueful amusement just as the butler caught sight of Nell. All expression was wiped from the butler's face, but something in his stoic expression reflected the brief flash of amusement in his master's eyes and Nell didn't know whether to be relieved by this first sign of some softer human emotion from the man she was engaged to.

'Tea. Oh, and send Hidgins to the Peacock and ask him to retrieve—' He broke off and turned to Nell. 'Let me guess—you gave them your real name, didn't you? I thought so. To retrieve Miss Tilney's baggage. Discreetly, Biggs. But first have him drive by Miss Amelia to tell her to wait up for me; I will be by within an hour with a guest for the night.'

Nell started protesting, but the butler merely nodded and withdrew.

'I can't stay with you!'

'Don't worry; I never invite women here and certainly not my betrothed. I will take you somewhere a damn sight more respectable than the Peacock is for a country miss with no more sense than to try to stay at one of the busiest posting houses in London without a maid or chaperon. You may not want to marry me, but I'm damned if I am going to have the woman whose name has just been publicly linked with mine create a lurid scandal through sheer stupidity. I admit your father and I agreed on the engagement four years ago, but I understood he would discuss it with you and inform me if there was any impediment to proceeding and that in any case it wouldn't be relevant until you came of age.'

'Because I wouldn't inherit Bascombe until then, correct?' she asked, not concealing her contempt.

He breathed in, clearly clinging to his calm.

'Correct. I don't see anything outrageous in wanting to ally the Bascombe and Hunter estates. I admit I should have probably discussed the matter with you myself, but since you disappeared from Tilney and since I was in mourning at the time, it seemed sensible to let your father discuss the issue with you. I had no idea he hadn't done so and I had nothing to do with that gossip in the *Morning Post*. Believe me, I am suffering as much as you from that nonsense.'

Nell shrugged, her anger dimming, but not her depression.

'That was probably my father's heavy-handed way of trying to force my submission, but it won't work. If I have to personally demand the *Morning Post* issue a retraction, I shall do so.'

'No, you won't, not unless you wish to escalate this into a full-scale scandal, which I, for one, prefer to avoid. We will deal with this discreetly and that means if you want my co-operation you will go to my aunts and once you are rested we will discuss our options. Until then I suggest we put a moratorium on this discussion. I never decide on important matters when I am tired, hungry and upset. I suggest you adopt this policy, at least for tonight.'

Nell didn't answer and the tense silence held until the butler entered with a tray bearing a pot of tea and a plate of sandwiches.

'We don't have any sweetmeats, I'm afraid, sir,' he

said as he placed the tray in front of Nell and she smiled gratefully.

'Never mind. I don't like sweetmeats. This is perfect.'

The butler's brows rose, creating a row of arched wrinkles on his high forehead. Again she saw the glimmer of amusement in the glance he directed at his master.

'You don't like confectionery, miss?' he asked as he poured the tea, and both the action and the question surprised her. 'Such a distaste is uncommon in young women, if you pardon the impertinence, miss.'

The scent of steaming tea was heavenly and her mouth watered. It occurred to her this particular servant was allowed a great deal of latitude, which surprised her given Lord Hunter's controlled demeanour.

'If my aunt is to be believed, my not liking sweetmeats is the least of my peculiarities. Thank you.' She took the cup and saucer he held out to her.

'You're welcome, miss. But eat those sandwiches, do. Anything else, sir?'

'No, thank you, Biggs. That is more than enough.'

Nell once again heard the mocking note in Lord Hunter's voice.

'Very good, sir. Shall I also send a message that you are…otherwise engaged?'

A flash of annoyance crossed Hunter's face.

'Yes, do that.'

Biggs bowed and withdrew.

'I'm sorry I ruined your plans, but really there's no need…'

'It doesn't matter. Eat something and I'll take you to Amelia.'

'I really don't think…'

'We've established that already. Eat up. And next time

you plan to stay alone at major posting houses, use an alias. I suggest "Mrs Jones, widow". Widows are granted more leeway.'

Nell was tired in body and soul, and disheartened, and miserable, and his brusque, matter-of-fact approach pushed her over the edge. Even the sight of the food wasn't enough to counter the fury that caught her. She put down her cup and saucer with more force than grace and stood up.

'What useful advice. I will apply it at the next hostelry. In fact, I will try it right away. Goodnight, my lord. Have a lovely life and when you speak with my father tell him to have a lovely life as well.'

He blocked her path, his hand closing on her arms firmly but without force.

'Don't be a fool. Come, I will take you to my aunts and tomorrow we will figure out what to do with you.'

'You will *not* figure out what to do with me. I am not a…a witless dummy to be manipulated. I promised myself years ago I will *never* again be bullied and I don't care how tired and hungry and upset I am, because if you say just one more nasty thing to me I will walk out of here and if you try and stop me I will scream at the very top of my lungs and enjoy every second of it!'

Once again his fleeting smile flashed.

'I'm certain you will, for a moment. But it's not very practical, is it? You would probably call the Watch in on us and you look done in and I don't think you want to spend the next hour explaining the whole story to magistrates and strangers, do you? Can we compromise?'

'Compromise how?'

'You eat up and I take you to my aunts and then tomorrow we discuss this. Calmly.'

'That isn't a compromise since I still do what you want,' she said, well aware she sounded like a resentful child.

'Yes, but tomorrow you can send me to the devil and I will not lift a finger to stop you.'

'That's still not a compromise.'

'Well, it feels like one to me. What on earth are you thinking of doing? You can't go to the Peacock, especially now I've sent Hidgins for your baggage, and if you are contemplating doing something so rash, I just might choose to communicate some interesting information to the landlord that will make your stay more uncomfortable than it already appears to be.'

'You wouldn't!'

'Try me. I'm damned if I'm going to have someone whose name has been tied with mine in an unfortunately public manner make a fool of herself in one of the busiest hostelries in the city.'

'So you are threatening to compound my folly with yours? That doesn't make much sense.'

'Don't start preaching sense to me, young woman. Well?'

She raised her chin, trying to find a better solution and failing.

'Fine. For one night. Your aunts will probably think you drunk or mad and I won't blame them.'

He smiled.

'Not them. They're used to my eccentricities.'

Nell felt a snide comment wavering at the edge of her tongue, but held back and sat down again. It felt so very good to lose her temper, a luxury she rarely indulged, but the truth was that he was right—she was hungry and tired and upset and more than willing to postpone coping with the consequences of her actions until tomorrow.

'Fine. And please stop swearing at me. It is very improper.'

'Fine. Eat up.'

Hunter watched as she finally did as she was told and took one of Biggs's bread and cheese creations. He walked to pour himself a glass of port so she wouldn't see his smile. Admittedly when he and Sir Henry had agreed on the betrothal four years ago he hadn't been at his best, but he wondered how his memory could be so seriously flawed. He knew people changed a great deal in four years, he certainly had, and not for the better, but the contrast between this young woman and that girl was extreme. Despite her height she had struck him as rather mousy, all long limbs and very little else, her pale hair showing a distinct tendency to fall out of its pins and obscure her face. She hadn't been ugly, just… awkward. He remembered her expressions more than her face, from the joyful light after that incredible gallop on Petra to the sheer terror when she had come under her aunt's attack. Then, in that last minute when she had marched out of the drawing room, there had been something else—for a moment she had taken full advantage of her height and looked almost regal.

She wasn't a beauty, but mousy or gawky were definitely not the right words to describe her. He wasn't quite certain what words were applicable, but those blue-grey eyes, sparked with the fire of temper and determination and with a faint catlike slant, were anything but plain, and though she was still lean and athletic, as her limber recovery from the fall on his steps indicated, even under her countrified cloak he could see that her girlish slimness had filled out quite nicely.

In fact, as far as looks went, she was much more appealing than he remembered. But what she had gained in looks, she had lost in temperament. He certainly hadn't remembered she was such a prickly thing, though now he could recall some of her critical comments during that ride four years ago which should have forewarned him. It appeared he had as thoroughly misread her character as he had been mistaken about her appearance.

It hadn't taken him long to regret his agreement with Tilney, but he had comforted himself that at least he would be gaining not only Bascombe but a docile, compliant wife grateful to be saved from her less-than-satisfactory life, content to stay in Hampshire and leave him to pursue his work and other interests in London. Well, that conviction was clearly nothing more than a fantasy. There was still something skittish about her and her words about bullying were telling, but she was about as docile as she was mousy.

He savoured his port as he watched her. She might not like sweets, but she was certainly doing justice to Biggs's sandwiches. She put down her empty plate with a slight sigh and he smiled involuntarily. She was a strange little thing. No, not little.

'Better?'

Her mouth wavered, as if she was contemplating holding on to her anger, and then settled into a rueful smile.

'That was the best sandwich I have ever eaten, I think.'

'I will inform Biggs of your appreciation. He takes bread and cheese very seriously.'

'A sensible man.' Her smile widened and he could see

that girl again who had slid off Petra after her gallop, confident and confiding, but then she was gone again.

'He is. Now that you are fed, I have a suggestion to make. When I go to Wilton I will confer with your father and when I return we will all sit down—'

'Wilton? You're going to the breeders' fair?' Nell asked, leaning forward.

Hunter raised his brow at the interruption. Her face had transformed again and was now alight and eager.

'Yes. I've gone for the past couple of years. I'm looking for a stallion to breed with Petra. Why?'

Her gaze remained fixed on him, but he could have sworn that for a moment she wasn't there, had left her body and travelled to some place lovely and warm because her cheeks and lips lost their pallor, warming to a shade of a very edible peach, and her pupils shrank, turning her eyes more silver than grey. For a split second he thought this is what she might look like after she climaxed, full of warmth and light, afloat. Then it was gone; she looked down at her hands and pressed them together as if about to pray.

'I will agree to your compromise. On condition.'

Oh, hell. Somehow he thought he wouldn't like this.

'What condition?'

'I will come with you to Wilton.'

It was not a request. This girl was definitely not turning into the biddable bride he had thought she would be.

'I am not saying that I agree, but may I ask why?'

She shrugged and tugged at her gloves.

'Well, clearly we need to speak with Father about repudiating this rumour and if he isn't in London he has most likely gone to Wilton early. Surely there is no harm in merely driving with you since we are, for the moment at least, engaged. Well?'

Well, indeed? Why should every one of his instincts be on alert? Ever since Kate had shoved the newspaper with that blasted gossip at him he had known his life was going to take a distinct turn for the worse, but somehow he had hoped he could put off dealing with this particular commitment for a little while longer. He was used to the occasional sniping column about his affairs and activities and accepted them as part of his choice of lifestyle, but the deluge that had appeared in today's papers following the appearance of those two sentences about his purported betrothal was trying his patience. It didn't help that Biggs had indulged his sense of humour by acquiring several newspapers and spreading them around the house carefully folded open to the most damning, including one entitled 'Wild Hunter Bagged at Last!', which had been borderline libellous and peppered with the initials of the women reputed to be mourning his removal from the field.

All told he had been looking forward to confronting Tilney at Wilton and telling him what he thought of his management of this affair. What he had not counted on was that Tilney had clearly never told his daughter about the arrangement or that she would descend on him from the wilds of the Lake District demanding a disavowal. He walked over to the fireplace and shoved in another log. She wanted conditions, fine.

He stood and brushed the slivers of wood from his hands.

'Very well. As long as you meet my conditions as well. Unfortunately, as far as the world is concerned we are betrothed and to deny that now will cause precisely the scandal we're trying to avoid. So while at Wilton we present ourselves as such until we can consider how to end this engagement without turning us into a laughing stock. In addition, my co-operation is conditional upon reaching some reasonable long-term agreement about the water rights. I'll be da—dashed if I have to negotiate yearly fee agreements with my once betrothed or your bridegroom of choice when eventually you decide to marry.'

Hunter trailed off as she blushed so hotly she might as well have been wearing her heart fully emblazoned on her sleeve. No wonder she wanted out of this betrothal. His forced fiancée clearly already had a bridegroom in mind.

As the blush faded she canted her head to one side.

'Somehow that amounts to quite a few more conditions than mine.'

'I'm not negotiating. Well?'

She gave a brisk nod and he relaxed.

'Good. Off we go, then. Just keep your hood pulled low. I prefer not to be seen abroad with such a reckless character as yourself at this late hour.'

She laughed and stood, pulling on her hood, and he felt a twinge of regret. He reached out and arranged her hood so that it better covered the silver-gold glints of her hair. Her eyes rose to his in surprise and he didn't immediately release the soft fabric. Her irises were an interesting combination of shades of grey and blue—from slate to ice to a rim of darker blue. This close he caught her scent, something warm, like a field of wildflowers in summer. His eyes glided down towards her mouth, slightly parted in surprise. A very generous mouth. For a moment he was tempted to taste that lush curve. The memory returned of her coming towards him on Petra, her hair tumbled and her face alight, except that now his imagination embellished, it was no longer a girl but this young woman coming towards him, and now he was drawing her down onto the grass, spreading that fairy hair out on the wildflowers her scent evoked…

He didn't move, noting with cynical amusement the enthusiastic response of his body. Trust it to show interest now that he was within arm's reach of escaping this engagement. Whatever the case, he had no intention of acting on the urge. He stepped back and held out his arm.

'Shall we?'

Chapter Two

Nell obediently kept her head down as they descended from the hackney cab. At least that had been her intention, but a quick glance at the building they approached made her look up in swift surprise and her hood slipped back. She grabbed at it, but stood staring upwards. She had expected a house similar to Lord Hunter's or like her father's more modest town house. This looked more like a rambling school and took up half the road on this side.

Lord Hunter noticed her shocked expression.

'I know, not ideal, but it's the best I can do at such short notice. Aunt Sephy and Aunt Amelia live in a separate apartment. Their entrance is down this alleyway.'

He took her hand and placed it on his arm, leading her towards a narrow gap between the building and a row of modest-looking houses scantily lit by a single oil lamp at the corner. His arm was very warm under her gloved hand and it spread a pleasant heat through her, like the comforting animal warmth of leaning against a horse in a cold stable.

She smiled at the thought. Lord Hunter would probably not appreciate being compared with a horse. In fact, she had no idea what he might appreciate. He was not at all what she had expected. Neither the perplexing young man she remembered nor Mrs Sturges's debauched rake. There was still that rather irreverent amusement hovering in the background, and sometimes not so far in the background, but she certainly didn't feel threatened by him. Perhaps just a little when he had helped her with her hood; something unsettling in his eyes had set off alarms, but it had come and gone too quickly for her to act on her need to draw back.

Still, it wasn't wise to trust this man and she shouldn't presume that she understood him simply because he was so unfashionably blunt. As someone who kept most of herself firmly out of public view, she had a good eye for identifying people whose surface differed from their interior. She could see beyond painfully shy or boisterously loud exteriors and she had used this skill time and again helping Mrs Petheridge with the schoolgirls and even with recalcitrant or challenging horses. Not that he appeared to be masking vulnerability or fear, but there was definitely something behind the urbane façade that outweighed it, and until she understood what it was she would do well not to take him at face value, no matter how charming the face.

As they weaved their way into the gloom she realised she was being all too complaisant about being led into a dark alley by a man she hardly knew. Admittedly the mention of an Aunt Sephy and Aunt Amelia didn't exactly invoke images of rape and pillage, but still…

'What is this place?' she asked in a whisper, slowing her steps, but just then the alley curved into a small courtyard set around a single tree. The cobblestones glistened with the remains of the drizzle and light shone through curtains which were definitely pink and embroidered with flowers. Even in that weak light Nell could see the façade here was well tended and the tree surrounded with chrysanthemums. It was so far removed from the dour impression of the front of the building that she couldn't help staring.

Hunter stopped as well and his hand covered hers where it lay on his arm. He stood with his back to the faint light from the window, once again a dark-on-dark shape like that first moment he had opened the door, but this time it was a different kind of shock that spurted through her. There was enough light to infuse his eyes with a startling burn of gold and his smile was so enticing that her hand began to turn under his. She froze before she could complete the gesture, but she was incapable of doing anything else but waiting for his move, as surely as if this was a game of chess and these the iron rules of a game they had engaged in.

He wasn't doing anything, just looking down at her, but in her weary and overwhelmed state he seemed to grow, take on the dark of the night, expand and envelop her. She had never been fanciful but she imagined Lucifer might look like this the moment before he claimed a failing soul for his own. It would feel like this, too: hot, terrifying, all encompassing, seductive. If she leaned forward she might fall into that heat and be consumed by it, claimed and changed for ever. It would be inescapable.

Then he spoke and the moment broke.

'A bit of a surprise, isn't it?' he said and there was nothing in his voice to reflect the swirling heat of the moment. She stepped back, pulling her hand away. It must be the weariness and the confusion, that was all.

More proof that she should not trust him, even if that moment had been merely her imagination.

'I can't go in there!' She heard the panic in her voice, but couldn't help it.

He took her hand again, layering it between his own. This was no longer Lucifer, and though the warmth flowed through her, now it was soothing.

'It's all right. You will like them and they will like you, I promise. There is nothing to be afraid of.'

She tried to resent being spoken to like a child except that it wasn't the patronising tone of some of the schoolmistresses. It was an offer, but the decision would have to be hers. She glanced at the pink curtains and nodded. She had little choice, after all.

He tapped lightly on a lion's-paw knocker and the door was opened immediately by a round little man who bowed and stood back.

'Good evening, my lord. Miss Amelia is waiting for you in the parlour. Miss Sephy has of course retired.'

Lord Hunter urged Nell up the stairs into the well-lit hall.

'Thank goodness for that, Bassett.'

The butler's mouth relaxed as he opened the door into a room at the back of the house and stood back to let them enter.

'Indeed, my lord. May I bring refreshments?'

'You may. Tea for Miss Tilney and something stronger for me.'

Nell cringed at the trouble she was causing and almost began apologising, but Lord Hunter ushered her into the parlour where a woman moved towards them with a smile in honey-brown eyes that clearly were a shared family trait. She also had her nephew's strong brows and slightly aquiline nose. It was a formidable face, but contrarily Nell didn't feel at all intimidated. In fact, and very uncharacteristically, Nell liked her on sight and met the woman's smile with one of her own.

'Amelia, this is Miss Helen Tilney. Miss Tilney, this is my aunt, Miss Amelia Calthorpe. She lives here with my other aunt, Miss Seraphina Calthorpe, who is thankfully asleep because her rampant curiosity would keep you awake until dawn if let loose. Amelia, we have an emergency. Miss Tilney needs a place to stay for a few days until she decides on her future path. May she stay here? I've sent Hidgins to collect her luggage from the posting house, but if he's delayed she might need to borrow some gear from you.'

Nell was grateful for the soft light, though she was sure her flush of shame was still as apparent as in broad daylight, but Amelia's face betrayed none of the shock and scorn Nell had expected.

'Of course you may,' Amelia said without hesitation, holding out her hand to Nell. 'And you needn't worry about your baggage. It reminds me I once lost my trunk and I was miserable because I had just bought the loveliest bonnet. Do come with me and we will have something warm to drink while Bassett is preparing the guest room. Did you travel far today?'

Nell followed her in something of a daze.

'I…from Keswick…'

'Oh, of course. I just realised who you are! I am not very good with the papers, but Sephy did show me the column in the *Post* today, or was it yesterday? I have been meaning to write you a note, Gabriel. Why didn't you tell me this is the woman you are engaged to?'

'Not any more. Miss Tilney plans to jilt me as soon as we can do so with minimal fuss.'

'Dear me, what a pity. Was it something you said?'

'I think it might be something I didn't say.'

'Of course. I quite understand, Miss Tilney, and I must say that though I personally adore Gabriel, I can see your point. From the age of four he was always one to go his own way and let the world follow if it can. Oh, thank you, Bassett. Just put it on the table. I will pour.'

Nell accepted the cup of tea Miss Calthorpe handed her, trying very hard not to give in to the urge to giggle at this increasingly improbable scene. She looked away and met Gabriel's eyes and the lazy invitation to share in his amusement evoked an involuntary response in her. If ever a look said 'I told you so' without exciting the least resentment, this was it. She drank her tea, answering Miss Amelia's questions as faithfully as possible, but without much awareness of what she said. She laid down her cup on the small round table by her chair, but it tilted alarmingly and the cup and saucer slid away as she watched, too tired and sluggish to even realise what was about to happen. But Lord Hunter leaned forward with a swiftness that made her jerk awake and caught the cup and saucer with a smooth motion.

'Thank you,' she murmured, flushing, and his eyes moved over her, intense and questioning.

'You're tired. I'll go see if Bassett is done.'

'Please, don't bother…' she began, but luckily Bassett entered.

'Miss Tilney's room is ready, Miss Amelia.'

'Thank you, Bassett. Come along, Miss Tilney. May I call you Helen, or is it Nell? Leave your cloak. Bassett will give it a good brushing. Goodnight, Gabriel. You may come by tomorrow.'

Nell allowed herself to be propelled out of the drawing room and up the stairs, resisting the childish urge to remain with Lord Hunter. It was a sign of how shaky she was that she was beginning to consider an irreverent rake a safe haven.

Chapter Three

'He wandered, lost and dreaming of his love…'

Hunter turned with a resigned sigh as a tall dark figure crossed the street towards him.

'And so it begins. Want to lampoon me out here, Raven? Or shall we wait until you can entertain Stanton as well?'

'Both, thank you. This merits quite a bit more ribbing than can be accomplished on a doorstep. Besides, I need a drink. I just walked over from Jenny's and I'm frozen through.'

'Didn't she warm you sufficiently? Either you or she is slipping, Raven. Good evening, Dunberry,' Hunter greeted Stanton's butler.

'Speaking of slipping, I frankly never thought you'd take the plunge; it was a bit of a shock to have that gossip in the *Morning Post* pointed out to me.'

'For me, too.'

'You don't remember proposing? And here I thought you had a hard head.'

'I remember proposing. Her father and I settled it four years ago but I thought common courtesy would require he speak with me before discussing it with gossip columnists. I didn't appreciate Kate bringing it to my attention.'

Ravenscar winced.

'I suppose she was peeved?'

'I was too distracted by being "peeved" myself to notice and it rather ruined the mood, so I didn't linger to chat…'

They entered the library and Stanton glanced up from the book he had been holding, but didn't bother rising from the sagging armchair by the fire.

'You're late.'

'May I have something to drink before you begin the catechism?' Hunter asked politely.

'Help yourself.' Stanton waved towards a decanter on the sideboard. 'What happened? You two having a hard time finding your timepieces amidst the tangle of sheets?'

'Good God, Stanton, tell me you've read the papers these past two days,' Ravenscar said with disgust.

'Of course I read the papers. A great deal more closely than you do, Raven. What does that have to do with your mistresses?'

'Other than the political pages,' Ravenscar corrected, taking his glass and settling in his usual armchair, his long legs stretched out to the fire that shot his black hair with a jet sheen that made his name singularly apt.

'In that case, no. Why, has something happened?' Stanton's blue eyes narrowed in concern.

'Hopeless,' Ravenscar murmured. 'Shall I tell him, or shall you, Hunter?'

Hunter took his usual seat as well.

'I wouldn't deprive you of the pleasure for the world, Raven.'

'Thank you. It appears we are to wish Hunter happy. He is betrothed.'

'What? When? To whom?'

'I think "Why?" might be more to the point,' Ravenscar replied and Hunter sighed.

'She's Sir Henry Tilney's daughter and heir to the Bascombe estate. Her father and I agreed on the engagement when I went to negotiate the water rights after old Bascombe died.'

'Wait, I remember now. You bought Petra and Pluck from Tilney. Right after Tim's funeral.'

Eventually this reflexive stiffening of his muscles at the mention of Tim would fade, Hunter told himself for the umpteenth time.

Stanton continued, his controlled voice far worse than Ravenscar's jibes.

'You've been engaged for four years and never once mentioned it.'

'I didn't mention it because the engagement was… conditional. The girl was just seventeen and Bascombe's will stipulated she inherit only when she turned twenty-one. If she died before that, married or not, the property went to some cousin. Her father agreed that it would be unreasonable to expect me to commit to a public engagement until the inheritance was legally hers.'

'And she accepted this cold-blooded arrangement? Well, you definitely have reached the mecca of complaisant and biddable brides, Hunter. I salute you.'

'Not quite. I presumed her father would discuss it with her, but it appears she didn't know about it until recently, and when she balked her father decided the best way to force her hand was to make it public.'

'Just so I understand,' Stanton said carefully. 'You entered into this engagement without ever asking the girl to marry you?'

Hunter rubbed his forehead.

'I couldn't very well make any announcement at the time anyway because of Tim. So it made sense to wait until the main reason for marrying her became valid. She was only a child, for heaven's sake, and the last thing she was ready to cope with at that point was someone else imposing their will on her. Her father and I agreed she would be better off remaining in the care of her schoolmistress as a boarder until she inherited. The corollary was that for the past four years we've enjoyed the best terms on the Tilney waterways in generations. I thought it was a damn good arrangement at the time.'

Stanton stood up himself and moved with uncharacteristic restlessness around the room.

'Are you saying you asked her to marry you because you felt sorry for her?'

'I told you, there were also the water rights. Put like that I know it sounds foolish...'

'Foolish doesn't begin to cover... Hunter, didn't it occur to you that making such a decision just days after Tim's death wasn't very wise?'

'You do have a talent for understatement, Stanton,' Ravenscar mocked.

Hunter rose as well and went to stand by the fire, watching the flames dance cherry and gold in his brandy.

'Very well,' Stanton said carefully. 'Now that her enterprising father has forced your hand, what do you intend to do?'

'Since I am honour-bound to stand by my offer, my intentions are irrelevant. She, on the other hand, intends to jilt me.'

Ravenscar grinned.

'This keeps getting better.'

'I still don't see anything wrong in principle with marrying in order to ally my land with Bascombe,' Hunter replied defensively. 'It's been done since time immemorial. Now you can take ten minutes to rake me down and then I suggest we get down to the business of finding a property for Hope House in the west country.'

'More important than my friend making a monumental mistake?' Both Hunter and Ravenscar straightened at the uncharacteristic bite in Stanton's voice. He rarely used his *last-chance-to-negotiate-surrender* voice with them. 'The only sensible thing about this whole fiasco so far appears to be Miss Tilney's reaction! I make every allowance for your original decision having been made in rather trying circumstances, but do you really mean to tell me that for four years it didn't occur to you once to seek out this girl and find out whether your decision was a wise one? I don't give a damn about what people have done over time immemorial! I know you've lived your whole life thinking you can rescue people and depend on no one, but you are not as clever as you want to believe and this, let me tell you, is sheer, abject stupidity. Ravenscar I could understand cold-bloodedly deciding to marry an heiress, but you don't even need the funds; the Hunter estate is one of the wealthiest in Hampshire...'

'Yes, but we depend on Bascombe for the water...' Hunter raised his hands placatingly, trying to stem Stanton's rising outrage. It was clearly a mistake. Stanton, renowned for the lightest of diplomatic touches on the most sensitive affairs of state, rarely allowed himself to descend into blasphemy but he did so now, with all the thoroughness he applied to his diplomatic concerns. When he was done the silence was of the calibre often experienced in the studies of the better tutors. The moral point having been made, behaviours examined and condemned, silence remained to let remorse and counsel rise to the surface and prevail. Hunter had had to share quite a few of those moments at Eton with both Stanton and Ravenscar by his side. Predictably Ravenscar broke first.

'What is she like? Ugly as nails? Heiresses usually are. When can we meet her?'

Hunter hesitated. Before this evening he would have known what to answer. After seeing her again he wasn't so sure. She was certainly no beauty like Kate, but she was…different. Unpredictable. Intriguing. He decided to keep it simple until he knew what he himself thought. Not that it would make any difference. If he could convince her to hold her course and withstand her father's ire, she would be someone else's problem.

'Not that it matters since I am about to be jilted, but she is neither ugly nor a beauty. More…unusual. I've never seen a woman with a better seat on a horse. On the other hand, she had a brutal harpy of an aunt living with them who reduced her to the state of a quivering blancmange, which when you're as tall as a Viking looks just a bit bizarre. Then halfway through one of the most tedious dinners I have yet had to plough my way through she suddenly transformed into an avenging fury, told the aunt to go to the devil with biblical panache and the next day she ran back to her school without a word to anyone but the cook and groom. Then tonight she appeared on my doorstep unchaperoned and determined to consign *me* to the devil. I'm glad you find this so amusing,' he concluded a bit sourly as his friends sat with various degrees of grins on their faces.

'You would too, man, if it wasn't happening to you,' Ravenscar replied. 'And I think you could call it a very auspicious beginning. Since marriage is a fate worse than death, it sounds as though you are getting a very fair preview of your future if you can't convince her to sheer off.'

'Thank you, Ravenscar. I can always count on you for perspective. I admit she wasn't quite what I had bargained for when I was resigning myself to the benefits of a modest, country-bred wife who would be happy to live at the Hall tending to children and horses and leaving me to my concerns in London.'

'Ah, the sentimental musings of today's youth…'

'You can be as caustic as you like, Raven. You're one of the least sentimental people I have ever met.'

'I have my moments. Luckily none of them involved an offer of matrimony.'

'So what are you planning to do?' Stanton interceded practically. 'You need to find the girl's father first thing.'

'He's likely at the Wilton breeders' fair and the girl is raring to go there, which is lucky because the sooner I hand her over to her parent, the less likely we are to turn this fiasco into an outright scandal. If she is serious about jilting me, I will need to manage this carefully.'

'Do you really want to nip this affair in the bud?'

Hunter shrugged. It was probably the wisest course of action. He had worn out his chivalric fantasies trying, and failing, to save Tim and his mother. Even before Tim's death he, Ravenscar and Stanton had acquired a reputation for wild living and for accepting any and all sporting dares. After a particularly difficult midnight race down to Brighton, society had delighted in dubbing them the Wild Hunt Club. Since Tim's death he had more than earned his membership rights in that club. He often spent his nights wearing himself down to the point where sleep captured him like the prey of the mythical wild hunts he and his friends were styled after. Whatever still remained of his chivalric impulses he channelled into his work at Hope House and he didn't need anyone outside his friends, his work and the uncommitted physical companionship of women like Kate. The thought of being saddled with a frightened, easily bullied near-schoolgirl was so distasteful he wondered why he hadn't just gone down on his knees and thanked his lucky stars the moment she had sent him to the devil. He had certainly been dreading the moment Tilney would come demanding his due.

It was just that he had been surprised. He had done a very effective job of putting her out of mind since that day at Tilney and coming face-to-face with her had disoriented him. She certainly didn't act like a frightened girl, despite a few moments when he had seen alarm in her silvery eyes. As for near-schoolgirl…those lips and that body were anything but schoolgirlish.

He sighed. None of this mattered. The key was to grasp this reprieve with both hands. He would take her to her father and see if he could extract himself from this fiasco without too much damage.

'Well, whatever you decide, I have faith in your ability to talk her into your way of thinking,' Ravenscar said. 'I've yet to see anyone get by you when you bend your mind to it.'

'Tim did.'

The words were out before Hunter could stop them. They would have been completely out of place, except that these two men had also risked their lives to rescue Tim from France during the war and they knew what caring for Tim until his death had done to Hunter. Ravenscar's cynical smile disappeared.

'Tim was lost the moment that French devil of an inquisitor got his brutal hands on him. We might have managed to salvage his body, or what was left of it, but five months in that prison was five months too long. It was damn bad luck the French were convinced he knew something of value simply because he was on Wellington's staff. They should have realised a boy of nineteen was unlikely to be privy to staff secrets.'

Hunter's stomach clenched as his younger brother's tortured, scarred hands appeared before him as they did in his nightmares, and his face—staring, shaking, wet with tears, begging for the release from mental and bodily pain that the opiates gave him and which Hunter had been forced to ration as Tim's dependency grew.

'That bastard would have continued torturing him anyway. But it was my fault allowing him to join up in the first place.'

'That's nonsense,' Stanton said curtly. 'You took better care of Tim than your parents ever did since the day he was born and he wouldn't have lasted a day after we rescued him if you hadn't nursed him. If there is anyone in this world who should feel no guilt over Tim, it's you. I'm damned if I know why you do.'

Hunter's shoulders tensed as the memories flooded back. For two years he had tried everything he could to help his brother heal, but nothing but laudanum had succeeded in dimming the daily agony of his pain and his attacks of terror. Hunter would never be certain if that final dose was intentional, but he was as certain as he could bear to be. He remembered Tim's words that night before climbing the stairs to his childhood room for the last time.

'You've always been so good to me, Gabe. If there is any way to stop anyone else from going through this, you'll do it, won't you? You promise?'

He would have promised Tim anything at that point, if only he had made an effort to... It was pointless. After the initial shock of finding Tim dead the next morning he had spent a year full of guilt and self-contempt that he had failed his younger brother, or worse, that he had somehow willed Tim to finish it because his agony was too much to bear, and yet worse—because he could only look ahead to years of servitude to a broken boy. Eventually he had dragged himself out of that pit with the help of Ravenscar and Stanton and their work at Hope House. But his grief and guilt and sense of failure clung. He had enough distance now to know that his pact with Tilney had been formed from the ashes of his failure with Tim. Bascombe, water rights and a young woman who was clearly in need of salvation and therefore likely to be grateful for what she could receive had been presented to him on a silver platter and he had taken them, platter and all, more fool he.

'Are you still having nightmares?' Stanton asked, dragging Hunter's thoughts back with unwelcome sharpness. He could feel the sweat break out on the back of his neck and he rubbed at it, but nothing could erase the sick feeling of helplessness. He knew Stanton meant well, but he wished he hadn't asked.

'Sometimes.'

'Since this piece of gossip showed up?'

'Yes.'

Both nights. The dreams were one reason he never stayed the night with his mistresses and another reason, if he needed any, why the thought of marriage was so distasteful. It was one thing keeping this secret from the women he chose to visit on his terms. He couldn't imagine the strain of keeping his fatal flaw a secret from a woman living in his own home. The realisation that he would have to go through with this marriage was probably bringing the worst of it to the surface. It was bad enough having his friends know about them, but he could trust Stanton and Ravenscar with his weaknesses. The thought of that girl...of anyone seeing him while he was in the throes of those moments that left him soaked in sweat... It was unthinkable.

'All the more reason to extract myself from this mess. I don't think my bride would appreciate finding out about my less-than-peaceful nights. She'd probably run for the hills.'

'If you found someone you cared about, you wouldn't have to hide this from them,' Stanton replied.

'That will never happen.'

'What? Loving someone or sharing your weakness?'

'Either. What the devil are you talking about anyway? Love is just another name for dependency or lust and I've had enough of the former in my life and I'm quite content with what I have of the latter. I have no intention of aping my mother or brother by letting myself depend on anyone as they did on me. It didn't do them any good, did it? Or me either.'

'It doesn't have to be such an unequal equation. I

liked Tim and your mother, too, but they drained you dry, man. I don't call that love.'

'You go too far, Stanton!' Hunter said and Stanton raised his hands in surrender.

'Fine. I've no right to preach anyway. Aside from my parents I've never seen evidence of the fabled beast myself.'

'You're too cold-blooded to fancy yourself in love, anyway, Stanton,' Ravenscar stated, swirling his brandy as he watched them. 'And I'm too hot-blooded. So let's put that topic to rest and leave Hunter's Viking bride for the morrow and focus on our business. You'll be pleased to hear I have found a reasonable location for a new house near Bristol. It belongs to a relation of mine who has seen the light and wants to go succour the poor in warmer climes than Gloucestershire. The only problem is that it is distressingly close to Old Dame Jezebel's lair.'

Hunter gratefully accepted the reprieve.

'Your grandmother? Good Lord, she would never countenance a charitable institution within a hundred miles of her domain. She'll never include you in her will if you do this.'

'Since I am already permanently excluded from that honour, her outrage will be well worth it.' Ravenscar winked.

Chapter Four

'You are early, Lord Hunter,' Bassett said as he took Hunter's hat and cane.

'Is that an observation or a hint, Bassett?'

'An observation, my lord. Miss Seraphina is having her cocoa in bed, and Miss Amelia is not yet awake, having read late as usual. Miss Tilney, however, is awake and Sue has gone to tell her breakfast is served. Is there anything I can bring you?'

'Just coffee, thank you, Bassett.'

'Right away. Oh, the newspapers are on the table, my lord.' He nodded at the pile on the breakfast table.

Hunter glanced up in suspicion at something in Bassett's tone, but the butler was already on his way out, so he turned to the dreaded society pages in the rag Aunt Sephy adored. He found his name quite readily and sighed again as he read through the latest creation of the columnists who were clearly having a great deal of fun at his expense.

'Bad news?' a voice said next to him and he whirled around. Nell was standing just beside him, frowning at the paper. She had entered so quietly he had not even realised she was there. He held back on a childish urge to tuck the paper behind his back. Very casually he turned the page.

'Good morning, Miss Tilney.'

'Good morning, Lord Hunter. May I see that?'

Hell.

'It's just the usual nonsense. I ignore it. So should you.'

Nell didn't look up from the paper, even though it now merely showed an advertisement for a cream to counter the ravages of the outdoors.

'Lady F. That's Lady Katherine Felton, isn't it?'

Double hell. How would she know that?

'You shouldn't believe everything you read in the newspapers. Not that this is a newspaper, just a glorified gossip column. Aunt Seraphina lives on a diet of gossip and cocoa.'

The silvery eyes rose and he felt an uncharacteristic heat prickle in his cheeks, throwing him back to the experience of standing before Nurse and a broken window, desperately trying to hide a cricket bat behind his back. He drew himself up. This was ridiculous.

'Shall we...?'

'You needn't be embarrassed you have a mistress. Mrs Sturges assures me most dandies in London have mistresses.'

'I'm not a dandy!'

'Aren't you? Oh, right, she said you were a Corinthian, not a dandy. Though there doesn't appear to be a great difference between them and I suppose they have mistresses, too.'

'There is quite a gulf between a dandy and a Corinthian,' he replied, annoyed at her dismissive tones and momentarily distracted from the fact that the last thing he should be discussing with his betrothed was mistresses.

'I suppose so, but they both are rather profligate and slavishly obsessed with things that matter to no one but themselves. There isn't anything in that column I didn't already know. Mrs Sturges told me all about you and your exploits.'

'My exploits!'

'That's what Mrs Sturges called them. She is very Gothic and talks in capital letters. I rather thought she had exaggerated, but the columnist obviously shares her opinion. She told me all about midnight races and something called the Wild Hunt Club, if I remember correctly. Strange—you don't seem like a dissolute rake. You certainly didn't take advantage of me yesterday, though I suppose that is not quite a criterion since I can't imagine anyone, even if he was a rake, making advances to every woman he comes across, especially if she isn't in the least pretty. It would be quite wearying, wouldn't it? Particularly if he already has a mistress and Mrs Sturges said that Lady Felton is an accredited beauty. In fact, by that logic rakes would be less likely to make advances to all and sundry, wouldn't they?'

Hunter struggled to find a reasonable response to this barrage, or even to manage his own response to her. Out of all the improper and thoroughly damning statements she had let loose with such insouciance, the one that caught his attention was her condemnation of her own looks. It was said with such matter-of-factness and with just a touch of wistfulness that he almost protested. But the need to contradict her statement was submerged by the same confusion he had experienced when facing her last night. In the light of day the difference between this woman and the girl he had thought he was engaged to was even more pronounced. The sun-kissed face looking at him in uncritical interest, though not beautiful, was remarkable in its way. Her wide grey eyes were slightly slanted and framed by the most amazing eyelashes he had ever seen, long and silky and definite and, like her brows, several shades darker than her hair. Her mouth, too, was remarkable—generous and lush and there was a faint white scar just below its right corner. Without thinking, he reached out and touched his finger to the line.

'I don't remember this when I saw you in Leicestershire. What happened?'

Her lips closed tightly and she stepped away from him and he could have kicked himself not only for his insensitivity but for his irrational reaction to that imperfection, a surge of concern and protectiveness that only arose with regard to the very few people he considered under his care. But if his intention had been to deflect her from her inquisition, it worked.

'I was thrown from a horse. It was my fault. But Juniper—the horse—is fine. I know it's ugly.'

'What? No, it's just—' He broke off. There was nothing he could say to explain, to her or to himself, why he had reacted that way. Why he had wanted to touch it and the line of her lip as it curved in. He looked down at the newspaper, trying to find his footing. Then he turned back to her resolutely.

'Why don't we sit down, have something to eat and then talk this over sensibly?'

Her eyes glinted at him.

'There is a pattern forming here. You appear to think I will be more amenable once fed.'

'I certainly will be. I'm useless without my morning coffee.'

Her smile widened, but she nodded and went to the sideboard. He kept the conversation light as they ate, telling her about Petra's and Pluck's successes at the racing meets, a topic which she clearly was happy to explore until she had finished her last finger of toast.

'I'm so happy they are content with you. I still miss Pluck, but I knew Father would never let me keep her, so I'm glad she is with Petra. Well, now that we've eaten I admit to being impatient to hear what you are planning.'

'What makes you think I am *planning* anything?'

'I don't know, but I'm quite certain you are. You have a look.'

Hunter, who had a reputation for being unreadable at the piquet table, barely refrained from asking what this 'look' was, drummed his fingers on the table and wondered how to play his cards. This was not precisely how he had imagined his dealings with a near-schoolgirl would progress. For better or worse she was a bright young woman and he had better start treating her as such.

'May I ask what you plan to do once you are freed of this engagement?'

She considered him, clearly debating whether or not to confide in him.

'I will probably go to Bascombe, but first I will find someone respectable to act as companion or Father or... or my aunt will think they have a duty to come...'

Her voice faded and the haunted look he had seen at Tilney returned. The last time he had seen that expression before her had been on Tim's face. Every day since he rescued him from that French hell and until the day he killed himself. Hunter uncurled his hand from the cup before it shattered. He was right to run. He didn't need this.

'Bar the gates, then,' he said, a bit more roughly than he had intended. 'Bascombe's gates are flanked by two portly gargoyles which make the point quite vividly.'

Her eyes focused back on him and he relaxed as the edge of a smile returned as well.

'Gargoyles?'

'Your grandmother's idea. At least if they were decent sculptures it might be forgivable, but they look like drunken gnomes about to fall off toadstools.'

The smile widened.

'Then my first order of business shall be to remove them. I don't think they would intimidate Aunt Hester anyway. She might even like them. She has the most awful taste.'

'I remember she told me the horrific banquet room at Tilney Hall was her design. Send her the gargoyles as a gift, then.'

She half-laughed and covered her mouth to stop the sound.

'I'd just as happily drop them on her,' she said daringly and he smiled. 'Meanwhile I shall write to a schoolmistress I know to come stay with me.'

'And then?'

She smoothed the tablecloth with her finger.

'I haven't decided yet. But I do know I don't want a marriage of convenience without affection or love.'

He managed to stop his expression from exhibiting what he thought about that last statement. Of course the girl would be dreaming of love. She came from a girls' school, for heaven's sake. The place must be a hotbed of silly novels and soulful sighs.

'Those are two very different qualities. What people call romantic love is not much more than a glorified term for mundane physical passion and tends not to outlive it.'

She flushed, but met his gaze squarely. 'I concede that passion is important, but love is an entity in itself. You are completely wrong to dismiss it so cavalierly.'

He raised a brow at her dismissive tones.

'Of course I am, being so very green,' he said quietly. There was a limit to the abuse he would take from this young woman.

'No, you're not green, just wrong. I may have had very little experience of the world, but I have also been very lucky. When I lost my mother I thought I would never find anyone else who would care for me as much, but now I have other people I love, really deeply love, like Mrs Petheridge and my best friend Anna, and it would be devastating to lose them. I may not expect to find that depth of feeling with a husband, but there must be elements of that for it to be worthwhile marrying. That is what I mean by love. Working in a girls' school where children can't help but mirror the joy or pain of their families is a fairly good arena to explore that particular topic. I have had excellent opportunities to observe the products of the kind of union this betrothal might lead to and I have excellent reasons for refusing. I grew up knowing what it is like to be insignificant and powerless and I will never put myself in that position again.' She leaned back, her Nordic sea eyes narrowed and challenging. 'But this discussion is pointless. Why don't we discuss what you are really interested in—the

Bascombe water rights. Well, I promise I won't be in the least unreasonable. I don't want to be at war with my neighbours. There is no reason why we cannot come to an agreement that is fair for all parties.'

Hunter shifted in his chair, battling the urge to give her as thorough a lecture in return. It would be cruel to take from her anything that had been so painfully won by pointing out that relations between men and women were substantially different than the kind of familial friendships she had thankfully developed away from Tilney. He knew the value of friendships all too well and he knew the pain of loss that came with loving someone who was brutally snatched out of reach, and those, thankfully, had nothing to do with the institution of marriage. To point this out would not only be churlish but counterproductive. He focused instead on her statement about the water rights.

'Though I appreciate your good intentions, if you are indeed set on finding your perfect prince, once you wed it will be your husband who decides on such matters. I suggest you keep that in mind because once it becomes known you have inherited Bascombe Hall some very skilled fortune hunters will be lining up and professing precisely the kind of emotions you appear to value so highly.'

He winced at the harshness of his words, but she just stared coldly back at him.

'I dare say I should be grateful you didn't bother to do the same in your quest to secure Bascombe for yourself. I rather thought you had enough wealth already, or is it never enough?'

He supposed he deserved that.

'I admit my concerns were practical. I never made

any pretence that this alliance wasn't primarily one of good sense. You might think me a profligate fellow, but I take my role as custodian of the Hunter estate seriously and of course I thought it made sense to ally our estates. But I have no intention of forcing you or your father to stand by your engagement, and though if I chose to be unpleasant I could have both of you before a court of law for breach of promise, I prefer to settle this peaceably. So I suggest we try to resolve this like adults. Is that reasonable?'

'Quite. I'm not very happy about the implied threat, though. Are you one of those litigious individuals like Father, who are always suing people over imagined grievances? I find that very self-absorbed people are very quick to find offence at the most absurd things.'

'It was not a threat, but an observation,' Hunter replied, his composure beginning to wear thin. 'And though I have never sued anyone in my life, I would be tempted to begin with you if you insist on continuing with your insults.'

She surprised him, the anger melting away from her eyes as she smothered a ripple of laughter.

'But I didn't insult you. Those were all general statements. You are far too sensitive.'

'Unbelievable. I think I will retire from the lists before I suffer further damage. But before that I just want to make my position quite clear—I went to Tilney Hall to negotiate terms with your father and having met you I thought an alliance between Hunter and Bascombe Halls was a perfect solution. I wouldn't have contemplated it if I hadn't liked you.'

'Don't bother lying! There was nothing to like! I was

pathetic!' Her words were so fierce he physically drew breath. The ice kept getting thinner and thinner.

'Your *aunt* was pathetic,' he replied quietly. 'Your father was almost as bad, and the worst is that they had no redeeming qualities. I don't remember you being pathetic. I remember a girl who was pushed to the edge of her endurance, but who still managed to be the most fearless rider I have seen and who showed more courage that night standing up to her oppressor than many men who went into battle. Don't let that harpy win by perpetuating her poison in your own mind.'

She brushed her fingertips over her eyelids and then rubbed her eyes like a tired child.

'Thank you. I was right that you are kind. You're clever, too. I won't marry you, but I will talk to the lawyers and see if there is a way to sell you some of the riverfront, which is what you obviously are truly interested in, so you needn't worry that my naïveté will land me with a fortune-hunting husband who will make you suffer like Grandmama did.'

He let this manna from heaven settle in the silence between them.

'You would sell me part of the water rights?' he asked cautiously.

She dropped her hands. Her eyes were red and her lashes stuck together like the spikes on the Bascombe gates, and she looked both very young and very adult.

'None of the land is entailed or obviously I wouldn't be able to inherit. I asked for the estate maps when Grandmama passed and I remember the river has a curve near your land before it branches off into the canal that feeds your fields, so if we split ownership of that portion of the river then you could build a canal from there instead. It would just be another, what, fifty yards? And then neither the Bascombes nor the Hunters would be able to control the flow and river traffic. So if I do marry a nasty fortune hunter, or if I don't marry anyone and eventually my cousin or his children inherit, they wouldn't be able to change anything. Correct?'

It was a perfect solution. Talk about keeping his cake and eating it, too. He would happily pay for such a concession. It wouldn't even be taking advantage of her youth—it was actually a sensible solution. The ongoing squabbling over those rights cost both sides funds and unnecessary anxiety and acrimony.

'That's a very sensible solution,' he said slowly and was rewarded by the same smile she had tossed at him last night after Biggs's sandwich. A mix between satisfaction and the dispensing of well-being. 'I will even happily concede Pluck to you to sweeten the deal. Meanwhile we go down to Wilton, sit down with your father and discuss how we are going to proceed. Agreed?'

'Agreed. I'm very glad you are being so reasonable about this. If I had to become engaged to and unengaged from anyone, I'm glad it was you.'

Hunter burst out laughing and stood up.

'That might be the nicest thing anyone has said to me in a long time, sweetheart, and I happily return the compliment. I will send word to your father and the Welbecks that we will drive down tomorrow.'

'But I can't stay here. Your aunts…'

'Will be delighted. They aren't very fond of society, but they love company. Do we have an accord?' He held his hand out and after a moment's hesitation she stood and held hers out as well.

'Yes.'

Hunter took her hand. It was a little cold and he could feel the calluses at the base of her fingers. Clearly she still rode, even up in her rainy mountains. Her hand warmed in his, the stiffness seeping out of it, but the pliancy that did nothing to mask the strength in her long fingers brought a responsive surge of hunger and a curiosity to see if he could make the rest of her warm and pliant. There was fire here; he was certain of it. She might not be aware of it, but it was there, just waiting for someone to show her precisely what she was capable of.

Not that it was his concern any more, he told himself, holding still as his body rode out a wave of physical awareness. Then he let go of her hand before he spit in the eye of providence and succumbed to the need to do something foolish.

'Come, Miss Tilney. There is something else we would like to show you,' Amelia said with the tone of someone who had come to a decision.

It was already well into the afternoon and Nell was tired but glad the sisters had allowed her to join them on their rounds at Hope House. She had had no idea that so much suffering continued to linger so long after the wars. If it wasn't the ravages of physical and mental damage it was the destitution and lack of employment that faced the men who had returned from the wars, having given their souls for King and Country, only to find that King and Country had made no provisions for their return. At least not alive.

Now Nell followed the sisters into one of the most peculiar rooms Nell had ever seen. It might once have been a library, because two walls were lined with shelves and the other two with framed paintings and drawings and there were chairs and two tables. But unlike the libraries at Mrs Petheridge's schools, there were very few books and the objects on the shelves reminded Nell of the pawnshop in Keswick. There were figurines, mugs, pipes, rolled-up belts, small metal boxes that might have been for snuff, some tinderboxes and a multitude of other objects. She turned, puzzled, to the hanging pictures and there the confusion deepened. These weren't family portraits or the tame landscapes and botanists' prints she was used to either. They were sketches of men, some serious and some caricatures. The landscapes were raw with minimal colour, of mountains, of a village market with a man leaning over a stall piled with fruit, of soldiers by a campfire… She stopped in shock by a small portrait of a handsome young man in an ensign's uniform looking directly at the painter with a smile that was surprisingly sweet. He might have been fifteen or sixteen and she recognised him. She shook her head. No. It looked incredibly like Lord Hunter, but not quite.

'Who is this?' she asked Amelia, who had come to stand behind her. For a moment the sisters were silent. Then it was Seraphina who spoke.

'That is Timothy, Gabriel's younger brother. He was never strong, but he was the sweetest boy you could imagine, full of light. He adored Gabriel most of all, perhaps because Anne, their mother, never fully recovered her health after the birth and because their father was so rarely there.'

'Thankfully!' Amelia added with a dismissive snort.

'He was not a good man,' Seraphina conceded. 'It was always a worry Gabriel might take after him, but though he was so very self-sufficient and has a tendency to be…well… It was quite clear he did not take after his father in any way that mattered.'

'Most certainly not,' Amelia interceded. 'Gabriel had that household in order before he was off leading strings. When we came to stay after Timothy's birth he made it very clear we were welcome but not needed.'

'He was always a trifle high handed,' Sephy conceded. 'But he took such good care of poor Anne and Tim. We would, of course, have preferred that his protective nature towards Tim not manifest itself in terms of violence towards offenders, but he was, after all, a very physical little boy. In others that might have lent itself to disdain of a brother who clearly did not share any of his outdoor interests, but it was quite the opposite. He had more patience for Tim than anyone. Especially those last two years.'

Her voice thickened and she raised a handkerchief to her eyes in a gesture that might have looked theatrical, but just squeezed at Nell's heart.

'Timothy died almost exactly four years ago,' Amelia added and Nell's mind shot back to a memory she hadn't even realised had lingered, of Lord Hunter, his face worn and serious beyond his age as he inspected Petra.

'I'm so sorry,' she said uselessly, but her mind struggled to understand. Four years ago the war had already been over.

'Timothy was taken prisoner and badly wounded in the war,' Amelia replied to the unspoken question. Then she nodded at the wall. 'This is the memory room. Those that come here or work here can bring mementoes of those they lost to war, or even just for themselves. You might think it ghoulish, but I find it is a beautiful room.

It is better to share pain than hug it to yourself. It binds us as surely as love.'

They stood for a moment in silence, absorbing the weight of those present in the room. The immensity of it sank in very slowly and Nell looked around the room again, her own words to Hunter the previous day coming back to her. There was so much about love she had yet to learn. At least she was open to it. She must not give up on that.

'You are right. It *is* beautiful.'

Amelia smiled and took her arm and as they left Nell glanced back at the small portrait in the corner.

Chapter Five

'**M**y dear, you look lovely, quite like one of *La Belle Assemblée*'s prints,' Sephy chirped as Nell entered the parlour the following morning. 'That shade of fawn is particularly becoming with that ivory trim and those blue ribbons.'

Amelia inspected Nell from head to toe and gave a brisk nod.

'Most becoming. I have a weakness for bonnets myself, and the trimming, I see, is particularly fine.'

'It was shockingly expensive,' Nell admitted.

'Quality usually is,' Amelia concurred approvingly and Nell smiled, wondering how she already felt so comfortable with the two vastly different ladies after such a brief stay. Sometimes bonds like that were immediate and inexplicable and it was best not to dissect the whys and wherefores.

'Thank you so much for allowing me to stay with you, especially under such irregular circumstances.'

'My dear, it truly was our pleasure, but please remember not to tell Gabriel about joining us on our rounds. He might be upset that we exposed you to such sights…'

Nell straightened.

'Lord Hunter does not decide what I can or cannot do.' As she saw the worry on Miss Sephy's face she relented. 'I shan't tell him if you don't wish it. But I do hope you will allow me to visit again.'

'Ah, that is no doubt Gabriel now,' Amelia said at the sound of the knocker. 'Do come in, Gabriel. You have arrived just in time to stop our goodbyes from turning maudlin.'

'I am very glad to hear that. The thought of conveying a watering pot to Wilton does not appeal.'

He spoke lightly, the faint smile curving his lips taking the bite out of his words, and she smiled back before she even realised she was doing so. She looked down to the gloves she was pulling on, suddenly shy. She had managed to convince herself over the past day that the unsettling sensations she had experienced in his presence were the result of nerves and weariness rather than anything intrinsic to Lord Hunter. This conviction received a much-needed boost by the excitement that rose in her at the thought that she would soon finally, *finally* see Charles again, a thought which bubbled as happily as water on the boil throughout the day. Therefore it made little sense that her anticipation should stutter and turn as flat as a tarn in midsummer when Lord Hunter entered the parlour.

It wasn't that he was too large and out of place in the frilly room with its embroidered cushions and baskets of darning and wool, but that he actually wasn't. He was completely at his ease as he went to kiss each aunt on the cheek, stepping back to inspect Miss Calthorpe, his hands on her shoulders.

'Aunt Sephy, surely that fetching cap is new? Is that

for my benefit or is some gentleman about to be very lucky?'

Nell watched with amusement as Miss Calthorpe giggled and tapped Lord Hunter playfully on the arm with her knitting needles.

'It is indeed new and you are shameless, Gabriel. What your sainted grandpapa the vicar would say about you I do not know. Off with you now. I know you don't want to keep your precious horses standing.'

'My precious groom is walking them, love. But we should be off so Miss Tilney can arrive there in time to rest before supper. Shall we go, Nell?'

Her friends called her Nell, but somehow in Hunter's deep voice it sound different, gliding down at the end and giving it a foreign ring, something more connected to myth and dusk than to her. She turned to the mirror to make certain her bonnet was straight and for a moment she had a peculiar sensation of seeing a stranger and expected her to move out of the way to reveal the real Nell. She raised her chin and the feeling dissipated.

As they exited the alleyway her attention was caught not by the elegant carriage, but by a perfectly matched team of chestnuts harnessed to a sleek curricle. She moved towards them instinctively, running her hand down the leader's neck.

'Oh, they're beautiful! Where did you acquire them?' she asked in awe, completely forgetting her constraint.

Lord Hunter came to stand behind her. 'They're Irish bred. I bought them from a friend of mine who went to India. Do you like them?'

'They're absolutely perfect. Can I drive them?'

The groom standing at the horse's heads choked and tried to mask it with a cough. He didn't look much like a groom. He was too large, for one thing, and he looked as though he had been in one too many stable brawls, with his broken nose and rough-knuckled bare hands.

'What is your name?' she asked him and the groom's eyes flew to hers with alarm and then darted past her shoulder to Lord Hunter.

'Tell Miss Tilney your name,' Hunter said, his voice low and amused.

'Hidgins, miss.'

'You don't think I can drive this team, Mr Hidgins?'

'It's just Hidgins, miss. And I wouldn't be so bold as to think anything, miss. Would I, sir?'

'I'm not sure you should apply to me to back your word, Hidgins. Miss Tilney is convinced I'm a sadly frippery fellow. Sorry, I believe the term profligate was employed.'

'And overly sensitive,' Nell added. Somehow everything was always easier around horses. 'Obviously I was right if you remember my comments so faithfully. So how would you like a wager, Hidgins?'

The look he sent Lord Hunter went beyond alarm to entreaty. But she had clearly hit a sensitive nerve and she could see the groom's interest awaken.

'A wager, miss?'

'Yes. I will engage to drive this team on the first stage towards Wilton without any aid either from you or Lord Hunter. If I fail I engage to pay you ten guineas…within one month,' she added, conscious of her need to spread out her funds until she met with the Bascombe banker in Basingstoke.

'Ten guineas, miss? A bit steep, don't you think?'

'Not at all, because I shan't lose. Done?'

Lord Hunter cleared his throat.

'I hate to point out the obvious, but these are my horses and neither of you has the right to make any wagers regarding them. So if you don't mind, we should be going.'

'But ten guineas, my lord!' Hidgins practically wailed.

'Surely you're not frightened of being driven by a woman, are you, Lord Hunter?' Nell asked, trying not to show how very, very much she wanted to drive these beautiful animals. 'I presume you could always come to my aid if you see I can't hold them. Or are you worried you might not be able to bring them under control if they bolt with me?'

'Now that was shamelessly transparent, young woman. You must think I am very easy to manipulate. Into the carriage with you.'

Nell sighed and let him lead her towards the carriage. It had been worth a try, but she wasn't surprised. Most men did not like anyone else driving their cattle and certainly not women. It was the one area where she had always appreciated her father's open-mindedness. As long as he judged she was physically strong enough to control a particular horse or team, he had never stopped her from riding or driving anything, and though these chestnuts looked very powerful indeed, she could tell by their stance they were so well trained their power could be directed and checked with skill, not brute strength. Mostly. All she needed was to feel them.

Halfway to the carriage Lord Hunter stopped.

'You can come with me in the curricle as far as Potters Bar.'

She glanced at him in gratitude as he led her back to the curricle. 'And drive your team?'

'Don't push your luck. Up you go.'

She settled in and sighed again as Lord Hunter took the reins and Hidgins jumped onto the perch behind with something very close to a huff.

'Are you both going to sulk all the way to Wilton?' Lord Hunter asked politely as he set the curricle in motion. 'If so, I won't bother trying to make conversation.'

'I am not sulking. I am disappointed,' Nell said with dignity.

'And you don't pay me to sulk, sir,' Hidgins added with equal dignity.

'Very true, Hidgins. Are you comfortable, Miss Tilney? Would you care for a rug?'

'Yes. No. Is this a custom-built curricle? It feels very light on the road even with the two of you in it.'

'Do you hear that, Hidgins? Miss Tilney thinks we are fat.'

Nell glanced over her shoulder at Hidgins with a complicit smile.

'No, no. Large boned. There are benefits to that, like the difference between an Arabian and a cob. Keeps you more firmly on the ground. But I'm not sure I'd like to race with you in the curricle.'

'As the saying goes, no one asked you; and annoying me is not likely to convince me to let you drive my horses.'

'Are you saying there is something I could do that might?' she said hopefully and he glanced at her. There was always a mix of rather cynical amusement and calculation in his honey-brown eyes. As if he knew something that explained the game they were engaged in and was toying with the possibility of letting her in on the secret. It should have intimidated her, but it had precisely the opposite effect. He was like one of Mrs Petheridge's little puzzle boxes. Nell had always been quickest at solving them and now she felt the same as when facing one of those wooden conundrums—confused but tantalised and very much on her mettle. Right now trying to make sense of all the disparate pieces of what she knew of Lord Hunter was stretching her intellect, which only made the pursuit all the more fascinating.

'Perhaps,' he replied lightly, giving nothing away. 'I might ask you to forgo these charming insults for half an hour, but I doubt you could comply.'

'I'll try—really I will.'

He laughed and the heat touched her cheeks again. She was acting like an over-eager child. She should really try to be a little more refined.

'All right,' he conceded. 'Once we clear the worst of town traffic I will let you try. Hidgins, be prepared to abandon ship.'

'Not without my ten guineas, sir.'

'Who's being insulting now? How far is Piccadilly?' she asked.

'Just coming up. I hope you will be more patient with my horses than you are with me, Miss Tilney.'

'I'm always patient with horses. Is this Piccadilly? What chaos.'

'It is and I hope it makes you appreciate my decision to wait until we are out of this chaos to let you drive.'

She nearly responded to this provocation when she remembered her pledge.

'It is very gallant of you, my lord.'

He guided his horses around a top-heavy wagon.

'I think I prefer your insults. They are more sincere.'

She glanced at him, unsure of his tone, but at Hidgins's snicker behind them she relaxed. She was always so much more comfortable with people when around horses. Perhaps because they didn't judge or condemn. They just were and so she could also just be.

'Very well. Hidgins, remind me that I knowingly took my life in my hands if we end up overturned in a ditch. *Mademoiselle*, your reins and whip.'

She didn't bother answering. Horses with mouths this fine would sense the change in driver immediately and their reaction could be unpredictable. She had been watching Lord Hunter's driving carefully and appreciatively and she could tell she would have her work cut out for her. It wasn't just her anticipation of driving a wonderful team of horses, but the need to prove herself to these two men.

The horses were well behaved in the city, but were clearly used to fast driving, and the moment they had cleared the worst of the traffic they lengthened their stride, eager to pick up pace. It would take both skill and strength to convince them to respect their new driver. She could tell the wheeler would be difficult and almost immediately he proved her right, his stride becoming uneven. She gave him a very light flick of the whip and caught it again about the base and with a shake of his mane he fell back into pace. Out of the corner of her eye she had seen Lord Hunter reach forward, but he sat back and she kept her attention on the horses. After a few miles she had their measure and they had hers and she started enjoying herself. The roads were good and not too crowded and she even had the opportunity to execute a very nice pass by a lumbering coach that tested her passengers' nerves, looping a rein and letting it slide free. Once past she grinned at Lord Hunter and he shook his head ruefully.

'Keep your eyes on the road. You can gloat later. Thankfully we've almost reached Potters Bar.'

'Sorry. I didn't mean to scare you.'

'I thought you promised no more insults.'

'That was an apology, Lord Hunter.'

'We clearly have different understandings of the term. Here, take the right side of that fork.'

As they approached Potters Bar she reluctantly handed the reins over, still full of the pleasure of driving such beautiful cattle. Then she sat back with a sigh and turned to Hidgins.

'I won't say I'm sorry about winning, Hidgins.'

'I won't say so neither, miss. It was a right pleasure to be driven by someone with such light hands.'

'*Et tu*, Hidgins?' Lord Hunter demanded. 'Is there prize money out there for taking me down a peg?'

'Eh, sir? I weren't talking about you.'

'That's even worse, man!'

Nell laughed, amused by the unusual camaraderie between the two men, but then there was something about Lord Hunter that invited informality. He didn't appear to take himself—or anyone else, for that matter—too seriously. Perhaps that was why she had been comfortable with him all those years ago. And now. Up to a point. Because there was also that watchfulness that stood back from the world and the distant memory of his eyes sunken with strain until he had smiled. She shouldn't presume to know this man because he was choosing to be kind for the moment. She knew better than to relax her guard, especially not when so much was at stake.

He turned into the cobbled courtyard of the White

Hart posting inn and two ostlers in smocks immediately ran forward.

'Here we are, and thank goodness. I don't think my vanity could take much more abuse. That is not an invitation, Miss Tilney,' he added quickly as she opened her mouth. She laughed again.

'I was merely going to thank you for allowing me to drive your beautiful horses, Lord Hunter.'

'I should have known you would find a way to put me in the wrong again.' He sighed and jumped down from the curricle.

Nell scooted over to where he was waiting to help her descend, holding down firmly on a smile. She jumped lightly to the gravel drive, inspecting the bustling courtyard. It took her a moment to realise Lord Hunter was still holding her hand and a flush of warmth, like embarrassment, spread up her arm, tingling in her chest and cheeks. The urge to pull back to safety was so strong and so distinct from the heady feeling of freedom she had experienced during the drive that she forcibly resisted it and looked up to meet his eyes.

It wasn't just the impression that he was enjoying some private joke that struck her, but a considering look that found an immediate answering chord in her, a warmth that was deepening into heat as he assessed her. She wasn't used to men looking at her like that and she had no idea what to do with the tingling that was spreading through her like a rash, making her very aware of her skin, of the tightness of her pelisse, even of the uneven cobblestones under her feet. Then he turned away and she was released.

She had been right. He was not to be trusted.

Once inside he led her into a private parlour at the

back and through the mullioned windows Nell caught the view of a garden rich with flowering bushes and beyond it a glimpse of a stream lined with weeping willows.

'What a lovely garden,' she said and immediately regretted it. The look of slight surprise on Lord Hunter's face indicated one did not normally gush about the ambience at posting houses.

'Why, thank you, miss,' said a deep voice behind them. 'The garden's my wife's pride and she's always pleased to have her labour appreciated. Good morning, Lord Hunter. Some of the house best for you and some lemonade for the lady.'

The burly innkeeper placed a tray on the table and rubbed his hands on his apron.

'That's perfect. Thank you, Caffrey.'

'Do you know him?' Nell asked curiously once he left.

'I know most innkeepers on the posting roads,' Lord Hunter answered casually. 'It's useful.'

'For what?'

He pushed her glass of lemonade towards her.

'Are you always this inquisitive?' he asked and the sting of the implied criticism sent an inevitable flush of heat up her throat and cheeks.

'For racing,' he said and she looked up. He was regarding her thoughtfully. 'In answer to your question, and at risk of providing more grist for your critical mill, during my *profligate* youth I accepted any and all wagers for curricle races and Caffrey here was well recompensed by us flighty youths to turn our teams around with all speed and efficiency. Not to mention that he won quite a bit on the back of my successes and he never begrudged me my losses. Gambling builds bonds between men…and women, for that matter.'

Nell cradled her lemonade. She didn't know whether to be grateful for his attempt to smooth over the uncomfortable moment or annoyed that he saw through her so easily.

'Do women also gamble on curricle races, then?'

'Not in public, or at least not respectable women.'

'Sometimes I truly wish I wasn't.'

'That's because you haven't seen the other side of the equation. Believe me, not being respectable is no guarantee of a happy life.'

He would know, too, she thought with sudden rancour.

'Nothing is a guarantee of a happy life. I would settle for an interesting one.'

'I seem to recall you said you enjoyed the school you attended. Weren't you happy there?'

Had she said anything about the school? Perhaps she had, but she was surprised he would remember any details of that meeting years ago. That was rather bad luck because it probably meant he remembered her horrific behaviour during that dinner. People tend to remember the bad more than the good.

She sighed.

'I am very, very happy there and truly I have nothing to complain about. I know how lucky I am. Which is precisely why I want to go back there once everything is arranged at Bascombe.'

'You want to go back? To school? Aren't you a little old for that?'

'Not to study. Though I suppose one is never too old to study. It is like trying to empty an ocean with a teaspoon; there is always so much more to know. But, no, I teach.'

'You teach. I understood you were just boarding with your schoolmistress and that she has been paid handsomely for keeping you. Do you mean to say she has made you work?'

There was a sharp bite in his voice and it raised her own inner temperature. It felt very much like her father had been reporting on her to this man, as though she was an investment.

'She did not *make* me work. What on earth would I do there year-round? Stare at the walls? Or course I worked. If you must know, I am not only a teacher, but I have invested my pay and part of my allowance in the school and I am now a partner...'

The gold in his eyes darkened into amber.

'I see. She took your fees, your allowance, your salary and your labour and gave you an alleged share in a girls' school in the wilds of the Lake District. A very enterprising schoolmistress. There surely is a great deal to learn from her.'

Nell stared at the transformation from the easy-going rake to this man who looked as though he was about to pounce across the table and rip someone's head from their shoulders. As always, just watching anger gather was emptying her from the inside, draining her enjoyment of the ride, the horses, the freeing informality of his company. The only difference was that she was watching it happen, watching herself like a timid wren perched on the windowsill. She could almost see the colour fade from her face and lips; could see inside herself to the sand grating under her skin.

He must have also marked the change and he reached towards her across the table.

'Never mind. It's none of my business, Nell.'

But it was too late. The wren had breathed in, filled, and was fast transforming into whatever avian species strongly disliked having their nest threatened. It was one thing to poke fun at her, but the way he had spoken of Mrs Petheridge…as if he knew her, which he didn't. He had no right! She could feel the heat in her cheeks; it still grated, but this grating felt good. It felt like talons ready to rip into something soft and yielding. It felt *powerful*.

'You just know *everything*, don't you!' she interrupted, surging to her feet, bumping the table and sending lemonade sloshing onto the tablecloth. 'Let's just assume Nell is a naïve little girl who people can order about as they see fit. Well, I will not sit here while you make facile assumptions about me and the people I love. If this outrage is because you are worried I have frittered away what you very prematurely presume to be your property, let me tell you that I meant what I said— I have no intention of marrying you and I have, in fact, already made a substantial profit when we sold one of our properties to the Blaketon School for Boys. If you ever insult Mrs Petheridge again, who was the first person since my mother who actually *loved* me, I will…'

She groped futilely for a retribution sufficient to the offence.

'I'm going to see if the horses are rested. And I don't want any more lemonade!'

She stopped before she further ruined the grand effect of her tantrum. She wished he had yelled back because the way she felt now she just might have yelled some more herself, but he just sat there, looking at her with a strange look of concentration on his face, as if trying to understand a voluble foreigner. It wasn't quite as rewarding as she had hoped a tantrum would be. She turned towards the door but he reached it before her and started opening it. He didn't speak and his eyes were downcast, but in the firmly held line of his mouth she caught the faintest quiver and a different kind of outrage slammed through her.

'Are you *laughing* at me?' she demanded, her voice rising further.

He surprised her by closing the door again and leaning back against it. There was definitely laughter in his eyes and she began to flounder, desperately trying to cling to the firm boulder of her outrage as something stronger was doing its best to knock her off it and into a fast-moving current.

'Only at myself. Just telling myself to remember this when I am next struck by one of my now-rare chivalric impulses. My only defence is that I did mean it for the best. Forgive me?'

Her boulder turned out to be a soap bubble and it burst and she sank into the current. She tried not to, because although she wasn't used to cajolery as a means of getting her to yield, she still knew it for what it was. This was what this man did. He could charm an innkeeper and a groom just as he had once charmed a frightened and lonely girl, and now an angry and nervous young woman. She took a step back, finding the safety of the shallows, but still very aware of the current tugging at her.

'Of course. We should be on our way.'

She shouldn't have sounded so grudging because clearly he wanted more from her. He reached out and raised her chin, and she forced herself to meet his gaze, hoping she looked both forgiving and unaffected, whatever that looked like. There was a challenge in his eyes and even in the shift of his thumb on the slight cleft in her chin. Then it rose to briefly skim the scar below her lip and once again the rush of inner heat pulled at her, towards him, and she almost turned her head to catch the slide of his finger with her mouth when he dropped his hand and turned to open the door.

Hunter had had every intention of putting her in the carriage for the second part of the journey. But though the carriage had arrived he led her past it to the curricle where Hidgins waited, ignoring her surprised look and his own mixed feelings about subjecting himself voluntarily to another stretch of her less-than-complimentary comments and this increasingly uncomfortable physical urge to cross the line into her private domain. He was used to flirting, but only with women who knew the rules of the game where it was an equal exchange. Here he was crossing a strict line in the sand as if it was merely a polite suggestion. If he wasn't careful the next thing he would be doing was giving in to this foolish urge to kiss her and he would likely end up with a boxed ear or, worse, more firmly engaged than ever.

For the first few minutes of the drive the discussion was distinctly stilted until Hidgins broke the awkwardness by telling Lord Hunter he had met Lord Meecham's groom in the stables and had a good chat about that time they raced to Brighton overnight.

'Ah, those were the days.' The groom sighed gustily.

'You moaned the whole way,' Hunter reminded him curtly. He wasn't in the mood for Hidgins's attack of nostalgia. He didn't know what he was in the mood for at the moment. Or if he did, it wasn't likely to be realised. It was his fault for trying to soothe the chit when she had turned into a spitting kitten and her fault for shifting from one mood to another with a mercurial agility that would have done the most temperamental of his mistresses proud. She had surprised him in there, flying to her schoolmistress's defence as if he was bent on rape and pillage when all he had been thinking of was her own good. She clearly didn't want or need his protection, which was fine with him.

For once Hidgins didn't take the hint.

'It was December! It *rained* the whole way!'

'Oh, the poor horses! They must have been quite frozen through!' Nell said and Hunter tried to resist the way his muscles relaxed at this sign that she had obviously calmed down. It was one of his iron rules not to let women's moods rule his, but he was letting this woman...this almost-schoolgirl, he corrected...do just that.

'You needn't worry. The punch thawed them out quite nicely once we made it to Brighton.'

'You give your horses *punch*?'

'Don't you?'

Her outrage transformed into a delighted smile in another shift that caught him off guard.

'Oh, I actually believed you for a moment. Though I suppose if someone had placed a wager on it you might have done so.'

'You wrong me. There are some things I don't wager on, the welfare of my horses being one of them.'

'And what else?'

He glanced at her for a moment. All the haughty fury had flown and she now merely looked as curious as a schoolteacher's dream pupil and he had no idea why that should be just as unsettling as her surprising show of temper and why he actually felt he should be careful what he told her. This was no schoolgirl, however inexperienced. She was actually trying to catalogue and analyse him and he was damned if he was going to be the object of whatever academic exercise she was engaged in.

'What else what?' he temporised.

'What else won't you wager on?'

'What I consider to be certainties, like the probability that you will find some new and creative way of insulting me again before we reach Welbeck.'

'But I have never insulted you.'

'Quite right. It is just that I am sensitive—I forgot. Hidgins remarks on it all the time, don't you, Hidgins?'

'That I do, sir. It's a fair shame the way I have to tippy-toe around him, miss.'

Nell laughed.

'I promise I shall do the same for the rest of the drive. Especially if you let me drive again,' she added, her voice rising hopefully.

'After the next toll you can take the ribbons. For a stretch.'

As before she glanced quickly back at Hidgins with a complicit smile and Hunter didn't have to see his groom's face to know he was grinning. He relaxed, but kept his own smile at bay. She was actually right; he was being far too sensitive. There was no call for this instinctive need to repel her curiosity. Her inquisitiveness and over-sharp wit were just the signs of a young woman let out for the first time from a confining environment and eager to explore the world. There was no reason to let it unbalance him. He should remain focused on his objective of easing out of this engagement as smoothly and painlessly as possible, and for that he needed her co-operation and her trust.

Chapter Six

Welbeck Manor was a sprawling Tudor structure which each generation but the last two had added to with a great deal of vigour and very little architectural grace. It had been four years since Nell's last trip to Wilton, but the tingle of happiness as they crested the rise was wonderfully familiar. She sighed as the curricle rolled up the wide drive and the view of the house disappeared behind a clump of old oak. Before the fiasco of the betrothal she had fantasised about meeting Charles dressed in her new finery and, if not dazzling him, at least showing him that she, too, had attractions worthy of being considered, even if they were primarily pecuniary. But now she was arriving at Welbeck an engaged woman in the eyes of the world. Engaged to a handsome, charming man who by all accounts made Charles's mild flirtations look monklike by comparison.

She glanced at the striking profile of the man beside her. She had no doubt if she were to tell him what was going through her head those brown-gold eyes would fill with contempt. He might be easy-going on the surface, but with every light-hearted comment she heard the echo of another thought, something firmly with-held. She didn't know whether there was ruthlessness or pain there, but whatever the case, that side of him would probably have no sympathy for her childish dreams. He would certainly be contemptuous of her plan to pay for a bridegroom. If only Charles could come to see her as a woman. Maybe even as a desirable one...

Impulsively she placed her hand on Hunter's arm.

'Could you stop, just for a moment? There is some-thing I would like to ask you before we arrive.'

Hunter checked his horses and with a quick nod Hidgins went to stand at the horses' heads.

'Well? Cold feet?' Hunter asked with a quirk of his mouth, but his eyes held the same considering look she had seen before.

'Not precisely. I have a favour to ask. I was wonder-ing if you would... If when we arrive at Welbeck... Oh, this is difficult!'

'Come, it can't be that bad. Out with it. What would you like me to do?'

'Flirt with me.' As his brows drew together she hur-ried on. 'Just a little. I mean I know we aren't really en-gaged, but everyone will think we are and I don't want them to think...'

She rubbed her hand to her forehead, trying to chase away her discomfort.

'Look at me.'

His voice was calm, but there was an edge to it and there was no amusement in his eyes now.

'I would have thought that such a request goes against your plan of calling a halt to the engagement. Unless you have another reason...'

He trailed off as the blush that had started in her chest

flowed upwards like lava escaping Vesuvius. Still, she tried to sustain his gaze. She had foreseen contempt and it came.

'I see. The real reason why you wanted to come to Wilton,' he drawled. 'So, I am to earn my keep this week.'

She looked down, feeling childish and strangely hollow.

'You don't have to. I just thought…'

'It is quite clear what you thought, sweetheart. Very well. It's no hardship on my part. As long as we keep to our agreement, never let it be said I don't provide value for money. Now we should move on. Hidgins!'

Hidgins hurried back to his perch and they drew forward. Nell felt her anticipation dim. She hadn't meant to insult him and she wasn't precisely certain how she had done so.

They drew up in front of the house and she kept her eyes down as he dismounted and came to help her down. She started towards the steps, but he moved to block her path, raising her chin so that she was forced to look up. The contempt wasn't there any more, just that serious look.

'I'm sorry. You trod on my vanity and I reacted badly. You surprised me again, that's all. Forgive me?'

A weight slipped from her shoulders.

'It *was* foolish of me,' she answered quickly. 'Of course you needn't…'

'I shall flirt with you with great pleasure.' He surprised her by smiling and the relief was so strong she couldn't help laughing.

'If it isn't young Nell! And, Hunter, good to see you again, man. Welcome, welcome.'

They both turned towards the stairs as two men approached and Nell stiffened. She would have much preferred her first meeting with Charles to be in one of her new dresses rather than in an outfit dusty from the long drive. She turned instead towards the portly man who approached them, his hand extended in greeting.

'Good afternoon, Lord Welbeck, Mr Welbeck.' Her voice wavered on the last and she raised her chin.

Lord Welbeck grasped her hand between his own, shaking it vigorously as he addressed Hunter.

'M'wife received your note about Nell here. Glad to have her. Congratulations all around, eh? Tilney already told us the news when we met him at Tattersall's last week before he hared off north.'

'Tilney isn't here?' Hunter asked.

'Heard a tip that Buxted is rolled up and selling off his stables, so off he goes to steal a march on the market. Wouldn't have minded doing so myself, but the dibs aren't in tune just at the moment, eh, Charles?'

'You couldn't very well disappear now just as the fair is set to start, Father.' Charles smiled at Nell and held out his hand invitingly. After a second's hesitation Nell held out her hand as well and he grasped it.

'Hello, Miss Tilney. Your father did say he means to join us here when he closes with Buxted, so of course you must stay until he does. Mother is delighted to have another female guest to commiserate with. Congratulations, by the way,' he added, his eyes sliding momentarily towards Hunter.

'That's right,' Lord Welbeck continued. 'Fine work, eh? We didn't even know the Bascombe land was to come to you, lass, or I'd have made a push to snabble you for my boy. Your father kept that card mightily close to his chest, didn't he, eh? Well, I'm particularly glad you've come, gel. There's this new filly I could use some help with and you might be just the one to do the trick. Lovely legs, but won't let anyone near her. She's in the far paddock. Have a look at her first thing and let me know if there's a point in keeping her, will you? Well, I'm off to the stables to see all's ready for the week. Say your hellos, Charles, and join me when you're done.'

He strode away with a buoyancy that was in stark contrast to his weight, leaving them to sort themselves out. Nell detached her hand from Charles's a little reluctantly. There was a moment of awkward silence and then Charles turned towards the curricle.

'Are these your famous matched chestnuts, Lord Hunter? Beautiful beasts.'

Nell stood back as the two men turned, glad for a moment to recover. Charles was bending down to inspect one of the horses, his golden hair catching the afternoon sun already scraping the treetops to the west. In a second she was cast back years ago to a moment in the Welbeck stables when she had seen him very much like this, his attention on one of the mares, painfully handsome and wholly oblivious of her.

She looked away and met Hunter's eyes. She had no idea what he had seen on her face and how he connected that with her wholly regretted request, but she rather feared he saw right through her. For a moment there was a hard, contemptuous light in his eyes that sobered her, like the burst of cold air after stepping out of a warm house. Then the butler appeared in the doorway and everything moved again. Nell followed the butler up the wide stairway with a strange sense of fatality, like a prisoner being led before a judge and jury. It was fanciful, but she felt the course of her life would be decided between these walls, in this week, and she hoped she had the strength of character to be an author of that future, not just its subject.

Chapter Seven

‘Miss Tilney, wait...’

Nell’s heart hitched and she stopped halfway down the stairs. There was never much light in the low-roofed corridors of Welbeck Manor and as Charles descended the stairs towards her his face was cast in shadows, only his smile glinting brightly.

‘Has it really been four whole years since we saw each other last? I am sorry about your grandparents’ passing, by the way.’

He stopped on the step above her, giving him some extra inches and making her feel, for a change, almost normal. Except for her thudding pulse and the heat in her cheeks which she hoped the gloomy light masked.

‘Thank you, Mr Welbeck. But since I never met them I hardly mourn them.’

She moaned inwardly. She hadn’t meant to be so blunt. He blinked and his smile wavered, but returned.

‘Well, whatever the case, I am glad you came this year. That is quite a piece of news, your engagement. Congratulations.’

‘Thank you. We are very happy.’

Oh, help, what an inane thing to say. She didn't know whether to revel in the fact that Charles was actually talking to her like an adult or to wish someone would come and relieve her of her embarrassment. No, it was now or never if she meant to impress upon him that she was indeed an adult. And a woman.

'Lord Hunter can be very…persuasive.' She smiled, trying to invest the word with all manner of meaning, and Charles's affable smile stiffened.

'Yes, I've heard that about him.'

There was no mistaking the undercurrent in those words. What would an experienced woman do? Nell thought. Anna would probably turn up her nose and march off, but that didn't suit Nell. Besides, any reaction other than amused condescension was good, wasn't it? She wasn't fool enough to believe Charles might be jealous, but perhaps he wasn't indifferent to her engagement. Or perhaps he just didn't like Hunter. That, too, was highly possible. She imagined Hunter rubbed many people the wrong way. Before she could think of an answer he smiled.

'Now, that was uncalled for, wasn't it? If you like him I'm sure he's a capital fellow. Forgive me?'

'Of course, Charles… I mean, Mr Welbeck.'

'If memory serves me right, we called each other Charles and Nell since before you put up your hair. I think we can dispense with such foolish proprieties, don't you?'

She smiled, warming from the inside out.

'Of course. Charles.'

'Oh. Good evening, Mr Welbeck.'

They both turned as a husky voice slid down the stairs. Nell wouldn't have been surprised if the woman's appearance was accompanied by trumpets and the strewing of petals—even in the gloom her beauty glowed. In colouring she was Charles's twin, with golden hair and sky-blue eyes, as if she had been created to stand by his side in the illustration for a fairy tale. She descended with leisurely grace, her eyes smiling into Charles's. She came to stop just a step above them and her tongue briefly caressed her lower lip in a gesture Nell had never seen before, but which must be universal because if ever there was an invitation, this woman was extending one to Charles.

The woman finally descended the last step, increasing Nell's agony. She was beautiful and perfectly rounded, her bodice cut as low as decency allowed, and worst of all, she was tiny, accentuating how awkward Nell's inches made her. Charles's mild gallantry towards her just a moment ago, which had filled her with such hope, just deepened her despair. As long as a woman like this wanted Charles, what chance had she?

'Won't you introduce me to your friend, Mr Welbeck?' the vision said and the prompt just made it worse. Charles introduced her as Lady Melkinson and somehow Nell answered, aware she was being as gauche as a child, and they moved towards the drawing room. Inside she scanned the room for Hunter, but he was nowhere to be seen and so she mutely moved towards the corner where Lord and Lady Welbeck stood speaking with Lord Meecham, feeling lost and hopeless.

Hunter entered the drawing room, stifling a resigned sigh. In past years he had avoided most evening events at Welbeck, preferring the conviviality of the horse breeders at the local inns to the stuffiness of the Welbeck drawing rooms. His reputation as one of the Wild Hunt Club always made respectable hostesses somewhat wary of his presence in their drawing rooms anyway. But with Tilney absent he couldn't disappear and leave Nell to cope alone, though judging by her strange request and by her blush when they had arrived, she might be glad to have the opportunity to spend this time with young Welbeck.

It was hardly surprising such a sheltered girl would fancy herself in love with a young man who looked like a storybook hero, and though he doubted Welbeck would fulfil any of the criteria she had championed so hotly, that wasn't his concern. What was his concern was that from his experience of the extravagancies of the Welbeck stables they would be only too happy to grab Nell's inheritance and were unlikely to honour her generous offer regarding the water rights. In fact, he didn't particularly want the Welbecks laying waste to Bascombe simply to feed the bottomless pit of their stables. She wanted to flirt? He had no problem with that. He might even enjoy it and Nell might come to realise she had better things to do with her life than moon over a fundamentally weak vessel like Charles Welbeck.

He scanned the room in search of her and his gaze paused on the woman standing in the centre of the room. It had been quite a few years since Lady Melkinson had tried to add him to her impressive list of wealthy lovers, but she hadn't changed much and was still doing her best to command male attention. Almost every man in the room was at least partly focused on her décolletage as she leaned to inspect a flower arrangement, holding the pose just long enough for conversation around her to sink and fade.

'Oh, aren't they lovely?' she asked no one in particular. There was a rumble of shared assent among the men, though no one was looking at the flowers, and Hunter had a hard time holding back a laugh. Then she held out her hand to her husband, but her eyes briefly caught and held Charles Welbeck's and Hunter's mood brightened. Well, well, apparently Nell's shining prince was otherwise engaged. What a pity Nell hadn't seen that telling meeting of eyes.

Hunter scanned the room again, wondering why Nell hadn't appeared yet, when he noticed her, half-obscured by Lord and Lady Welbeck and watching Lady Melkinson with an expression as telling as the act put on by the lady herself, though less intentional. She was pressed against the wall, using her hosts' impressive bulk as a shield. Someone smaller might get away with the wall-flower manoeuvre, but in her case it was a futile effort. Against the dark old wood and in her long silvery dress she looked as dramatic as Lady Melkinson, but from a very different kind of play. Not a rococo farce with frills and tossed-up skirts in the rose garden, but a Saxon princess about to be bartered to an enemy tribe. Someone predatory like Lady Melkinson could have made mincemeat of a rival's petite plumpness if she had possessed Nell's attributes, but it was becoming clear Nell was completely unaware of her charms. He was tempted to show her she had no reason whatsoever to be envious of someone like Phyllida Melkinson, but that lesson wasn't his to give.

Hunter moved towards her and when she saw him her face relaxed into a smile. Clearly she already regarded him as a safe haven, which was a good sign. He never flirted with marriageable misses, but in this case there was no harm in fulfilling his part of the bargain—since her affections were firmly focused on Welbeck she wasn't at risk of taking his attentions seriously and she could probably use a boost of confidence. When he reached her he took her hand as he let his gaze move over her, taking his time.

'It's quite lucky you taught in a girls' school. I can't imagine any boys being able to concentrate on their declensions with you by the blackboard.'

She flushed a little at his examination, but her eyes lit with amusement, dispelling the tragic Saxon. She twitched her skirt, setting off a silvery wave on the gauzy overskirt.

'It's not me—it's the dress. It was shockingly expensive, but Mrs Sturges insisted. She has very strong ideas about fashion.'

'And about gossip, if I remember correctly. But it is unfair to blame the dress; the culprit is most definitely you, sweetheart. Do you mean to tell me there are no mirrors in a girls' school?'

'Not many, but Mrs Sturges has two full-length mirrors in her room set so you can see yourself fore and aft, as she says. She made me exhibit all the dresses as soon as they were delivered. It was excruciatingly embarrassing, but she was so excited I couldn't say no.'

'And to think I missed it. I might have to request a private viewing.' He dropped his voice, watching her closely. She hadn't even appeared to notice he still held her gloved hand and was gently caressing her palm with his thumb. Standing this close to her also made it clear there were distinct advantages to tall women. She would fit against him so easily and all it would take was a gentle lift of her very determined chin… He gave in to the urge to just touch it lightly and finally an edge of awareness entered her silvery eyes.

'There is a perfectly serviceable full-length mirror in my room,' he observed softly.

Her breath caught and a gentle flush warmed her full lips to a soft peach colour. He watched it, fascinated by this quite unique and very appealing transformation; then he looked up and met her eyes and was surprised to see that they were brimming with laughter.

'I think I might actually enjoy this,' she half-whispered.

'What?' he asked, confused.

'Flirting. I think I'm starting to understand how it works.'

A slap might have been more painful, but no more sobering. For a moment he had actually forgotten what he was doing this for.

'That's good. Feel free to experiment. Despite my name, I don't mind being hunted.'

'I'm not sure how. I don't think I could ever do what Lady Melkinson does.'

He caught the hopelessness in her voice.

'You won't know until you try,' he said lightly and this time her eyes were assessing. Then she half-lowered her long lashes so that the silver irises glimmered through them.

'Like this?' she asked huskily, leaning towards him, the tips of her fingers just making contact with the sleeve of his coat. Then her lips parted and the tip of her tongue touched her lower lip, drawing it in gently and letting it go. As far as seductions went it was very mild, as hesitant as a girl dressing in her mother's finery. There was no reason it should have felt like the blood was reversing course in his veins.

'A very good start,' he managed and was rewarded with another smile.

'I'm not the only one working on my flirting. Betsy, the maid, is already quite sweet on Hidgins. You should warn him he is a marked man.'

'She told you that?' he asked, surprised.

'Well, they used to assign her to me when I came as a child, so she and I know each other quite well and she tells me things. I was even thinking of asking Lord Welbeck if I might take her to Bascombe when I leave. I will need a personal maid.'

'You're still determined to live there on your own?'

'Of course. I've already written to ask Mrs Calvert to come to Bascombe. She is lovely, rather like your aunts.'

'There is no one quite like my aunts. I don't know how comfortable someone like Sephy would be for a young woman living on her own. Every time I come to dine she remembers she is a parson's daughter. Serving up the late Reverend Calthorpe's views on my unlikely prospects for redemption with the syllabub tends to wreak havoc with the digestion. I suggest that if you must employ a companion, find someone who teaches progressive topics such as geology or biology, perhaps with a particular interest in crustaceans.'

'I hate syllabub anyway, but sermons will definitely be banned from the supper table. As would be any discourse on crustaceans. Mrs Calvert taught music.'

'Will I still be welcome to visit you once you are settled at Bascombe? Or are we to play this along tragic lines of jilted lovers, smiting brows and scowling darkly when chance meetings occur.'

Her laugh, tumbling but quickly checked, made him want to shake it free, just as he wouldn't mind seeing her silky hair shake free again as it had four years ago.

'Of course you will be welcome! You must come and give me advice on my stables and of course you will come when you bring me Pluck.'

'Ah, I see you won't forget that offer.'

'Are you reneging?' she challenged, raising one brow at him in an impressive golden-brown arc.

'I never break my word. If I can help it. Giving you Pluck will give me even more reason to visit because Petra is certain to miss her.'

Her expression shifted so rapidly it was almost comical.

'I hadn't thought... Perhaps it isn't a good idea after all.'

He took her hand and gave it a little squeeze, touched by her concern. Mother–daughter relations were obviously a sensitive point for her.

'Nonsense. They will both be fine. We can do it gradually if you like.'

She nodded in relief.

'Yes, that will be best.'

'You know, it just might be that Pluck will miss me more than she will Petra. I have a way with mares,' he mused and she laughed. He caught her hand as it rose to block the laugh.

'Why do you do that? You have a beautiful laugh.'

She shook her head, her eyes catching on his with a flash of fear. Then she shook her head again and her eyes cleared.

'It is silly, isn't it? Anna makes fun of me for doing that. Not in a bad way, I mean. My aunt always said laughing aloud was ill bred, and so if I ever found my-self laughing when she was about, which wasn't often, I would hide it. I still do it when I'm nervous.'

'I see. So I make you nervous?'

She tilted her head to one side, considering him.

'Actually, no. Which is strange. I should be more ner-vous around you than around anyone else here prac-tically. Perhaps it is because you don't take yourself seriously.'

'I beg your pardon. I take myself very seriously.'

Her smile returned, sunny and intimate, and he re-alised it *was* strange that she was treating him with such friendly ease on such a short acquaintance. Especially someone as sensitive as she.

'No, you don't,' she said easily. 'I think the list of things you take seriously is very short, but perhaps you regard those things as very particularly serious so that might atone for the rest. Oh, dear, that sounds very pa-tronising, doesn't it? I didn't mean it like that. It's just to say that I'm glad you decided to let me come to Wilton with you. I'm usually quite nervous the first day here until I settle in. It's different having you here.'

Hunter took a moment to work through his reaction to her casual but rather brutal dissection of his character. In anyone else he would swiftly discourage the freedoms she was taking, but beyond a reflexive rejection of any-one's attempts to come too close, he really didn't mind her less-than-complimentary observations.

'You know the Welbecks and you must know some of the other regular guests as well. It's rather strange that you would need someone who is essentially a stranger in order to feel comfortable.'

If he had been fishing for compliments at the expense of the Welbecks, he came up empty.

'Well, ordinarily after the first day I do begin enjoying myself, but I promise I won't drop your acquaintance when that happens.'

For a moment he nearly took her seriously, she looked so sincere.

'Do you know,' he said slowly, assessing her, 'you may not have much experience flirting, but you certainly know how to tease.'

This time she laughed openly and Hunter noted, and not completely with satisfaction, that as many eyes strayed to her as had followed Lady Melkinson's manoeuvre. The main difference was that his betrothed clearly neither expected nor noticed the attention. One of those observers headed towards them and Nell's smile wavered.

'Hello, Charles.'

'Hullo, Nell. You look like a princess in that dress.'

Hunter watched in disgust as Nell blushed.

'Meecham has agreed to let me take his bays for a turn tomorrow,' Charles continued. 'Will you come with me? That is, if Lord Hunter doesn't mind?'

'I'd love to.' Nell nodded. 'And of course he won't mind, would you?'

'Not at all,' Hunter lied.

'Perhaps we might even organise a friendly race with your team.' Charles smiled, clearly extending an olive branch.

'I think that would be up to Meecham,' Hunter replied and Charles's cheeks reddened at the rebuke, but the boyish smile held.

'Obviously. Just getting ahead of myself. Well, there's

Mama come to herd us into dinner. You're sitting next to me, Nell, so you can tell me everything you have been doing these past four years.'

Hunter hoped that the Welbecks' ploy in seating her next to Charles was as obvious to her as it was to him, but by the glow in her eyes he doubted it.

After dinner the men remained to savour their port and cheroots, but as soon as they joined the women in the drawing room Hunter watched as both Charles and the young man who had been seated on her other side during dinner headed towards the sofa where Nell was seated next to Lady Welbeck by the windows opening to the veranda. The evening was unseasonably warm and a set of long doors at the end of the drawing room had been opened and the lawn and gardens lit with hanging lanterns so the guests could stretch their legs and digest their meal.

Hunter was tired and he was tempted to leave her to her little victory, but when the two men fell into a laughing rivalry over who would take Nell for a turn around the gardens, Hunter's patience faded and he moved towards them. There was a limit to the leeway he was willing to grant her—having his betrothed, real or not, make a laughing stock of him by wandering a darkened garden with another man was just such a limit.

'I believe in such cases the third option is often considered the least controversial.'

'Are you willing to come in third? That isn't what one hears of the members of the Wild Hunt Club,' Nell said daringly, her shining look still very much in evidence, and his resentment faded. She looked very different from the timid girl he had seen when he first entered the drawing room that evening.

'In this case the prize for third is well worth throwing the race.'

She laughed and shook her head, but gave him her hand with an apologetic smile to the other men.

'Don't forget we are to go driving tomorrow morning, Nell,' Charles tossed in with a smile that had lost some of its exuberance.

'Now that your morning is so pleasantly accounted for, you are free to dedicate the rest of your evening to me,' Hunter said, holding her gaze, and she pressed her full lips together like a child trying not to laugh. Behind her he spotted Charles Welbeck already moving towards Lady Melkinson, her coral-pink dress and gold curls glinting in the crowd like a tropical fish strayed into a village pond. He didn't want Nell to have any illusions about Welbeck, but neither was he anxious to see her smile extinguished, so he guided her towards the terrace. Outside a large group of the younger guests were already gathering, the men laughing and the women flirting with their fans, and he led Nell down the lantern-lit path to a spot where they were caught in the shaded darkness of a yew hedge. He knew he shouldn't risk their absence being noted, but he could use a moment of quiet.

She didn't speak, just waited with a look he was becoming very familiar with. Direct, curious and making it very clear that though she might be cowed in certain circumstances, there was an inner core of steel he wondered if she was even aware of herself. He sighed and shrugged out of his coat, draping it over her shoulders.

'I know it's not really proper to be out here like this,

but I can't stomach any more drawing-room conversation,' he said truthfully.

She tucked her arms into his sleeves and smiled as the ends flopped over her hands.

'I'm not surprised. You must be exhausted after that long drive and I admit I have had enough for tonight as well. We should probably go to bed.'

Watching her efforts to roll up his sleeves, Hunter wanted to agree wholeheartedly.

'Wouldn't that be a little improper?' he asked politely.

She glanced up, her dark gold brows gathering in confusion. Then realisation dawned and she burst out laughing.

'Are you never serious?'

'I am very serious. Very often. It just doesn't always show.'

Her face was still alight with amusement, but even in the gloom he could make out the return of her assessing look.

'I think that was one of your honest moments, whether you meant it or not. Aren't you cold? I feel guilty about taking your coat.'

She moved to slide it off, but he caught it, holding the lapels and gently easing it back onto her shoulders.

'I'm not in the least cold.' That, too, was very honest. He wasn't certain what was wreaking more havoc on his self-control, her comments or the sight of her wrapped in his coat, the dark cloth bracketing the pearly rises of her breasts above the silver and ivory bodice, their juncture marked by a single-tear pearl pendant hanging from a long chain.

She might not be abundant like Lady Melkinson, but her breasts were perfectly shaped and they would fit marvellously in his palms… He must indeed have been more tired than he thought because it didn't make any sense that he couldn't just slide his hands under his coat to her waist and pull her towards him and do something about this rising ache, like stripping away that silvery sheen of a dress, leaving her in nothing but his coat, her hair against the dark fabric, her skin like moonlight and shadow underneath…

Without giving himself time to consider, he gently plucked the pearl necklace from its resting place, the backs of his fingers skimming the silky skin that curved enticingly into the lace-lined bodice. The pearl was warm and he balanced it in his palm, feeling the heat rise from her skin not an inch from his, wondering what he was doing. She seemed to be wondering the same thing.

'Is this significant? This necklace?' he managed, just to say something, waiting for her to pull back, but she nodded.

'Yes. It was my mother's. Her father gave it to her when she married and it is the only thing I have from her that meant something to her. She never cared for jewels or fashion. She liked animals.'

'Like her daughter.'

Her alarm faded, replaced by her sudden smile. It was a wholehearted smile, full of love and the warmth of memory, and it pressed further at the edges of his control.

'Not really. Or rather, much more than I ever did. She was only ever comfortable around horses. I like animals, but I like people more. Some people, at least.'

'Some more than others. As with animals I would

just advise you are certain they genuinely like you back before approaching them with overtures.'

He should have kept quiet. Even in the dark he saw the flush of colour spread upwards from her bodice and she stepped back and he let the pearl slip out of his fingers and it snaked its way back down between her breasts. He stopped himself from following her, trying to ignore the thud of desire that was spreading through him.

'I know I must appear very foolish to you,' she said. 'But I'm not as naïve as you think me. I saw him go to Lady Melkinson just now. I'm not surprised he is attracted to her; they're both so very perfect, after all.'

She was trying to speak lightly but he could hear the anguish in her voice. The need to reassure her battled with the need to maintain his distance. Whatever pretensions to save people from themselves that remained in him after his disastrous failures should be firmly confined to people he could ultimately walk away from like the veterans at Hope House. If this conceit that he could protect her was what had drawn him to this girl four years ago he should be thanking the stars she wanted none of him. He was no one's champion. In fact, if he ever did decide to marry, he should probably choose one of those spoilt, shallow society misses London excelled in producing who needed nothing more from him than his title, an open purse and the chance to lord it over society. They would leave him alone much more effectively than his fictitious biddable country-bred wife.

'Perfect? Are they? You have a rather shallow understanding of that term.'

Her mouth parted in surprise at the mockery in his

words and even in the dim light he could see colour rise on her cheeks. He waited for the hurt to push her away. Let's just finish this.

'I suppose I do.' She frowned. 'Beauty has a mesmeric effect, doesn't it? The lakes are beautiful and when I look at them everything I see is tinged with a sense of well-being, but when you break down the landscape it's just rock and ferns and water and people's houses with regular lives. I suppose it's a matter of perspective. But I don't think my feelings for Charles are based on his looks. I've known him for years, you see, and he is a kind man, even if he is beautiful.'

Her calm acceptance of his condemnation just raised his tension.

'If we are talking about perspective, do you really think you have any on Welbeck? Not that it is really any concern of mine if you want to tie yourself to him, but you were a child when you knew him. Are you really willing to stake your entire future on a childish infatuation?'

She raised her chin.

'Perhaps I am. Children are not necessarily fools and their intuitions about people can be very sound. I was a child when I met you and I think my intuitions about you, despite our short acquaintance, were just as sound.'

He wasn't going to rise to that bait. This was just what was wrong with this girl. She didn't stay where she was put; she had to go turning tables all the time. He barely resisted the childish urge to demand she hand back his coat.

'We should go inside now.'

She nodded, her mouth curving in a rueful smile. 'You see? You really are better off taking my offer of the riverfront and being grateful you aren't saddled with me after all.'

She began slipping off his coat and he grasped the lapels, stopping her again. He shouldn't ask. He knew he was going to regret it.

'All right, what were your intuitions about me?'

Her laugh was just a quick intake of breath.

'Nothing bad. That you were a good person. That you were too aware of people…not just of people; that's why you were so good with Petra… You thought of her before you thought of your own needs. You can tell a great deal about people from the way they are with animals. But I also remember not knowing if that calm you had with her wasn't covering something else.' She hesitated. 'I didn't know about your brother then. I do remember thinking you looked tired and very sad. I'm so sorry.'

Nothing bad. All in all it was a rather kind, if damning, assessment. He should be flattered, not flicked on the raw. It was also confirmation that he was right— she was precisely the wrong combination of clever and needy. She was already tempting him to step back into his old and futile role of protector, except that in time she would probably see his pretensions for what they were. He didn't need this schoolmistress dissecting him like a specimen at the Royal Academy. He didn't want to live his life with someone like her constantly reflecting back his failures. She wasn't one to let things be, and much more than he wanted to bed her, he wanted quiet. He wanted to be left alone.

'We should go back inside,' she said and handed him his coat and he put it on, aware of how her warmth lingered in the pliant fabric in a way that he knew was ridiculous.

'You're right. Let's go in.'

Hunter woke with his fingers still digging into the mattress. He loosened them slowly, but otherwise didn't move, letting the sweat cool on his skin which always felt pinched and raw after the nightmares. Eventually he turned and groped on the floor for the blanket he had thrown off.

It had been worse this time. No, not really worse, just different. For the first time since the nightmares had started four years ago the images had changed. Not just Tim writhing in pain as their mother serenely plummeted off a cliff into a river of blood fed by Tim's wounds. This time a new figure had been standing there, watching his futile efforts to stop the tragedy, her long hair streaming out and colouring the grey cliffs a silvery gold.

Actually, it *was* worse. The curious, watchful pressure of her eyes had added shame to his agony and his sense of failure, but at least this time he had woken before he himself had been dragged down into that chasm as he tried to cling to Tim's disintegrating body. That anomaly was also her fault—she had started walking towards them and he had tried to stop her and both Tim and his mother had slipped away before he could grab them and then he had woken, their names choking in his throat. It was a small mercy that he didn't make too much noise during these nightmares, that the primary damage was to the bedclothes he scattered around the room and sometimes to his own skin.

The house was very quiet, enough to hear the creak-ing of the wood and the distant cry of a night bird. He closed his eyes. His pulse was slowing, but the familiar sluggish mix of despair and disgust was taking the place of the frantic fear of the dream. He was so tired of this. There was nothing he could do about the guilt of failing his family, but he kept hoping he could at least, finally, be rid of these nightly accusations. Perhaps one night he might manage to stop them from destroying themselves. And him. Not likely, though.

He wished he could just rest.

He was so tired…

Chapter Eight

Nell raised her face to the sun. It was still cool as Charles guided the curricle out the gates, but the bite of autumn was more than recompensed by a perfectly blue sky. She smiled in wonder that she was here, being driven by Charles, looking as good as Betsy could make her in a lovely pale peach jonquil pelisse over a sprigged muslin dress. All she needed to complete her happiness was the nerve to ask Charles to let her drive Meecham's lovely team. After all, she had had no such qualms about demanding to drive Hunter's horses and he was practically a stranger. It was peculiar to feel so much less comfortable with Charles, whom she knew so much better.

'So, Nell, tell me what you have been doing these past four years. Breaking hearts in the Lake District?'

Nell's attention was on the way his whip snapped at the leaders as they came over a gentle rise, resisting the urge to tell him not to hold the reins quite so tightly.

'Hardly. I have been too busy teaching.'

'Teaching? As in schoolmistress?'

Nell tried very hard not to stiffen at the shock in his

voice as she had yesterday with Hunter. Apparently this concept was hard for some people to grasp.

'Yes. I happen to enjoy it. Very much.'

Charles looked at her briefly and then smiled.

'That's nice. Will you miss it when you're married?'

'I won't stop teaching just because I marry. I am even planning to open a school. Not right away, I will need to find the right people and, well, there are a lot of considerations, but eventually.'

His eyebrows disappeared beneath the tumbled locks of golden hair on his brow and she forced herself to change the subject before she completely scared him off.

'How are your stables faring?'

He sighed and guided the horses around the village green where workmen were already busy preparing for the upcoming fête, which was the highlight of the breeders' fair.

'Hopefully the fair will go well. I don't know how your father does it, honestly. I would swear our stock is as good as his, but… Anyway, let's talk about happier things. Your engagement, for example. When is the wedding?'

Nell's heart gave a great big thump and then settled into a rapid tattoo in rhythm with the horses' hooves.

'We haven't settled on a date yet. After all, we have just become engaged.'

'But we understood from your father this was a long-standing arrangement?'

Trying to convey availability while not revealing that Hunter had no interest in anything other than her inheritance was a stretch of Nell's flirtation skills. What would Lady Melkinson do?

'It is, but I was very young at the time. I'm afraid I still don't know my own mind.'

Oh, dear, that sounded dreadfully missish. Anna would probably start giggling at this point. Hunter would probably say something unrepeatable.

'I see. You deserve better, Nell.' Charles's hand squeezed hers briefly and she flushed in a mixture of excitement at the gesture and shame at her perfidy. It wasn't that far from the truth.

She looked at his perfect profile, at the soft line of his cheek and the way his wheat-gold hair curled over his forehead. The memory of that day he had defended her came back sharply and she spoke before she could think.

'I always wanted to thank you, Charles, for that day you defended me against Papa. I know it was years ago, but it meant a great deal to me.'

'I did?' He looked surprised.

'Oh, it was years ago, at the jumping course. I think I must have been fourteen at most.'

His frown cleared after a moment.

'Goodness, I remember that. He was ranting about you cramming your horse. No offence, but he was always foul-tempered. I remembered we had Lord Davenport there to look at some stallions and your father was embarrassing everyone. Luckily Davenport didn't shy off; bought Jade Dragon that year, which was a good sale. Your father should have known better than to put you on the course at that age in the first place. Why, you were nothing but a child.'

Nell watched him flick his whip at the horses as he urged them up the incline turning into the drive and felt as if the leather had stung her as well. It made no difference, she told herself. Of course that moment had meant more to her than it had to him; there was no reason for her to feel so let down. It was a miracle he remembered it at all. It was her own stupidity for even mentioning it. This was Charles, here and now, with her, listening to her with that gentle smile. She should be grateful, not disappointed. Still, she was relieved as they approached the house. Make one last effort, Nell, she admonished herself. She tried out the smile she had practised on Hunter last night, up and half through her lashes.

'Nevertheless, it was very kind of you, Charles.'

The only problem was that he was watching the horses. She held the smile resolutely as he pulled the horses to a halt and finally he turned to her. Apparently it was not a bad effort because his cheeks tinged with colour and his sky-blue eyes settled on her mouth. The sheer absurdity of what she was doing made her smile falter and she looked down at her gloves.

'Thank you for inviting me.'

'I'm glad you came, Nell. Good morning, Lord Hunter.'

Nell swivelled in her seat to meet Hunter's gaze where he stood by the curricle, waiting to hand her down. She had been so focused on Charles she hadn't even noticed the curricle standing by the stairs. He had probably seen her laughable attempt at being seductive.

'Good morning, Welbeck. You have timed your arrival well; I was just looking for Miss Tilney. Shall we go look at the filly Lord Welbeck mentioned, Nell?'

Nell nodded as he helped her alight, trying to read his expression, but he was giving nothing away. There wasn't even the cynical but tolerant amusement she was becoming used to—still, her shoulders tightened with unease and her face heated under the force of his golden-brown eyes. This was ridiculous—she was mounting a defence and she didn't even know if she was under attack.

Hunter watched Welbeck reluctantly climb the stairs as the groom drove the curricle to the stables. He knew drivers like Welbeck—he had raced their type often enough—they were skilled but commonly lost in the end because they wore their horses out too soon. It gave him a little satisfaction, but not enough to counter the effect of the sunny smile on Nell's face as she had sat staring at her prince or the intent look in Welbeck's eyes, as he finally began seeing her clearly. He was tempted to tell her what he thought of such a blatant display of juvenile adoration, but he was aware it would not only put up her back, but smack of jealousy, which was ludicrous. He wasn't going to marry the girl, so there was no need to play dog-in-the-manger.

'Do those bays drive as well as they look?' he asked, searching for a neutral opening. She looked at him and he grimaced in annoyance as her smile sparked the increasingly familiar kick of lust.

'They really are beautiful steppers, though the wheeler is just a little short in the shoulders, so it's not a perfect match. Did you see?'

Hunter felt his antagonism melt at her obvious excitement about the horses.

'Don't tell Meech that. He doesn't have your discerning eye and he'll be devastated.'

'Still and all, the lady's right,' Hidgins assented behind them. 'Just a little short. Fine forward action, though. I'd like to see their paces up a hill.'

'Charles took them over the rise once you pass the

village and they took it, crest and all, as if it was a walk.' She glanced over at Hunter. 'Your team is just as evenly paced and perhaps have a little more staying power, though.'

Hunter resisted the urge to smile, barely, and some more of his tension faded. 'Are you placating me, by any chance? Precisely how old do you think I am?'

'Ancient,' she replied promptly and with all seriousness and Hidgins gave a snort of laughter, hastily subdued. 'I wasn't trying to placate you. It was just that you looked a little annoyed just now. I know it's never easy to see a team you know is just as good as your own.'

'I would debate that they are quite their equal, but in the end it is also the driver that wins the race, not merely the team.'

She clasped her hands in front of her and nodded, eyes wide.

'What the devil does that expression signify?' he asked, trying to hold on to his annoyance.

'That's how I look when Elkins, our head groom, tries to teach me something about horses that is painfully obvious, but I don't want to offend him. It is supposed to convey interested attention.'

'Well, you just look like a dyspeptic owl.'

She laughed and walked over to Hidgins and stroked the lead horse's sleek neck.

'I was going to tell you Charles mentioned that Meecham is bringing a stallion here for sale, too. A grey. I saw him when he was just a foal and he's probably a beauty now.'

'Meecham?' Hunter enquired politely and her smile glinted at him over the horse's neck.

'Meecham is a darling, but I don't think anyone

would call him a beauty. My point is that I remembered
you mentioned you were looking for a horse up to your
weight and he stands over sixteen hands.'

Hunter came to stand on the other side of the leader.
She had taken off her gloves when she approached the
horse and he watched as her hand moved with calm
rhythm down the horse's neck.

Hers weren't the plump pampered hands of a society
miss, nor the carefully soignée, white hands of someone
like Lady Felton. They were warmed to a pale honey
and looked strong, and when she brushed her fingers
along the horse's mane he saw the pucker of calluses
on her palm.

He pulled off his own gloves and placed his palm on
the firm muscled neck between them. The short hair was
warm and vibrated with the blood and life beneath. It
was ridiculous to be envious of a horse simply because
a young woman was petting it. To be reduced to stroking the same horse simply to approach her was a tactic
he would have thought had gone the way of his schoolboy days.

'Are you making fun of my size again, by any chance?'

That won him another teasing smile which gave him
far too much satisfaction.

'I'm not one to say anything about being too big, unfortunately. But it is worth looking at him. Apparently
his name is Courage, which is a bit pompous, but he's
too old to change it, I would think. Or perhaps you could
call him Coleridge, which is close enough, no?'

'There is no possible way I would name a horse after
a poet.'

'What's wrong with Courage?' Hidgins asked. 'Fine

name for a stallion. We have a good strapping gelding named Valiant, don't we, sir?'

'Don't give her grist for her mill, Hidgins. There is only so much abuse I can take before noon.'

'Valiant is a very charming name,' Nell said, her tone blatantly propitiating. 'I'm sure many medieval knights named their steeds Valiant and Intrepid and…and Fearless.'

'How about Impudent? Or Shameless?' Hunter replied, edging Hidgins out of the way. She was getting all too comfortable poking fun at him and that came at a price. Hidgins, good man that he was, took the hint and moved towards the curricle. Hunter completed the manoeuvre, boxing Nell in between the horses. She glanced up in surprise and tried to pass him, but he didn't move.

'Don't run away just yet. You did ask me to flirt with you, didn't you? And I presume Welbeck won't be able to resist taking a peek on our progress from the windows. Besides, all this talk about medieval knights and steeds makes one want to do a little marauding. You might think,' he continued, stroking the horse's neck and stopping just short of where her hand rested, 'that it isn't easy to maraud in broad daylight in full view of the front door of a country home, wouldn't you?'

She did the same thing with her lips, that faint lick and tug, but though this time it was completely unconscious, the gesture and the coral-coloured flush, that winter sun–coloured hair between him and those lovely, firm little breasts…

'I would have thought it is close to impossible,' she murmured as the silence stretched.

He slid his other hand down this time so that his thumb just came to rest against her wrist, then very slowly slid under it until he could feel her pulse, warm and fast, against the pad of his thumb.

'Be you ever so close to impossible, you remain in the realm of possibility.'

'Who said that?' she asked, her voice husky. She raised her wrist almost imperceptibly, so that his fingers could slide under into the warm cavern between her wrist and the horse. He found it hard to believe she had no idea what she was doing. In anyone else he would have considered this behaviour to be a blatant invitation to take this flirtation to its natural conclusion. If she were anyone else he would do just that.

'I did.'

'It sounds impressive. Rather like a heraldic motto. Ours is *Qui edere vult nucleum, frangat nucem.*'

He frowned, momentarily distracted.

'"If you want to eat his centre, break his nuts"?'

'Dear me, you would have failed my Latin class. It means "he who wants the kernel must crack the nut".'

'I would have failed your Latin class because I would have found it very hard to concentrate. On the other hand, if you taught anatomy...'

He slid his hand between hers and the horse, his fingers tracing the dip at the heart of her palm up to the rasp of the calluses at the base of her fingers and then on until his hand laced with hers. She still didn't pull back. He almost wanted her to because he was beginning to feel very much like that schoolboy he had described. He knew she was enjoying this exploration of what he suspected was a very passionate nature, but it was also obvious she trusted him to set the boundaries and keep her safe. She was here to learn theory, not practise. And he...

A distinct throat-clearing from Hidgins made them both turn their heads. Just as a day earlier, a group of men were coming around the house and Hunter moved back. Impossibility had won this time. She looked suddenly much younger and quite shy, reminding him precisely what she was. He placed her hand on his arm and he led her away from the horses.

'Porridge,' he said decisively and she looked up in surprise. 'Sounds just as much like Courage as Coleridge does, no?'

'Porridge?' Her voice shook with laughter and the shyness faded. 'You would never call a horse Porridge.'

'I'd sooner call him suet pudding than Coleridge, darling. Now we'll let Hidgins take the horses to the stables and we can go see this filly Lord Welbeck mentioned yesterday. Unless you would like to ask young Welbeck to take you?'

She actually had the audacity to consider his question for a moment.

'No... I don't think I should seek him out again so soon. I prefer that he sue a little for my attention. Is that awful of me?'

'It is in the finest of feminine traditions, at least.' He tried to keep the edge out of his voice.

'I don't think you are in a position to accuse anyone else of being flirtatious. Certainly not me. This is my first real taste of it.'

'Then you are an extremely precocious pupil.'

'Some credit must go to my teacher, then,' she conceded gallantly. 'Is it terrible to admit I enjoy it?'

'Appalling. Up there with necromancy and slave trading.'

'I just knew I was a hopeless case,' Nell said with

relish and he couldn't help laughing. It might not be very comfortable, but he could surely survive a little misplaced attraction, and it appeared to be doing her a great deal of good, so it was churlish to resent her artless enjoyment.

The path separated a collection of buildings that surrounded the stables from the paddocks and they had just come to the last of the buildings when a snort and the sharp strike of hoof against wood made Hunter turn abruptly.

'That's probably Griffin,' Nell said. 'They keep him in the small stable away from the other stallions. He's a beauty, but he's the most ill-tempered horse I've ever seen. He's just not meant to be domesticated.' She paused. 'You're curious, now, aren't you?'

Hunter laughed, not surprised she had seen through him so clearly.

'A little. Let's go take a look.'

The stable was a small one, with just four large loose stalls, all of which were empty but the last. The moment they stepped in, a large bay head surged over the stall door which squeaked in protest as the stallion's body hit it with a thump. Hunter took a step forward, but stopped as Nell grabbed his arm. He closed his hand on hers reassuringly, rather pleased she was concerned for his safety.

'Don't worry; I won't go too close.'

The stall door creaked again as Griffin pushed against it, tossing his head up, ears flat and eyes wide. Then his meaty lips pulled back, displaying very large teeth, and he surged forward again, his teeth closing with a sharp snap on the air.

'Well, that answers that question. We're definitely not welcome here.'

'I'm afraid it might be too late to help him. Some people are like that, too. There was a girl at school who enjoyed hurting other girls. Nothing we tried made the slightest difference. I was very glad when she left.'

'Did she hurt you?'

She looked up at the tension he hadn't even realised had entered his voice and her brows drew together.

'No, not me. She was quite little and she went after smaller girls. She did try to bully my best friend Anna once, but that earned her a nosebleed. Anna has six sisters, you see.'

'That would teach anyone survival skills. Anna is your best friend?'

'Since we were ten. She lives near Windermere and I spent all my holidays with her family. Her parents even have me call them Uncle Arthur and Aunt Ginnie. They are more family to me than my own.'

'They sound nice.'

Again the careful glance at him.

'You would probably like Anna. She's small and quite as lovely as Lady Melkinson, but she has black hair and eyes. All the boys always fall in love with her.'

'Are you jealous of her?'

He expected a denial, but she just sighed.

'That's awful of me, isn't it? I love her dearly, but I can't help wishing I was also tiny and dark and her hair has a lovely natural curl. It really bounces. Not very nice of me, is it?'

He took her hand, turning her towards him. They had reached the folly, a small brick tower around which a copse of old oaks created an intimate and private cavern.

'It's honest, but misplaced. I wouldn't be surprised if she was envious of you.'

Nell shook her head.

'She did say she wished she was tall and pale, but she was just being nice. She is like that.'

Her full lower lip was curved in a soft smile and it occurred to him that this strange girl had made a completely new life for herself away from her cold and damaging home. She spoke of her schoolteacher and friends with more warmth and protectiveness, and even with the expectation of being loved in return, than most people he knew spoke of their own families.

Her insecurity always centred on her height and looks, which was nothing short of baffling. It was true that at seventeen, aside from her performance on the horses, she had shown all the gawkiness of a girl grown too much too fast. But the woman who stood before him, because she was definitely a woman, might not be conventionally pretty like the petite china-doll girls she admired, but she was far more attractive and exciting than someone as transparent as a Lady Melkinson. It was clear she had no idea of the damage she could do with her elegant body and quicksilver eyes. Part of him wanted to teach her, but another part didn't want to give her any more help in her aggravating plan to capture Welbeck.

As he remained silent, her smile dimmed.

'You would probably like her, too.'

'I'm not sure; my taste runs along different lines.'

She half-snorted.

'I know. Lady Felton and opera singers.'

His mouth quirked and he stepped forward, moving his hand lightly up her arm.

'Longer lines. Much longer. There are distinct advantages to a woman who fits against you…perfectly.'

He took another step, moving his hands to her waist.

'See?' he asked, trying to keep his body in pace with his mind. 'And I happen to appreciate Saxon princesses with North Sea eyes. They tend to bring out the medieval warrior in me.'

Her lips parted and their colour warmed to the lovely pink peach that kept tantalising him.

'Do you know many Saxon princesses?'

He liked the way her voice, already deep, sank and thickened, increasing the feeling of being lost and isolated in a fog-bound moor.

'Just one,' he answered, letting sensible considerations slip away. She was clearly ready to carry her experimentation a little further—she wouldn't stop him. No, she *wanted* this, and he...needed this. For a moment the truth of that alarmed him but he shoved it down hard, touching the tips of his fingers to her jawline, to her cheek, raising her chin with his thumb, very slowly. 'But she's not a princess—she's a queen. Princesses are soft and middling; queens are strong and weak in equal measure. And fascinating. And worth fighting for...'

He was using his voice like his hands and body, but the words rang true even in his own ears. Her mouth bowed a little and her eyes fell away.

'That's beautiful,' she breathed. 'Thank you.'

It took him a moment to realise she thought this was part of their charade of flirtation and another moment to remind himself that it was. But it didn't stop him. His hand tightened on her waist, closing the distance between them. Her hair, sliding between his fingers, was hot and silky, soft as liquid, and he twisted his hand in it, raising her face the last inch towards him.

'Nell,' he murmured, feeling the flush of his breath

against her cheek and then against her mouth. Finally. His mind was still struggling to describe just what it felt like when with a small sigh that sucked the breath out of him she opened her mouth under his, just canting her head a hair's breadth so that the fit was...perfect. He stopped thinking, at least with his mind, and let every instinct take over, talking with her and listening to her by all other means.

And she was a symphony of contradictory and conflicting answers. Her hands moved first in feather-light, tentative brushes against his coat that reflected the light teasing slides of his mouth over hers as he waited for a sign she was ready for more.

He shouldn't have been surprised that the surrender, when it came, would be so thorough. The moment his tongue lightly caressed the silk of her inner lip, where the skin was warm and full and smooth as mother-of-pearl, her arms rose to wrap around his neck with a sigh and her body sagged against him with the abandon of a collapsing marionette.

For a moment he froze, holding her to him, his hand deep in her hair as she clung to him like to a mast in a storm, waiting. Then forces of nature won out over the strange surge of fear and his hand moved down to the rounded rise of her backside, pulling her against him as he indulged the urge to lick and tug at the soft and lush lower lip that had done so much damage to his control.

This time her sigh was more a moan and her muscles gathered with purpose as she dug her fingers into the hair at his nape, pulling herself against him, opening her mouth for him, her lips catching against his, and it was his turn to groan. It was obvious she wasn't used to being kissed and it was even more obvious that she liked it. She didn't even pull away when he deepened the caress, his tongue finding hers, stroking it slow and long. She just moved against him, tasting and seeking and rewarding him with little whimpers of pleasure that were as devastating to his control as the urgent movements of her body.

He had been so right about how perfectly she fit against him. It would take so little to push her against the wall, pull up those skirts, warm and heat and dampen her until she was ready for him and then…

'Hunter…' It came out a whisper and a plea and his whole body contracted as if he was about to climax just at the sound of her and the slide of her breath into him. He leaned one hand against the wall of the folly, holding her tightly to him with the other, aware at some level that he was in the act of committing a folly of his own. That, madness aside, there was no possible way he could follow through on what body and mind were begging for. That he had to stop. Now.

He pulled back, registering with some surprise that his arm was shaking as it leaned against the stone surface.

'Nell, I don't want to stop, but we have to… Anyone might come by here.'

Her eyes opened slowly and he forced his gaze from the plump, reddened dampness of her lips to her eyes. Unfortunately, they met his with a dreamy, dilated shimmer that was almost as bad for his control. What did he care if someone saw them? The worst that could happen was that they would have to carry through on this engagement. But as he was about to lean back into her, her hands fell from about his neck and the dreamy look was replaced by one of mingled surprise and awareness.

'Is this how you kiss all women?' she asked huskily.

The introduction of other women into the moment was so out of place he struggled to even understand what she was asking. His brain, already in a losing position, told him to keep his mouth shut while his gut was demanding he answer a resounding 'no'. His other instincts, scrambling to recover lost positions, told him to tread very carefully.

'Of course not!'

Her mouth drooped.

'Did I do it wrong?'

A laugh escaped him at the absurdity of it all.

'If doing it wrong means taking me within an inch of losing all control, then yes.'

He was sober enough now for the admission to cost him, but he was rewarded by one of her sudden joyous smiles.

'I would have thought that meant I did it correctly. Must we stop?'

He leaned forward, pressing his lips against the soft hairs at her temple, breathing her in. Oh, he loved her scent. He had no idea what it was, just that it was the most beautiful…

'Yes, we must. For now.' He spoke against the tickle of her hair. He was so damn tempted to take her into the gloomy entrance of the folly, braving cobwebs and mice and headless spectres if need be just so he wouldn't have to take his hands off her. He let them curve one last time over her hips and behind, trying not to pin her to him again so she could feel precisely why they had to stop now.

'It doesn't feel done yet,' she whispered, turning so that he felt the last words flutter against his neck.

'Why not?' he asked. He was falling again. It was as though in a dream, watching himself do something he knew he shouldn't, but being incapable of moving to stop it.

'I don't know. I feel…awake and asleep. Buzzing. It doesn't feel right to stop now.'

'Oh, Nell. Please stop talking. I can't think.'

'I don't want to think…'

'If we don't stop now, we'll be exchanging vows by the end of the week,' he said desperately, as much to himself as to her, but apparently it was enough for Nell. He hadn't realised how pliant her body was against him until she froze; then her elbows shoved between them, pushing him away.

Without another word they turned and continued, their feet scrunching on the gravel path. It wasn't far from the folly to the paddock and the filly had obviously sensed them coming and retreated to the far end, her ears flat and her eyes wide. Nell stopped and leaned on the paddock fence, watching the filly, and Hunter did the same a yard away, his hands pressing against the sun-warmed wood as he tried to understand just how on earth he had lost all judgement.

For a while neither spoke as they watched the filly. The buzz and chirp of insects and birds and the gleam of the sun on the late summer wildflowers created an idyllic setting, but he just stared at it grimly.

She bent and tugged at a dandelion that was tapping against the fence.

'Well, at least I can see why you men do this all the time.'

He closed his eyes briefly, wishing her a thousand miles away until he was himself again and his body stopped dancing to the tune of her voice and her art-less remarks.

'We don't precisely do this *all* the time.'

'No, it would be quite tiring, I suppose. Still…'

The sound of hooves made both of them turn. Hunter realised that his half-prayer that something save him from his baser instincts had taken a distinctly unwanted form—the last person he wanted to see right now was Charles Welbeck.

Charles nodded to Hunter, but addressed Nell as he dismounted.

'Well, what do you think of her?'

Nell's smile shifted into the serious look she reserved for equine matters and Hunter was at least glad to see that in her master-of-the-horse mode she showed no inclination to blush in the presence of her prince. What amazed him even more was that she showed no sign of what had just taken place between them. She might not have much experience, but she was taking to this new sphere like a duck to water.

'She is beautiful, her head and shoulders are perfect, but it's not a good sign that she has kept her ears back ever since she sensed us, even though we are nowhere near her. Did something happen to her?'

'She had a hard birth and her dam rejected her early on. I told Father to sell her, but he said someone might pay a good price for her if we could calm her. I think it's a waste of time. She just doesn't have the makings of a good breeder.'

'I don't agree, but we shall see. Has she been named?'

'We just call her Buckminster's Filly after her sire. You name her, then, Nell.'

Nell's gaze followed the filly, her mouth softening.

'Daisy.'

Hunter watched with mute frustration as Charles's eyes skimmed from Nell's profile to her other attributes and his mouth bowed into a sweet smile as Nell turned back to them.

'Daisy, then,' Charles assented.

Chapter Nine

Nell slunk past the door of the drawing room as the women bent over the latest fashion plates. The weather was still lovely and the last thing she wanted to be doing was exchanging gossip with the matrons. She would take this opportunity to go see Daisy on her own. Perhaps without two very tall, very male individuals by her side, the filly might be more amenable.

She also could make use of some time alone after her inexplicable behaviour with Hunter. She was clearly taking this whole flirtation idea too far. It wasn't surprising that Hunter was very, very good at it or even that she enjoyed it so much. After all, she had always wished she could flirt like Anna, and to do so with someone so handsome and adept was an opportunity not to be missed.

Already it was making her much less affected by Charles's presence. She had actually felt quite his equal during that exchange down by the paddock and during the walk back to the house. It was very kind of Hunter to be so obliging, though kind was probably not the right word. He probably hadn't abandoned his plans for Bascombe, but she sensed that he was someone who would take his failures with good grace and probably be quite content with just the water rights in the end.

A sudden roaring cheer from the direction of the stables made Nell pause and then change course. On a grass clearing a large group of men, gentry, servants, grooms and stable boys stood shoulder to shoulder, clearly enjoying some spectacle at their centre. Standing back from the crowd, but with an excellent vantage point on stacked bales of hay, was Hunter's man, Biggs.

She stopped next to him. 'What on earth is happening, Biggs?'

Biggs, caught in mid cheer, gaped down at her.

'Miss Tilney! You oughtn't to be here.'

'Why not? Is there a fight? Help me up.'

Seeing he was too shocked to comply, she clambered up herself. Sometimes there were advantages to being tall. From the hay she could see over the crowd to the two men who were... Her hand flew to her mouth as Hidgins's fist drove itself into Hunter's middle.

'Oh, no! Why are they fighting? I thought they were friends.'

It was a strange thing to say of a master and a servant, but the words were out before she could consider their wisdom.

Biggs looked startled, but recovered himself.

'They are, miss. This has become a yearly tradition at the stables, so to speak. His lordship and Hidgins being proficient in the Fancy, they draw a fine crowd and excite not a little bit of wagering.'

'The Fancy?'

Biggs tore his eyes away from the fight and smiled reassuringly.

'It's just sparring, miss. Fisticuffs for pleasure.'

For pleasure! Hidgins stumbled back under a blow and the crowd shifted to give him room to rally, re-forming again as he propelled himself headlong into Hunter.

'You needn't worry, miss. They've been sparring since they were boys, Hidgins being the eldest of the old groom at Hunter Hall.'

'You knew Lord Hunter when he was a boy?'

'You might say we grew up together at the Hall, miss.'

'But you and Hidgins are older, I think, no?'

'We are, miss, but his lordship was always old for his age.'

Biggs glanced at her momentarily and then continued, his eyes fixed firmly on the fight.

'If you'll pardon the impertinence, miss, but don't let his lordship's manner fool you into thinking there's no substance there. I don't know how it was, but there wasn't one that didn't know who ran the Hall and saw to Lady Hunter and Master Tim long before the old lord passed. He never asked for help, always stood firm on his own two feet. There's no better man or master I know.'

Nell smiled at Biggs's obvious pride, but couldn't help a prick of annoyance at the way he regarded Hunter's self-sufficiency as evidence he didn't need anyone. Hunter's aunts had said something very similar. It was impressive that Hunter had taken such responsibilities on to his overly young shoulders, but someone should have interceded on his behalf. She had seen enough during her years at the school to know children should always have someone to lean on if they are to feel safe in the world; their strength shouldn't come from being strong for someone else, but from believing themselves valued and protected. Her mother had been her protector and, when she had died, Nell had luckily settled on Mrs Petheridge as another source of strength. Perhaps she had been luckier than Hunter after all. She tried to shrug off her sense of unease. She was clearly exaggerating. Hunter was a grown man and had obviously come through these imagined emotional privations with minimal scars, except those incurred by being bludgeoned by fists. He wasn't a pupil of hers to be worried over.

'His lordship wouldn't like you to be here,' Biggs said with great resolution, distracting her from her thoughts, but his eyes remained firmly on the fight.

'But I'm not here, Biggs,' she murmured, her own attention returning to the rhythm and force of the exchange. She could see now that Hunter's catlike grace and reflexes had distinct advantages when it came to beating opponents into a pulp. Hidgins's lunges and jabs were quick and brutal, but though Nell cringed each time they shot out, not many managed to make contact. But Hidgins was as broad and thick as a brick wall and just as hard to fell, and when his fists did finally make contact with Hunter her own body contracted with sympathetic pain.

'Do they beat each other until one of them breaks the other's nose?'

His thin lips quirked and settled back.

'No, miss. After the first year it was decided to establish some rules to ensure presentability after the encounter.'

Nell was used to schoolmistressy euphemisms.

'No blows to the head, then?'

Again the prim quirking of lips.

'Precisely, miss, and none below the…if you will excuse the word…waist, miss.'

She almost said that it was silly to be prudish about the mention of a perfectly everyday part of human anatomy, but her eyes dropped to Hunter's waist just before it was blocked from her view as Hidgins came forward with an impressive jab and blow. She winced at the rush of concern that coursed through her and a parallel rush of heat at that very brief and utterly inconsequential consideration of Hunter's waist. She had seen his waist and other men's waists before and it certainly had never been an issue. Perhaps the difference was that she had actually felt that waist against her, hard and urgent and making her disastrously aware of her own waist, her legs, the way her skin felt, the way her hands had wanted to touch...

She tightened her cloak about her and tried to focus on feeling disapproving at this very childish exhibit. Fisticuffs and betting in a stable yard! It was so typical of Hunter—he probably went to drink ale in the village inn afterwards and then to share his waist and everything else with whatever maid he could charm. Charles would probably never engage in such activities. She couldn't imagine him with his hair all tousled by rough handling and his shirt being mangled by Hidgins as the groom tried and failed to deflect a blow to his stomach. As the crowd sang out their approval and agony she turned resolutely to Biggs.

'Have you placed a bet yourself, Biggs?'

He shook his head mournfully.

'No, miss. It wouldn't be quite proper.'

'To bet against Lord Hunter?'

'Against Hidgins, miss. His lordship's pride is rather more...flexible.'

Once again the two men went down onto the grass.

'Those stains will never come out.' Biggs sighed.

The crowd had closed again and for a moment it looked as though they might all join in the fray and she lost sight of the two men on the ground. Then both a great concerted groan and a rival cheer stretched out.

'He has him pinned,' Biggs informed her and the groan and cheer scattered into laughter and the settling of debts. The knot unravelled, revealing the two dishevelled men who might just have well been rolled down a hill into a bog, Nell thought as her breath finally began to settle.

Then Hunter turned and saw her and her breath lost its rhythm again. He came towards her, his strides long and less graceful than usual. There was almost a bounce in them, as though he might suddenly leap from the ground. She tensed because his stride spoke of anger, but his face was still alight with laughter even though she could see he was trying to school it into disapproval. The combination was doing something to her and it wasn't just the saggy platform of hay under her feet that made her feel off balance.

He wore no coat or cravat and his shirt was untucked and marred by various stains which were likely, as Biggs had said, to resist extraction. It was also rent at the shoulder, revealing a triangular patch of skin which was almost the same warm tan as the skin at his neck. He must go shirtless quite often for his shoulders to be sun-touched like that, she thought. Where on earth could a gentleman do that? At Hunter Hall? If she had agreed to marry him, would she see him striding towards her just like that, but bare chested, with those powerful shoulders she had clung to and those arms that could control a four-horse team with less effort than it took most men to drive a gig?

'Biggs, why didn't you see Miss Tilney back to the house? It's not proper for her to be here.'

The words were perfectly sensible and in complete discord with the movement of his body and the brandy and honey eyes which were as hot and enticing now as the spirits they resembled.

'Who, my lord?' Biggs asked and received a quick sardonic glance.

'Subverting my servants, Nell?'

'I think that is a lesser sin than beating them up,' Nell replied. 'Are you all right, Hidgins?'

Hidgins grinned at her and pressed his hand to his ribs with a pitiful moan.

'I think you broke a rib, sir. I'll be laid up for a week, I will.'

'Oh, poor Betsy,' Nell said before she could stop herself and Hidgins dropped his hand and burst into laughter. Then, with a glance at Hunter, he and Biggs headed off towards the central stable. Nell realised she and Hunter were the only ones remaining on the patch of grass and she was still standing atop her perch as Hunter looked up at her with a very unsettling expression and resembling a pirate after a pitched battle. An incredibly handsome pirate. Most pirates would probably be grimy, with missing teeth and perhaps stunted from scurvy and not at all an object for admiration, she told herself, but the image clung. At least to her less-than-sensible imagination he did look like a pirate with the wind tangling in his warm chestnut hair with its shades of bay and cinnamon and flapping the edges of his shirt, threatening to lift it up so she might be able to see if his abdomen was also that colour as it dipped downwards into his buckskins, whether he was heat and warmth everywhere.

She tried to be sensible.

'It really is quite silly to be brawling like that. You two could have hurt each other!'

He grinned, tucking in his shirt and looking very much like a boy just returned from a successful raid on a neighbour's trout stream.

'Not really. This is what is called mere flourishing. After the first time, Hidgins and I agreed we would avoid blows to the head and below the waist. This way the only marks are easier to hide than a black eye.'

Another allusion to waists! She was not going to look or think about tucking in the ruined shirt herself and wondering if he would feel soft or hard there.

'So Biggs explained. Have you ever had a black eye?'

'Several.'

'Several. That is impressive; most people can only have two.'

His grin widened.

'Very amusing, Saxon. Now come down before I decide to put all this hay to good use.'

She really should come down, but she didn't want to, not yet. As she remained unmoving the raffish quality of his grin shifted, mellowed, his lashes dipping.

'You do look like a Saxon queen up there, about to bestow her favour on her knight,' he observed and Nell planted her feet more firmly as the bale quivered beneath them, or maybe that was just her legs that had wobbled. She was used to looking down at men, but very contrarily looking down at him made her feel dainty. Dainty?

'She would probably be a Norman queen if there were knights,' the schoolmistress corrected, and then, more to the point and in a less resolute voice. 'I don't have anything to bestow.'

'Yes, you do.'

How could three words turn a quiver into a blaze? He might as well have touched a match to the hay the heat was so intense. Also the sense of danger. He was making love to her in the middle of a stable yard without raising a finger and she didn't want it to stop. *This is not making love, just flirting*, the schoolmistress pointed out and was kicked off the bale of hay.

'I do?'

She would have preferred his hands, but his eyes were just as thorough and they left a scalding trail as they moved over her, a light shining and picking out the elements of her body, one by one, and she felt them as clearly as if he pressed his mouth to each point—to the skin just where her cheek sloped towards her ear, to the hollow below her chin, to the rise of her breast under the soft scrape of her fichu. All the way down her arm and so warm into the palms of her hands, telling her they could touch him, slide under that torn linen shirt...

'Your ribbon,' he said. He must have moved closer without her noticing. Now she could see the thick strands of his hair rising and falling against his forehead in the mounting wind, just touching the beautifully sculpted cheekbones. Was it ridiculous to feel envious of the wind that was doing what she so desperately wanted to do? It had to be.

'I will settle, for now, for your ribbon.' He spoke slowly, as if aware she wasn't quite listening.

'My ribbon.'

He nodded and took her by the waist and lowered her to the ground so gently and slowly she realised there must be even more strength in those arms than she had imagined. Now she was so close she could see the shading of his eyes. How could there be so very many shades of brown and how could they be so very warm? His scent, too, was composed of the same elements of sultry warmth, reaching her below the familiar scents of the stable yard and fields beyond. She had been cold a moment before, wrapping her cloak around her. Now it choked her, she wanted it off...

'This ribbon.' His voice was even slower now, treacle slow and warm, and when his fingers caught the fluttering end of the ribbon of her bonnet it became a thread of tingling, an extension of her dancing nerves.

'Why?'

'Your hair. I need to see it.'

Her hair, her hopeless, shapeless pale-as-dust hair, and he wanted to see it. Either she had no better charms or he actually, really did like her hair. He *needed* to see it. She could feel the truth of that word and it was very strange.

He didn't wait for her permission. The ribbon tautened, pressed over her bodice and down, and the slide of the satin fabric over the layers that kept her at bay was torture. She wished he could keep pulling and everything between them would unravel and peel away.

Her bonnet landed on the bale of hay and inevitably her hair, released so incautiously from its cage, slipped from its knot and settled on her right shoulder. The wind, scenting new prey, set about making as much of a tangle of it as possible. While he just stood there and watched it dance and flick about, his hands fisted on her cloak.

She shivered and it wasn't from the cold, but the sense of being bare though she was fully clothed. But it did make her think of him in his linen shirt. He must be freezing. She wrapped her cloak about his hands, drawing them into hers. They weren't in the least cold, but she chafed them anyway.

'You must be cold.'

'I am many, many things at this moment. Cold is not one of them.' But he didn't draw away his hands.

'Sorry, my hands are rough,' she said as she slid her palm over his, feeling his calluses and hers, regretting all those years of reins and harnesses and brushing down horses because at this moment she wished her hands were as silken and soft as his lovers' probably were. She wanted to be a woman in every sense of the word.

'The hands of a queen are never soft. They aren't passive. They take what they want. They are beautiful and elegant and strong. You can take what you want.'

She didn't know what she wanted beyond this pure present instant. She wanted time never to exist again so she could remain just there in the universe created around his voice throbbing inside her and her palm against his. But the moment the thought of time intruded, it began to rush again. She could hear horses coming along from the gravel drive. A curricle and riders. For a moment his hands moved deep under her cloak, catching her and pressing her the length of him convulsively, his face sinking towards her. It was seconds, but she felt the hard ridge press against the pliant skin of her stomach and her whole body clenched against a rush of heat that centred between her legs, making her squirm against him, seeking.

'Nell.' His voice was a warning as he whispered her

name against the corner of her mouth. Then his lips brushed up and against her and he was already a few steps away, taking his coat from where it hung on a railing. By the time the riders appeared he had knotted his cravat and was now marginally presentable but still looked like a pirate, just in rumpled riding clothes.

'What? Did we miss the match?' Meecham called out, his pug-like eyes crestfallen. He bowed and smiled shyly at Nell. 'Hello, Miss Tilney.'

'Did Hidgins win this time?' another man asked hopefully as he inspected Hunter's dishevelled state.

'Sorry, Walters. Maybe next time. Now, if you will excuse me, I need to see Miss Tilney back to the house.'

Nell followed meekly, still shocked at her own behaviour. With that light, humorous and wicked charm he kept slipping through her defences and she didn't even realise it until he was ready to make it clear, as he just had. This man was a walking, talking Trojan Horse.

They came around the paddock by the small stable and she caught sight of Charles holding Griffin's reins well near the bit. The great dark stallion was clearly being his endearing self, shaking his head, his hooves tattooing on the ground, his rear dancing even as Charles tried to control his front. In the neighbouring paddock a large bay stallion was tethered to the fence and he also didn't look overly happy at being so close to a rival stallion.

'Oh, no. Stop,' Nell cried out, but it was too late. Griffin ripped the reins from Charles's grasp with a great backward heave and shied away, bouncing off the ground.

'Charles, get out of the paddock. Leave him be.'

She kept her voice low, but either Charles didn't hear

her or he chose to ignore her because he kept moving towards Griffin. The stallion's movement was so quick it was over in seconds. He had stood with his rear to Charles, but in a flash he turned, lowered his head and charged like a bull, slamming Charles into the fence and dragging him along it before pulling away. Charles dropped and half-rolled, half-crawled under the fence and straight into Nell's arms as she knelt on the grass to pull him through.

'Don't move, don't move.' Her voice was tight with shock, but her hands moved swiftly and surely over his ribs and arms.

'I'm all right,' Charles croaked. 'I'm all right.'

'Well, you don't deserve to be,' Nell said, her voice still shaky. 'What on earth were you thinking, trying to discipline him when he is in full territorial mode with another stallion right there in the next paddock? You are lucky he didn't break your back and bite your hand off into the bargain!'

Charles's cheeks went from chalk to cherry as he shoved to his feet, brushing the dirt from his clothes, but before he could react she reached out.

'I'm sorry, Charles. I didn't mean to scold. I was just frightened.'

He laughed shakily and took her offered hand.

'Don't apologise—I deserved that. I let my temper get the better of me. I should be the one apologising, Helen. I've quite ruined your dress.'

Nell glanced down at the grass stains on her muslin dress.

'That doesn't matter. I'm just glad you're not hurt.'

'Yes, well, we had all best change. It wouldn't do for us to be seen like this.'

Nell flushed at the suspicious look he cast at Hunter's ragged state and the tousled hair escaping her bonnet. She should be happy at this sign of jealousy, but her shakiness just increased as Hunter took hold of her arm again, more stiffly than before, and they moved towards the house.

She cast a glance back at Griffin, who was still cantering around the small enclosure like a tiger pacing its cage. It might be foolish to be worrying about that devil of a horse, but despite what she had told Hunter, she did not really believe anyone was irredeemable. It was a matter of time and patience, and once she established her own stable, and her own school, she would do her best to reach precisely those who erected the most effective barriers against warm human contact.

As they approached the house she realised she had been distracted from her plan to go see Daisy. She would return once she was alone; she could use some time to sort through her own thoughts and she was always clearest when facing a serious equine challenge.

The small stable was empty, which meant Daisy was already out in the paddock, but with the clouds sinking lower and lower the afternoon fog had also rolled in over the low-lying field, obscuring most of it. She ducked under the paddock fence and leaned against it, rubbing her cold hands under her cloak. Then the fog shifted, swirled, and a dark figure came towards her with the speed of a hurtling stone. She held still as Daisy pranced close to the fence, her tail up, her thin forelegs high off the ground. Nell stood with her back half-turned, one hand on the top rung of the fence, her eyes on the ground, and waited. Again and again Daisy made the circuit, but even when her lovely tail flowed out, like hair in water, and grazed Nell's shoulder, Nell kept her gaze on the shift and eddy of the mist around her legs, waiting. Finally a whicker just behind her told her Daisy had stopped and when the filly's breath settled warm and moist against Nell's cold fingers where they lay on the fence she moved very slowly away and into the paddock, her head down. She could feel Daisy just a yard or two behind her at all times, her curiosity and need for contact battling with nervousness. Nell knew what that was like.

Once she completed the circuit she allowed herself a slow glance up. The filly stood quite close, her eyes a wide liquid brown. Very slowly Nell reached out and stroked her neck, just once. Daisy held still and then lowered her head, edging closer. Nell allowed herself another couple of gentle caresses and then placed her hand back on the fence. After a moment the filly nuzzled her hand and then turned away, rising on her hind legs and doing a strange little dance before bucking playfully and cantering off again. Nell burst into delighted laughter at the beautiful animal's surprising show of character and at her own success.

'I'm glad at least you find this amusing.' Hunter's harsh tones snapped her out of her reverie and she whirled around, raising her hands.

'Hush!'

'Lady Welbeck sent your maid for you and the poor girl enlisted Hidgins's help when she couldn't find you. We've been looking everywhere for you!'

She hugged her cloak to her, not sure whether the shivering was from the cold or his anger.

'I'm sorry I caused a bother. I should have asked

Betsy to tell Lady Welbeck I had a headache or something. I wanted to see Daisy.'

'Alone? And in this weather?'

'Yes, alone. I wanted to see Daisy without anyone distracting her. Stop treating me like a child!'

'You are quite right—you aren't a child. You're a damn walking provocation. You can't just go tramping around the stables and fields on your own with impunity. Anyone could have...'

He half-turned away, his jaw tight, and contrarily her resentment faded as she registered his tension. Just as Biggs had said earlier, he took his responsibilities far too seriously.

The wind shoved at them and when they still didn't move it flicked some needles of rain at them. Hunter took her hand and turned her towards the house.

'Your hand is frozen. These gloves are hardly any more than a scrap of cotton. Don't you know to put on real gloves before you go out in this weather?'

She laughed at the scold.

'I forgot.'

'Very childish. Come, we need to warm you up.'

She didn't answer. It wasn't so terrible after all to be treated like a child sometimes, being led by a very large and warm hand. She hadn't quite realised how cold and stiff she had become until his fingers forced hers apart and laced between them with his palm pressed against hers.

When they reached the door to her room she turned to thank him, but there was a burst of laughter from the stairs and she suddenly found herself inside her room with Hunter.

'You can't be here,' she whispered. 'What if Betsy comes?'

He turned the key in the lock.

'Problem solved. Besides, you need someone to light your fire.'

She frowned at his back as he took the tinderbox from the mantel and bent down to the grate. She nearly answered that she was quite capable of lighting her own fire, but that seemed the wrong response to his words. Instead, she unfastened her damp cloak and hung it from a peg by the wardrobe. When he rose from the burgeoning fire she stepped back.

'Thank you. Now…'

He took her hand and sat her down on a chair by the fire.

'Now we thaw you out. You're turned to ice. Little fool.'

He sank down on one knee and cupped her clenched right hand. Reality swirled and for a moment she thought of a knight presenting a precious offering to his sovereign. He took off her glove and gently rubbed and chafed her hand until it tingled and pulsed.

'Here, I think we've thawed this one out. Let me see.' He touched his mouth to the back of her hand, turned it over and gently smoothed out her clenched fingers before pressing the same light kiss to her palm.

'Now let's have the other hand,' he said, placing her warmed hand in her lap and holding out his own hand, his eyes on hers.

She gave it to him and just sat as he continued his ministering. Except that it wasn't the same. When he had propelled her into the room she had felt embarrassed and foolish and he had been in full imperious mode and she had hardly noticed when he had taken off her glove.

Now something had shifted. The fabric of her glove caught and pulled and slithered over her cold skin, and when he cupped her fist and very gently blew upon it, like a mother warming her child's hands, the heat was too intense, like hot water poured on a limb recovering from frostbite. She tried to draw it away, but he held it without force and it stayed there. After a moment he began the same calming ritual as before. His thumb moved gently over the bones of her wrist, the back of her hand and the sweep between her finger and thumb.

She watched his long elegant fingers move between hers, darker and more powerful and so gentle. She watched him, the dark chestnut gleams in his hair, the black lashes shielding the gold in his eyes. She wanted so much to touch that hair, the sharp ridge of his cheekbone. There was a little white scar there, a slightly tipsy letter L, hardly visible, and she remembered the way he had touched the scar by her mouth and she wondered she hadn't seen it before. He was slowly coming into focus for her. Element by element.

'What is this from?' She touched her finger to the scar and his hands stilled, his eyes glinting like a cat ready to spring.

'What?'

'The scar, the little L. Here.' She touched it again. She wanted to do more than that, place her now-warm palm to it, bend down to brush it with her mouth.

'I don't remember.' His voice was already closing down and she felt it in his hands, too, as they gently placed her left hand in her lap, but she turned it and caught his wrist and he didn't immediately draw it away.

She was walking the edge of his pain and any moment now he would repel her, either with mockery or teasing or anger.

'I was trying to rescue my brother's cat. It wasn't grateful,' he said after a moment and she thought of that sweet boy's face in his ensign's uniform and of Hunter as the fierce little warrior protecting his domain and subjects.

'Your brother probably was.'

His eyes flicked to hers again, the danger more evident now. Even his breathing had changed. Her insides started to grate with the inevitable reaction to anger, but she wouldn't stand down. Hunter wouldn't hurt her. Not like this, anyway.

'It's unusual for a boy to have a cat,' she said into the silence. 'Did he like animals?'

He pushed up from his knees and turned towards the door, but then walked towards the dresser.

'He was often ill and bedridden as a boy, so I brought him the kitten to keep him company when I went away to school. Why he ever went into the army I'll never know. I told him he was a fool. I should have stopped him.'

'Maybe he had something to prove.' It must have been hard having an older brother who was so very good at everything male.

'He had nothing to prove. Everyone that mattered loved him. It was my fault for thinking it was a good idea he be sent to school. It took me months to realise he was miserable there and I only found out by chance because one of the boys there was the younger brother of a friend of mine. He never complained. The fool even apologised for making me come all the way there to bring him home. He was just like that. He gave back a hell of a lot more than I could manage to give him. He was the last person on earth who should have had to prove anything to anyone.'

Nell watched him pace the room.

'He sounds as stubborn as you in his own way. You probably couldn't have stopped him.'

'I should have found a way. I knew it was wrong for him, but I never thought... I should have stopped him.'

'He was a grown man by then. Even if you considered yourself responsible for him, you couldn't live his life for him.'

'I didn't want to live his life, just try to prevent his death! I failed him when I let him join and I failed him when I couldn't stop him from taking his own life. Don't you understand? When he came to me saying he wanted to join up, I actually encouraged him. I thought it would finally force him into the world. I never thought they would send someone like him to the Peninsula, let alone put him on Wellington's staff. I knew it was wrong, but he was so damn proud of himself I allowed myself to believe he was finally ready to stand on his own two feet. That's the worst. I was so damn relieved he was finally growing up, that... What a selfish fool I was...'

The room itself was thudding with the restless energy of his pacing and she held herself very still, wondering how to keep him talking.

'How long was he in the war?'

She wasn't certain he would answer, but she waited.

'Just under a year. Six months before he was captured and then five months in that hell. He was so broken they had to move him to a monastery because the gaolers couldn't stand his screaming every night. The abbot was so horrified he actually helped us… He woke up screaming to the end.'

Her mind worked away at the pieces even though her heart was wholly caught in Hunter's agony and guilt and loss. She could feel them as palpably as if each was a living, beating organ on its own. But it was her mind that spoke, too shocked to hold back the words, because the threat to Hunter felt real and present.

'Helped you? You went to rescue him yourself? During the war?'

It was a mistake. He turned back to her and she could see him gathering in and carefully shutting down. Pain and guilt were returned to their drawers and the door firmly closed on her.

'It's already past six. You should dress. I will see you downstairs.'

She stood, trying to think of something to bring him back.

'Gabriel, you aren't to blame for what happened to him…'

'I will see you downstairs.'

He reached the door and turned to her and she had never heard him speak with such a bite of ice in his voice.

'I am not one of your homesick little schoolgirls to be soothed and mollified. You don't know me and you certainly didn't know Tim, so I would appreciate if you would refrain altogether from discussing the subject. I don't like meddlers.'

Chapter Ten

Hunter watched Charles bend over Nell's shoulder as he leaned to turn the page of the *Illustrated Collection of Thoroughbreds* balanced on Nell's lap, his hand so close to a flaxen curve of hair resting on her nape that if she breathed in deeply the man's fingers would tangle in it. From the easy intimacy of Charles's posture it was obvious Nell's scold after Griffin's attack had shifted the balance between them and for once Welbeck's eagerness in her presence didn't appear at all forced.

His own absence today had probably helped as well. He hadn't joined her or the Welbecks the previous evening and had spent the morning down in Wilton, but he had known he had to show his face eventually, if only to tell her he had decided to return to London. She was safe enough with the Welbecks until her father came for her. Safer than she was with him. It hadn't taken the recurrence of his nightmare that night to remind him that he was still paying the price of allowing himself to care for people who were too weak to care for themselves. It was only getting worse. This time she had also been at the centre of his dream, walking blithely towards a rearing, raging black beast while he tried to stop her, weighed down by Tim's pain-racked body. He had saved neither of them and had awoken shivering, his nightshirt soaked in sweat.

He should have left right away, but he had gone to Wilton instead and now it was too late to drive to London today. Besides, he had to face her and tell her he was leaving. The problem was he had no idea what to say to her after his outburst the previous evening. He had never lost his calm like that, not even when the pain and guilt at failing the one person in the world he needed to protect above all had still been so raw he had thought it would submerge him. He still didn't understand why he had lashed out. So what if she had seen through him and shown him a little compassion? That was her nature, the same impulse that drove her need to worry about Daisy or her schoolgirls. Nothing more. There was no reason for it to have felt like danger. Not from her, but from something inside himself. Something dark and sluggish had stirred in response to her warmth and the invitation to share, something he knew very well was not to be set loose.

He shouldn't have gone into her room in the first place. He was already raw when he reached the paddock, worrying that she might have gone to see that devil Griffin, or perhaps been accosted by someone. She was far too trusting when around horses and someone might misread her warmth as an invitation. The relief of finding her safe by the paddock had been overtaken by something else as he stopped to watch the peculiar courtship between her and the filly. He had been mesmerised by her stillness, the calm and calming presence that drew the nervous filly towards her, closer with each circuit, the young horse's whole body easing until it had finally come to a stop. When the filly had nuzzled Nell's hand on the fence, a thunderclap of lust so powerful had struck him and he had almost moved after her as well when she began walking. But he kept still, waiting for it to pass like the first shock of a bee sting before it settled into a persistent ache and itch. By the time she and the filly completed the calm, companionable circuit and climbed out of the paddock, he thought he had regained some control. But he had been wrong. The sting had subsided, but the ache had only deepened.

He watched her and Welbeck's golden heads bent close together. He might not think much of Welbeck, but there was no denying the man was a damn sight more respectable than him and it was beginning to look like her dream of having her prince fall in love with her might not be so far-fetched. All the more reason to step back. The only problem with this resolution was the heat that was even now simmering in him as he watched her; his attention kept snagging on elements of her—on the shadows and lines marking the winged perfection of her collarbone, on her elegant fingers as they turned the pages, on the slope of her shoulder that Welbeck kept hovering over, adding the burn of anger to the mix of snapping desire. It must be because he was unused to dealing with innocents, but just sliding his fingers over the ridge of her wrist bone, into the soft valleys between her fingers, had packed a greater erotic punch than a full naked display. By the time he had moved to her second hand he had been harder than he had ever been with Kate and that was without Nell even touching him. Then she had touched his cheek, her finger as soft as a raindrop on his skin, falling on painfully fertile ground—it had taken all his will not to accept that invitation and make use of the bed behind him.

It was just Nell being Nell, he told himself. There was nothing to read into it, certainly less than the shocked panic she had exhibited running towards Charles in the paddock. He could forgive her for her unintended seductiveness, but it was harder to forgive her for the way she had made him reveal things about Tim—treacherous things, showing Tim in his weakness and his dependency and raising the edge of the cover on Hunter's lifelong frustration with his younger brother. He could never have explained to anyone why he had always been envious of Tim. He had told her that Tim had never asked for anything and it was true, but from the day his brother was born he had received a full measure of love and a cocooning care that no one had ever thought to offer Hunter.

His mother had told him that he had come out ready to fight and had taken whatever he wanted without waiting to be offered. She had actually been proud that he had never needed shielding, not even from his drunken libertine of a father. Far from it, he had become her champion at the tender age of six and it had been as natural as breathing to extend that shield to Tim, who had always been dreamy and fragile and who had looked up to Hunter as a demigod at least. He hadn't even known there was something wrong with his mother's and Tim's dependency on him until he had brought Tim back all broken and had to come to terms with their weakness. In the end he had shattered along with Tim and he hated being reminded of it. Nell had blindsided him in there, taking advantage of that moment of weakness to make him betray Tim and his own perfidy. He was losing control of the situation to an inexperienced virgin.

It was a stark reminder it was time he returned to London. She was safe enough here with the Welbecks. Depending on one's definition of 'safe', he thought, as he watched Welbeck laugh at something she said and lightly brush the curve of her shoulder as he turned the page. Hunter saw her shoulder hitch just a little and his fists closed reflexively. He might not want to marry her, but he was damned if he was going to let them paint him a cuckold while he stood just two yards away.

'Do let the girl have some fun, Hunter.' Lady Melkinson glided into his path as he began to move towards Nell, her childish blue eyes raised to his in the sweetest of smiles. 'She's been aching for it for *soooo* long, apparently.'

'Phyllida. Engaged in procuring now? Aren't you concerned your swain might stray?'

'Darling Hunter, always so distressingly direct. You cannot seriously think I find that long meg a rival? I am fond of Charles and he has his heart set on expanding his stables. If it's the land you want, I am certain some agreement can be reached without you having to abandon your hedonistic lifestyle. He has no interest in Hampshire and you can more than afford it.'

'I'm curious—has he sent you to negotiate or is this your own initiative? In any case, it is rather late in the day for that. She is, after all, engaged to me.'

'Well, precisely, my dear. To you. Had it been a love match naturally Charles would concede defeat. But apparently Tilney in his cups was quite revealing. Charles knows this engagement is mercenary on your part and everyone at Welbeck knows the chit has held a candle for him half her life, and though you are admittedly a very handsome and charming rake likely to appeal to women of more…mature tastes, Charles is the epitome of any girl's dreams, isn't he?'

'Apparently not just girls.'

Lady Melkinson laughed and tapped his arm with her fan.

'I do admit there is something scintillating about waking next to a man quite as beautiful as I. I simply knew I must have him when I saw him.'

'All those mirrors in your rooms no longer satisfying, Phyl?'

'The pleasure is thus doubled,' she replied with a mock-innocent fluttering of her lashes.

'I'm not sure I can stomach the image. Now, if you will excuse me, I will go and relieve your pretty prince of his chivalric duties. I wouldn't be quite as certain as you that he is not enjoying himself far more than you would care to admit, Phyl. There is a saying—be careful what you wish for.'

He walked around her, barely refraining from walking through her. Not even her quick frown of doubt gave him satisfaction. Nell and Charles looked up as his shadow fell across the illustrated plate of the stallion they were examining, and though Charles straightened, he didn't relinquish his position by her side. Nell's gaze flicked past him towards Lady Melkinson.

'Lord Hunter.'

He had been wrong that she was angry at him, he realised. Just wary. He had begun to forget how sensitive she was to anger. Another mark against him and another reminder of why he should stay away from her.

'Shopping for new inmates for Bascombe's stables?'

he enquired. 'I don't think Tiresias is for sale. Portland is quite attached to him. But he might be willing to part with Bull Dog.'

'I was just looking,' she said wistfully, her shoulders releasing some tension. 'He is quite beautiful. And look at this lovely brood mare, Lady Grey. Her stallion Gustavus won the July Stakes. I heard he's a perfect grey. Did you see him?'

'It was a wonderful run,' Charles interposed. 'I wish you would come to the races, Nell. Newmarket and Epsom are quite respectable and it is a great pity your father never brought you. Perhaps once you are married you will attend.'

His tones were both teasing and caressing and Hunter's jaw tightened.

'That's an excellent idea. If we forgo the banns and can track down a handy bishop we can make it to the Newmarket Meeting, Nell,' he offered.

'Attending the races is not a sufficient reason to rush into wedlock, Lord Hunter,' Nell replied primly, but the laughter had returned to her eyes.

'Certainly not. There are many better reasons, both sufficient and necessary. Excuse me, Welbeck. My betrothed apparently needs my help listing them.'

Hunter sat down by Nell and Welbeck was forced to retreat. Once he was gone Hunter turned to Nell.

'I'm sorry about yesterday.'

Her mouth parted in surprise and she shook her head.

'No, it was my fault. I shouldn't have pried. You had every right to warn me off. I just… You have nothing to apologise for.'

'Yes, I do. I am not accustomed to speaking about Tim and I reacted badly. Not even my aunts know everything, just the two men who were with me in France. I wasn't angry at you and I don't really think you were meddling. Forgive me.'

She shook her head again.

'I knew it wasn't really at me and it was foolish to expect you to talk to me about something so precious to you. As you said, we hardly know each other. I don't particularly like talking with people about what hurts me, either. Perhaps because I already told you things I only told my closest friends and I wanted to help and I didn't know how and I made a mull of it; I know it was presumptuous of me. Do you forgive me?'

Hunter reminded himself he was in a civilised drawing room under the very watchful and hostile eyes of his hosts. He had no idea what to do with the fist clenching around his lungs, but doing any of the things the rest of his body was clamouring for was strictly impossible. He took the book and closed it, allowing himself a light brush of his hand along her fingers, trying to ignore the dangerous heating in his groin. He was allowing this aggravating lust to dictate his actions again, but at the moment he was too unsettled to care. Besides, he had to tell her he would be returning to London and he preferred to do that without an audience.

'I hear the Welbecks have a very fine Stubbs of Diomed. Have you ever seen it?'

'Yes, it's in the green room,' she replied as he drew her to her feet, the telltale tinge of colour filling out her lips, and he held himself from tightening his hold on her hand as he led her towards the green room.

'Do you like it?' she asked, looking at the painting.

'Like what?'

The confusion in her eyes turned to laughter.

'You don't care much for art, I gather. Why did you want to see it, then?'

'I never said I wanted to see it. I am more interested in the green room.'

She glanced around with a frown.

'Why? Is there something special here?'

'Two very rare commodities. Privacy and you.'

She stilled.

'I see. No one has ever called me a commodity before. I am not certain I appreciate being categorised with corn and turnips.'

'The schoolmistress should know most terms have multiple meanings. In this case as something of value or necessity.'

'It's not that I am not impressed, but don't you ever become weary of always having a suave answer ready?'

Hunter considered various less-than-polite responses to his betrothed's impertinence.

'I certainly do if my efforts aren't being appreciated. I recall a very direct request that I flirt with you.'

'And you do it beautifully, but I think I was wrong to ask it of you. It is rather like harnessing your chestnuts to a gig.'

'Good God, woman! That must be the most insulting compliment I have ever received. You might try for a touch of suavity yourself.'

Her face lit with a surprisingly shy smile and he stepped forward and stopped. He had come here to tell her he was leaving, not to settle the debate in his mind whether this was just a girl to be handled lightly or a woman to be seduced to the point of mutual combustion.

'I sent a letter to your father yesterday care of Buxted.'

The laughter drained out of her eyes and she raised her chin.

'What did you tell him?'

'That you are here and the key points you and I have already discussed. That the three of us need to resolve this issue. Reasonably.'

'I see.'

He moved back towards the picture, not looking at her.

'I think it best that you stay here and I return to London until he arrives. My being here…complicates matters. Besides, you don't need me here.'

That sentence had sounded reasonable enough when he had formulated it in his mind. There was no reason to feel just as he did when he woke from his nightmares, shaky and emptied. It was ridiculous to feel guilty about abandoning… He wasn't abandoning her. This was precisely where she wanted to be with precisely whom she wanted to be. Simply because he was aching to bed her didn't mean he should subvert her whole life and his for a bodily urge. He was neither ready to assume a burden like her nor willing to expose his weakness to her, and that was precisely what would happen if he allowed himself to think with his body rather than his mind.

'I see,' she said again, but her voice sounded distant. There, it was done. Time for a swift exit.

'Perhaps I should stay until your father arrives. I don't want you to face the worst of his anger alone.'

She shivered or shook her head, he couldn't tell, but when she spoke her voice was clear.

'There is no need for that. He can't hurt me any more. You shouldn't stay because of that.'

The key now was to walk out and let her proceed

with her dreams, however flawed. She would probably discover soon enough that Phyllida wouldn't let go of Welbeck that easily, perhaps even less easily now that he was hankering after another, and very wealthy, woman. Phyllida would consider it piquant to deck herself in jewels purchased with another woman's money. It wasn't his business. He was probably being petty because the thought of anyone…

'Won't you stay for the jumping and the fête tomorrow?' she asked suddenly. 'It's the best day of the fair. I hate the thought that you feel you must leave because of me. It's just one more day.'

Just one more day. He shouldn't; he could do a great deal of damage in a day.

'Perhaps…one more day. But I would think you would rather remove me from the field now that you are doing so well with Welbeck, no?'

'I'm not quite that shallow. I don't know how to thank you for—'

'Whatever you do, don't start thanking me!'

She looked up, startled, but then she smiled.

'I forget sometimes how sensitive you are.'

'That's more like it. I was wondering how long before you started abusing me again.'

'I was trying to thank you!' She laughed.

'Your gratitude, like your compliments, leaves a great deal to be desired. Your abuse, on the other hand, provides a perfect excuse to punish you a little in turn.'

He moved towards her. He was surely allowed one more taste…

'That isn't punishment.' Her voice, quick, breathless, and both mischievous and touched with longing, cleaved through him and whatever shreds of suavity he still possessed incinerated in the heat that rose through him. God help him, he was blushing; he could feel the singe of fire in his face, everywhere. It was wrong. He had no business taking this any further when he had no intention to follow through. If he did one hundredth of what he wanted to do to her he would probably both terrify her and end up trapped...

He backed her against the wall and the silver-grey of her eyes darkened in an invitation as clear as the flush on her lips and cheeks and the arch of her back as her hips met his for a moment before pressing back, just enough to make him painfully aware of how hard he was. These teasing tastes were moving quickly from the realm of playful pleasure to sheer torture.

'Are you sure you haven't done this before?' he asked, tracing the line of her cheek with his knuckles, his voice husky and strange even to his own ears. 'You are far too good at this.'

'Mrs Petheridge always told me to insist on employing the best instructors if I wanted to excel.' Her own voice sank to the melodic rasp that did so much damage to his control. How on earth had she managed to make the mention of her headmistress erotic?

He gave in and sank against her, gathering her to him, moulding his hands down the dip of her back and to the soft round curve of her behind. He groaned, his hands tightening on the pliant flesh, and she rose against him, her hands twisting into the lapels of his coat, her hips arching against his again, and he held her there, trying to remind himself why it was not a good idea to toss up his virgin betrothed's skirts in the unlocked and very exposed drawing room of his hosts and discover if she was as damp as he was hard.

She pushed away so abruptly it took him a moment to notice the door opening.

'Hunter,' Phyllida Melkinson's silken voice admonished from the doorway. 'Not the hackneyed "come see the painting" ploy. So *déclassé*. You are usually much more original.'

Hunter resisted a powerful urge to toss her out, under no illusion she had just happened to enter the green room by chance.

'I think you have mistaken the room, Phyllida. We left your quarry in the main drawing room.'

She unfurled her fan with a smile, her eyes shining bright blue victory above the ivory sticks.

'Under the circumstances don't you think it wise to revert to calling me by my title, my dear Lord Hunter?'

Hunter held Nell's arm as she tried to pull away. He was definitely off form to have made such a foolish error.

'I was just taking a leaf from your book and leaving your poor husband out of it. Now if you don't mind, we are busy.'

'So I see. Appreciating the livestock. Such fine sturdy beasts, don't you think, Miss Tilney? I do believe I heard Lord Welbeck mention that you were wont to ride astride as a child? Very daring. I am almost jealous.'

'Of what, Lady Melkinson?' Nell asked and Hunter felt the tension in her arm. 'I would have thought you well versed in riding all forms of sturdy beasts.'

The fan dropped to dangle by its ribbon from Lady Melkinson's wrist and Hunter, too, slackened his hold in shock and amusement at the unexpected vulgarity of Nell's comment. But Phyllida recovered swiftly.

'Oh, most amusing. I see all those years in the stables have given you a certain finesse, my dear. Perhaps you might be a match for Hunter after all. He is quite worth-while, even if one has to share. Oh, don't bite my head off as I see you wish to, Hunter. I shall remove my presence so you can continue your campaign to secure the heiress, but really, my dear Miss Tilney, I assure you you have no need to buy yourself a husband as your equally horse-mad mama apparently did. You do see such alliances do not always prosper...'

Her words petered out as Nell tugged out of Hunter's hold and took three long strides towards her.

'You will not mention my mother, or I will...'

Lady Melkinson shrugged, but there was a flicker of fear in her eyes and when she spoke again she had put a *chaise longue* between them.

'Or you will what? Really, there is no need for such histrionics. Everyone knows Tilney married your mother so he could expand his stables, no pun intended.'

'Or I will have a tearful word with your husband about how you are throwing yourself at my betrothed,' Nell continued with resolution, the words grinding out between her teeth, but Hunter could hear the quiver of tension in her voice and moved towards her. 'Downstairs gossip has it that Lord Melkinson has already threatened to curtail your pin money after a certain scandal in London. If I hear one more mention of my mother's name on your lips, I will happily add wood to that fire and you might have to make do with whatever baubles you can cozen from your lovers. So I suggest you watch your words carefully from now on, you little...'

'Nell?'

They all turned to the door where Charles stood staring in shock.

'What on earth is going on here?'

Lady Melkinson sank onto the *chaise longue* with a small sob and drew out a lace handkerchief from her reticule, pressing it to her eyes.

'I merely remarked that Miss Tilney shouldn't be here unattended and she… I have never been so insulted in my life.'

'Somehow I doubt that,' Nell muttered, and Hunter crossed his arms, trying not to smile.

Charles entered the room, his hands raised placatingly.

'I suggest we all return to the drawing room. It really is quite improper for you to be here alone with Lord Hunter, Nell, engaged or not.'

'Please, Mr Welbeck,' Phyllida said prettily. 'There is no need to chastise Miss Tilney. She is clearly unused to polite society.'

Nell rounded on her.

'I may be unused to polite society, but I am very used to spoilt girls like you who think they can manipulate people around them with impunity. Certainly in the lower forms of the school where I work. As for you, Charles, I will accept rebukes regarding my conduct from your mother, not from you or Lady Melkinson. I certainly won't remain silent while she insults my mother.'

'I am certain Lady Melkinson did not intend to insult—'

'Are you, Charles?' Nell interrupted. 'On what precisely do you base that certainty?'

Charles's glance flickered over to Lady Melkinson, who dabbed her handkerchief to the corner of her eye. He held his hand out towards Nell, smiling.

'If she did, then naturally it was most improper and

I will ensure she will not do so again. You were right to chastise me as well, but I really did mean it for the best. Won't you please come in to supper with me, Nell?'

Hunter wondered that Welbeck had not realised how telling his words about Phyllida were. He could see Nell noticed the familiarity immediately and her mouth bowed, her eyes darkening. She shook her head.

'You are very kind, but I have the headache. I will ask for something to be brought to my room. Good evening.'

Welbeck moved towards her, but she evaded him and left the room.

Nell refrained from taking the stairs two at a time, but only just barely. Clearly the same considerations didn't apply to Hunter because he caught up with her halfway up and she wished it wouldn't be considered childish to shove him back down. First he raged at her, and then he disappeared for a whole day only to turn up and pull the rug out from under her with that apology, then to tell her he was leaving her to her fate. And after he had unsettled her once again with his flirting and his embrace he hadn't even come to her defence when that woman, who had also probably once been one of his endless succession of mistresses, tore strips off her. He was the very last person on earth she wanted to speak to right now.

'Leave me alone!'

'Presently.'

He took her arm and she tugged it away abruptly and nearly stumbled on the last step. He took it again, steadying her.

'It is a bit late to be offering assistance when I no longer need it!' she snapped, turning to glare at him.

He frowned down at her.

'If you had needed my help, believe me, I would have come to your aid. But you didn't.'

'Yes, I did. She just sat there play-acting in the most unconvincing way and he believed her...'

'Well, that's her stock-in-trade, isn't it? It's not surprising she does it well.'

'She made a fool of me.'

'No, she didn't. You were magnificent. You won that round hands down and she knows it.'

'What on earth are you talking about? I ranted like a demented schoolteacher and she sat there like a stricken kitten. I know you are just desperate to wash your hands of this whole affair, but you could have done something other than stand there smiling!'

'You had her against the ropes—can't you see that? That was precisely why she had to resort to such a cheap trick. You most certainly didn't need my help.'

'I may not have needed it, but I wanted it. Even if you don't want to marry me, I thought you were my friend.' She felt very foolish and young as the words came out, even more so because she was so raw and confused. Everything was moving too fast. She had been racked by guilt all day at hurting Hunter. She hadn't even been able to apologise because he had disappeared to Wilton in the morning. It had been almost a relief to have Charles seek her out during the day and she had even felt the warmth in his eyes was sincere and not just a manifestation of his usual offhand cheerfulness.

When Hunter entered the drawing room in the afternoon she had just hoped for an opportunity to apologise. His own apology had shaken her and probably contributed to her willingness to sink into the disturbing but increasingly familiar warmth of flirting with him, seeking to erase the traces of tension between them. But then that woman had to ruin it by practically parading both him and Charles like possessions, confident that all it took was for her to bat her lids in their direction and they would come running. Hunter's words, that she had had the upper hand, were ludicrous.

It was always hard to read Hunter's face; sometimes it was the light-hearted humour or the teasing that served as a mask, but now, like those painful and unsettling moments in her room, it was a forbidding blankness that came between them and reminded her he was far from the easy-going rake people thought him to be. She was beginning to distinguish shapes in the dark shadows in his eyes. She could see conflicting currents of anger and compassion and even resentment. When he spoke his voice was without inflection, but the calm unravelled as he spoke.

'If I had felt you needed to be saved from someone who could do you real damage, believe me, I would have had their face in the dust before they got within hailing distance of you. Why the devil do you think I made it a condition of the engagement that you board at that school and never return to Tilney? But interceding between you and that doxy would be more of an insult to you than to her. Four years ago I saw you take down a tyrant and, however hard it may have been, don't tell me you don't look back at that moment with pride. Now tell me you don't feel good about not being the one who collapsed in fake tears on the sofa.'

Her hand closed tightly on the knob of the banister.

'What do you mean you made it a condition?'

Chagrin flickered in his tawny eyes.

'That's not the point. The point is...'

'You forced Father to let me stay in Keswick year-round?'

He hesitated.

'I thought you wanted to? Was that wrong?'

She pressed her hand to her forehead and continued down the hallway, feeling rather dazed, all her anger against him fizzling. Present and past were all shifting and rearranging and her excuse of a headache looked likely to become a reality. With each passing day it was even stranger that her memory of Hunter's presence at that pivotal moment four years ago should be so tenuous. Her future had changed during those two days in so many ways and this man had been instrumental in most of them and she hadn't even known or thought twice about him except to occasionally cringe that she had disgraced herself so thoroughly in front of the handsome, troubled young man who had been so good with Petra.

He had been right about her. Again. As embarrassed and shaky as she was, it *was* a victory of sorts to stand up to someone so beautiful and experienced, and though she might have wanted a knight in shining armour or two to leap to her defence, she had done moderately well on her own. In fact, she had done quite well against someone with skills as finely honed as Lady Melkinson.

She stopped and turned to him.

'I don't know how to thank you, for everything.'

'I didn't say that to be thanked.'

His frown deepened, making her think of a proud little boy who had just been told how adorable he was and was finding the compliment vastly distasteful.

'I know, but I'm grateful anyway. You can't even begin to understand how much that changed everything for me. I was to come back to Tilney for good the following year and it would have been hell. Staying with Mrs Petheridge was one of the best things that ever happened to me.'

'Don't exaggerate my part in it. It involved no effort on my part, so all this gratitude is very cheaply bought. Besides, I think you underestimated your ability to deal with your aunt even if you had returned to Tilney.'

'Perhaps you are right. It wasn't just that one night, I was growing out of her power anyway, but it certainly was much more enjoyable staying in Keswick than waging battle, successful or not, at Tilney. But if you wish to cling to your selfish-rake façade and reject any token of gratitude, I shan't insist.'

'Don't start deluding yourself it's just a façade, sweetheart. Just to prove it I think I will accept a token of your gratitude after all. But not in the middle of the corridor.'

Before she could respond he pulled her along and opened a door by the servants' stairwell.

'The linen closet? Really?' She laughed nervously as much with anticipation as the fear of being discovered again. Her mind might be plagued by uncertainty and upheaval, but her body had a simpler view on matters and it was already tingling and heating as his arms rose to lean against the shelves on either side of her, caging her in.

'A very useful room, love. One should always know where they are located.'

'Someone might...'

'No servants will be engaged in changing the linen in the evening. Too busy with preparations for supper.'

'Also useful information,' she murmured, wondering why she wasn't more outraged. But it had been a difficult day and right now she just wanted…something. Something wholly for herself and without thought of consequence. She should want Charles here with her, but it was hard to imagine Charles in a linen closet. It was hard to imagine anything at all with the heat of Hunter's body seeping into her even though he hadn't touched her yet. She wanted him to. To start with his amazingly beautiful lips, that carved line around the lower lip was magnificent, as beautiful as any statue. She had to admit he had a finer mouth than Charles, but maybe that was because she had already felt Hunter's on hers and she knew to her core how wonderful it felt, so it wasn't fair to compare.

Especially when it was already on hers. Oh, heaven…

It felt as beautiful as it looked, she decided as she closed her eyes. Its beauty was spreading through her like dye in water, a hue of its own, colouring her as it went, making her beautiful. Powerful.

Her palms were cool against his cheekbones as she slid her fingers slowly into his hair, gathering sensations as they went, so sensitive she could feel that little scar puckered against her palm. She slid her mouth from his, rising on tiptoe to trace with her lips the line her hands had marked, the lean plane of his cheek, the scrape of stubble along his jaw.

When she lingered on that whitish L his breath shuddered in and out. Her body echoed that shudder, moving towards his heat, moulding to his length as her mouth was moulding itself to the ridge of his jaw just beside his ear. She was back in that wonderful *sleep-wake-buzz* realm except that she wanted more.

Apparently so did Hunter because his passive acceptance of her exploration gave way. His arms left the shelf, one hand tangling in her hair and the other wrapping around her back, pulling her even more firmly against him. Pins clinked on the stone floor and she felt the weight of her hair slide and roll off her shoulders, then the tug and pull as his hands sank into it, tilting her head back. His eyes were gathering all the last glimmers of light from the high window above them and turning them to tawny flames.

'Nell… I want to see you with just your hair between us…'

His voice rubbed against her like rough velvet and her legs pressed together involuntarily as if it had scraped against her just there. The thought of her hair, sliding pale and silky against the warm tan skin she had glimpsed in the stable yard, trailing down over his waist, his hips. The same hips which were now pressing against her, hard and bulging and rigid as a real statue. It was surely unthinkable to actually want to see his hips, to see his everything, to bare him as he was baring her, slipping the dress from her shoulder.

Her skin danced as his mouth moved down her neck, tasting, licking, lashing at her nerves and dragging little moans from her she couldn't silence. She wanted closer; she wanted to tangle her body with his, merge it, lose it.

She wanted more.

'Hunter, please…' That wasn't her voice; her voice could never sound like that. But it had a clear effect on Hunter. His body surged against her, pressing her back against the piles of linen, between her spread legs, his fingers biting into her thighs as his mouth opened on hers, moving from coaxing to consuming.

He was devouring her, burning her, absorbing even her breath. She didn't need to breathe. She gave back everything until he groaned as well, pulling away a little, his hands denying his withdrawal by tightening around her, and then he gave way and was kissing her again with an abandon that she instinctively knew was out of character and she revelled in the gift of it.

He might not be a knight in shining armour, but her body felt revered as his lips seared and teased and feasted on hers until it started happening again, that rising of her body, a gathering into a powerful, throbbing unity telling her there was so much more and she needed it now. She was so hot it was becoming unbearable; she needed to do something. She dragged his body towards her and the moment the hard muscles of his thighs pressed against her the chaotic heat gathered into a fireball between her legs.

'I don't know what to do,' she moaned, squirming against him, and his arms tightened around her, pressing his mouth to the soft skin of her neck, his voice shaky with laughter or something else.

'Yes, you do. God help me, you do.'

She didn't care if he was laughing because his mouth was suckling at the skin there and now the fireball had grown and she could feel it in the tingling, aching tips of her breasts. Was it mad to want his mouth there as well, doing just that, tasting, sucking? She must be mad because that was her hand taking his and pressing it there. Oh, heaven, that felt right...

'This is madness. We can't...' he groaned even as his hand tightened on her breast, his thumb finding and brushing that ache into a cascade of fireworks along her nerves.

She was about to argue that they not only could but must, when their combined weight proved too much for the shelf behind her and with a creak it gave way and tilted. Luckily the snowy mountain of linen hit the ground before them, but Nell's backside still struck the padded ground with enough force to wake her. They remained motionless for a moment, Hunter's arm still around her, his other braced on a pile of pillowcases.

Her eyes met Hunter's and she covered her mouth to stifle a laugh. Immediately the lines at the corners of his eyes crinkled in response.

'I told you a linen closet was a bad idea,' he whispered, his head canted as they listened to see if someone had overheard the fracas.

She smiled guiltily and reluctantly pushed him away.

'We need to put the linen back.'

'We need to return you safely to your room. You look as tumbled as the sheets.'

She didn't know if it was possible to flush further, but she certainly felt her temperature rise.

'We can't leave it like this. Apparently linen closets have distinct disadvantages. Has this ever happened to you before?'

His arms tightened on her as he drew her to her feet and for a moment his mouth settled lightly on the curve of her neck before he bent to pick up a pile of sheets that had somehow remained folded.

'Since this is my first time to ever make use of a linen closet, I have to say it hasn't.'

She swiftly picked up another pile.

'I thought you said…'

'Knowing where they are doesn't mean I have made use of them before. Now I know why it is better to employ one's own rooms. There, that looks almost respectable. Come, we should return you to yours before our luck runs out. You need to rest before the fête tomorrow.'

He was clearly in control of himself now, both the passionate lover and the vulnerable boy tucked away as neatly as the piles of linen had been before they had tumbled them. So she held back all manners of answers and thoughts and allowed him to lead her to her room and push her in gently but firmly, closing the door between them.

She stared at its blank surface. She had no idea what she would have done if he had chosen to stay. She hardly recognised herself any longer. How had she allowed this man, this…rake, to so undermine her plans and in a matter of mere days? He had just told her he was leaving; he had told her what he thought about passion being short-lived, and surely he lived his life like it was a game for him, one long wild hunt, without aim or object but his own pleasure. Even now he was, to all intents and purposes, betraying another woman, even if she was his mistress and not his wife. Somewhere in London was the beautiful and experienced Lady Felton, awaiting his return. At no point had he made pretensions of any deeper feelings towards her than lust. What she had always wanted from Charles was utterly different—she wanted companionship and trust. She wanted to feel safe. With Hunter she felt about as safe as a cork bobbing in a stormy sea and he made no pretension of offering anything more.

She slumped down on the bed. It was no excuse that this was all new to her or that Hunter was so very skilled. She had to remember that learning how to flirt and discovering her enjoyment of…of physical contact was all well and good, but it was not the object of her visit to Welbeck. The only problem, she thought as she turned wearily and went to ring for Betsy, was that having started down this path, she was no longer quite certain how to stop.

Chapter Eleven

Peony's powerful body shook with the thumping of hooves as they approached the fence in the middle of the jumping course. It was high for a horse of Peony's size, but Nell had her measure and breathed in, checking the mare's headlong speed and feeling the mare's muscles gather, and then they left the ground behind. Everything fell away—Hunter, Charles, the crowd watching the jumps, even her own treacherous body and confused mind. For those few precious seconds she knew exactly who she was.

She took the jar of the landing easily, laughing in pleasure as she guided the mare towards the exit. Hunter was standing there waiting for her and she let him help her down, forgetting her embarrassment and awareness.

'I can see why this is your favourite day of the fair,' Hunter said as they went to lean on the fence to watch the other jumpers. 'You made all us mere mortals look half-asleep. Especially on that last jump.'

'Nonsense. You took the black you were riding over with inches to spare.'

He turned to her with his half-mocking smile.

'Placating me again, Nell? I remember that about you even four years ago. I felt like a four-year-old being measured for my first pony. It was a very humbling experience.'

She flushed, but couldn't help laughing.

'Oh, dear, I'm so sorry. It's true I can be very condescending about the way other people are with horses. I do try not to be. My only excuse is that it is the only thing I am good at.'

'Just a middling teacher, then?' he asked politely.

She frowned.

'I am an excellent teacher. Mrs Petheridge says she has never had girls actually asking for more Latin and history lessons before I started teaching.'

'I see. And we've already established you are a precocious pupil. Therefore your excuse for being rude is hereby revoked.'

She considered him, trying not to smile.

'That was sneakily done.'

'I'm learning from an excellent teacher. I've yet to meet anyone who makes her insults sound so reasonable and her compliments so suspect.'

'I'm only like that with you, because you don't seem to mind.'

'That comment is a case in point. If you had been a man you would undoubtedly have been a solicitor. In case you were wondering, that was a knowingly suspect compliment.'

'It was still a compliment and I shall take it as such, thank you.'

'You're the only person I know who would think being likened to a solicitor is a compliment. They're just one step above that hawker over there selling horse quackery in glass bottles.'

Nell looked over towards one of the fête stalls already set up, this one exhibiting a colourful array of horse tonics.

'I used to spend all my pin money at the stalls in under an hour. I even bought a most horrid-smelling potion because that hawker promised it was a miracle cure for spavins.'

'I take that back, then; no solicitor would be so gullible. I wouldn't pour those on the grass, let alone down one of my horses' throats,' he said.

She laughed, about to respond in kind when she spotted Charles. He was standing with his father and Lord and Lady Melkinson by the enclosure, and with a strange sense of fatality she realised she didn't want him to see her. She turned back to Hunter.

'I think I would like to go back to the house and rest before the fête. Would you mind walking me back?'

Hunter nodded and took her arm, leading her through the stalls. He hadn't missed the way she had turned away from the sight of Welbeck standing near Phyllida. Surely, however painful it was, she was finally realising the man was utterly wrong for her? She couldn't possibly cling to her belief she cared for Welbeck while responding with such abandon to another man's touch.

Her problem was that she had the body and soul of the most gifted of lovers. Or rather, it was his problem. Every time he thought he was in control of the situation she kept swinging him between desire and pique and confusion with a skill that would have done a court flirt proud. It didn't help that her dark blue riding habit fit her lean figure like a glove, making his fingers itch to bare what lay beneath so he could finally satisfy his curiosity as to how she would look covered with nothing but the shimmering silk of her hair.

He opened his mouth to say something, anything to distract him from his thoughts, when a burly man came around a stall stacked high with apples and stopped in surprise.

'My lord!'

It took Hunter a moment to place the weathered face, but the name came before he even remembered it.

'Mr Pratchett!'

The man's face creased into a smile that brought to life a multitude of wrinkles and craters.

'What are you doing here all the way from Bristol, Mr Pratchett?'

'My daughter married into these parts, my lord, and my wife and I are here to see our first grandson. Pardon the liberty, sir, but when I saw it was you I had to come and speak. About Jamie.'

Hunter tensed, waiting. It shouldn't matter. He knew not everyone could be reached. It shouldn't grab at him like this. It was already emptying him, preparing him not to feel.

'He married early summer. A fine girl who never minded about his leg. There's to be a child come spring. If it's a boy they want to name him Timothy, if it's no offence to you, sir. He said as it was those talks with you in his dark moments and looking at that picture as kept him afloat until he reached land, so to speak. I don't mean to take liberties, but my wife and I know matters might have run a very different course but for Hope House and we're right grateful.'

'It's no offence. Tim…Timothy would have been honoured. Tell Jamie that. My congratulations as well.'

'I will, sir. Good day to you, miss.'

He nodded to them and disappeared between the stalls.

'He was talking about the portrait of your brother in the memory room, wasn't he?' Nell asked.

He had almost forgotten she was standing there. He was so tense he was certain she saw the danger, but she just waited for his answer. *It's none of your business and it has nothing to do with us.* He formed the words. Carefully, so they would be unequivocal, absolutely clear.

'Who told you about the memory room?'

'Your aunts showed me. That was how I knew he had passed away just before you came to Tilney four years ago.'

'He didn't "pass away". He killed himself.'

He had expected to shock her with his bluntness, but though her brows drew together, she just nodded and he found he was still talking.

'He was barely twenty-one. He drank a whole bottle of laudanum. I don't even know where he found it. I kept all the medicines in a locked cupboard in my room because he was already taking too much. But he was always in pain and he had nightmares and he was afraid to sleep. They had taken off his left arm because the wounds wouldn't heal and there were so many broken bones in his other hand they thought of taking it off as well, to stop the pain, but he wouldn't let them. He said his left hand still hurt him as much even though it wasn't there, so there was no point. He wouldn't go outside and he wouldn't talk to anyone but me and Nurse. My mother couldn't bear seeing him in pain and he couldn't bear seeing her suffer, so she stayed away. He had attacks where he would just sit there, white and shaking, and there was nothing I could do, not even hold his hand because it hurt him too much. He couldn't even escape into sleep. He kept dreaming the man who tortured him had found him again. I wish the English hadn't shot that vicious bastard so I could have done it myself.'

He dragged himself to a halt. There was no reason to tell her any of this. There were only two people in the world who knew and that was only because he would... he *had* trusted them with his life. What would this little girl know about anything, with her sheltered life and unformed dreams? He must be a little mad to be telling her any of this. She would probably run for the hills now and would be right to do so. Charles Welbeck would certainly never subject her to such an assault.

He waited for her to turn away. The last thing he expected was for her to take his hand and lead him out of the crowd towards the wooded path to Welbeck, drawing him with her like a child or one of her schoolchildren. He wanted to hold his ground, but his feet followed his hand. She didn't speak until they had reached the place where the path split off towards the pond by the lower paddocks.

'I wondered how you knew so well how to help me that day at Tilney Hall. You were so kind without appearing to be. That's a very rare skill. I'm sorry it was so dearly bought.'

He looked out over the pond, still trying to find the resolve to shake off her hand, feeling more and more like a child being taken on an airing for their own good. Except that it did feel good. Side by side with the usual roiling guilt and pain was the calm of moving through fields and paths that were as removed from devastation and pain as anything could be.

'It didn't work with him.'

'Didn't it?'

She stopped to look at him and he met her gaze for a moment before looking back out on the dark green water with its edges feathered by surrounding willows. The image of Tim's pain-racked face stretching into a sweet smile as he came out of an attack and his words, hoarse and unsteady, thanking him for 'being there'.

'I don't think I could bear anyone else, Gabe. Some day, maybe, but not just yet. I'm sorry…'

'*Some day, maybe*' hadn't come, but Hunter was free now. Except he wasn't really free. The person he had loved most in the world, who had been his to care for since they were boys, no longer existed. He had lost a limb himself that day and, like Tim's non-existent arm, it still ached just as fiercely and brutally shattered his nights.

'You were just three years older than I.' Nell frowned.

'What?'

'I just realised. You weren't much older than I when you had to care for him.'

'So?'

'That's very young for such a burden.'

'It has nothing to do with age. It has to do with accountability.'

'I see. Is that why you founded Hope House?'

'I don't believe it. My aunts told you that?' He was truly shocked. Amelia and Sephy knew they were never to mention his and his friends' involvement to anyone. It was no one's business. How had she managed to drag that out of them in one day?

'No, *you* did just now.' Her sudden smile glinted and he didn't know whether to feel like a fool at being tricked so easily or indulge the need to bask in the admiration he read in her eyes. He pulled his hand away.

'It's guilt money. For failing him. As you know I can afford it without even noticing.'

She nodded and took his arm.

'I know. And sitting with Mr Pratchett's son means nothing, either. Come, let's go see Meecham's grey. I heard it arrived last night.'

He followed, but didn't answer, his tension lasting all the way to the stables. He should never have told her anything. This was precisely why he had always insisted on keeping his part in Hope House as quiet as possible. He didn't want people prying and feeling sorry for him. At the stable doors he stopped. He was letting this girl manage him like a blasted nurse.

'Not all the world's ills can be salved with horses, you know,' he said, detaching his hand.

'Very few, I imagine. Come, I hear Courage is well over sixteen hands and very good-natured for a stallion.'

She opened the stable door and didn't wait for him to follow but he did anyway, telling himself it would be churlish not to see the horse now he was here; it would be to give too much importance to his discomfort or admit that any discomfort existed at all.

Nell crouched by the enormous grey, wondering what she was thinking to have dragged Hunter here when it was obvious the last thing he wanted was to look at the horse. At least being here was calming her, if not him. The urge to comfort and encompass which was always part of her existence at the school was out of place here, but she didn't know what else to do. Hunter certainly wouldn't appreciate if she did what she really wanted to do, which was wrap her arms around him and hold him until he softened.

She breathed in the familiar smells of the stables and disregarded her unladylike position and the straw that caught at her skirts. For a stallion Courage was very well behaved and merely whickered and turned his head to nuzzle her hair as she examined him.

'He's sprained his fetlock in the past few months, hasn't he? What happened?'

The dismay on Meecham's chubby face was so obvious she wished she had been more diplomatic. Meecham was a serious and conscientious breeder; of course he wasn't hiding the mild injury on purpose.

'Three months ago. George, my brother, tried to jump him. I thought he had completely healed. I never...'

She smiled reassuringly. 'I don't think there is lasting damage; there is no swelling I can feel. He just reacted a bit differently when I touched him there. He is a beautiful horse, Lord Meecham.'

Meecham's shoulders visibly relaxed.

'He is, isn't he? It's rather a shame to sell him, but I have Golden Boy and Spangles for breeding already and it is such a shame to geld him. You did say you were looking for a grey, didn't you, Hunter?'

Hunter, who had stood silently throughout her inspection, nodded and moved towards the stallion with the same calm and fluid movement she remembered from all those years ago, showing none of the tension that had flared in him just moments ago.

You could tell so much from the way someone approached animals. It wasn't just that, like the stallion, Hunter was an exquisite specimen of his breed. As she followed Hunter's progress, the slide of his hands over the silky, slightly dappled coat, the way his long fingers gently eased back the horse's mane and ran down the revealed neck, the beautiful grey stallion faded into the background. It was hard to look away from Hunter's hands; they suited him so well, sleek and powerful, and it was easy to see why women would want those hands on them. It was hard not to react to their calm and purposeful exploration, to imagine it was her own skin being skimmed and tested.

She forced herself to turn away, but the image lingered—of his strong profile outlined against the horse's shoulder, his mouth uncharacteristically soft as he murmured something soothing to the horse as he tested the injured fetlock. The stable suddenly felt too hot and oppressive and she wished someone would open the doors wider and let in a breeze.

'You are a beauty, aren't you?' Hunter said lightly to the grey before moving back towards them. 'I'll take him out for a ride, but as far as I'm concerned you can name your price, Meech.'

The words released Nell and she half-sighed and moved towards a mare stabled by the door as the two men began discussing terms, steadying herself as she stroked her, drawing calm from the familiar motions and sensations.

It made no sense, the way she kept reacting to his presence. How was it possible when it was Charles whom she had loved for years? When it was Charles who had always made her feel flustered and full of hope? Not that that was how Hunter made her feel, which should have reassured her, but it didn't. It was more inexplicable, uncomfortable. There was nothing magical about it. It was too earthy and low and it worked its way up from the ground like an encroaching vine. She felt restless and turned inside out and needing to act. To do something. Take something. Touch him.

'Shall we?'

His voice was so close it sounded as though he was speaking inside her, his very voice had become part of her. It ran rough and warm through her, like brandy. She almost asked 'shall we what?' until she realised that would be a deliberate provocation.

'Shall we what?'

He didn't answer immediately. Then he placed his hands on the stall door behind her, bracketing her body. The anger was gone, but this was worse, because this look was the one that had sent her heart thudding and tightened its merciless coil around her last night. His eyes were molten honey and amber, spilling heat over her. She forgot where they were, that Meecham was a few yards away fussing over Courage, that stable hands and guests might come by at any moment.

Then abruptly he took her hand and drew her out of the stable and down the path leading into the trees. She followed, matching her stride to his long legs, stumbling as they turned off the path and into a tiny clearing hedged by stunted oaks.

There was no pause, no discussion, not even a warning before he turned her and captured her mouth with his.

It was raw, punishing. His hands untied and pushed back her bonnet and dug deep into her hair, locking her to him while his mouth took possession of hers. It wasn't a seduction; it was a demand. It should have scared her, but it just opened a new door. If he could demand, so could she. She met the thrust of his tongue against hers, wrapped her arms around the hard expanse of his back under his coat and pressed herself against him. It felt so good. Surely this meeting of her body with the hard surfaces of his was her natural state. Almost. There was too much between them, her skin chafed at her dress, at his coat and waistcoat. She wanted to be as bare, as immediate as her mouth under his, to take and be taken as she was.

'You're driving me insane, Nell,' he muttered against her mouth, his hands skimming over her body, shaping curves and dips and reflecting the urgency and impatience that was plaguing her. She wanted something. She *needed* something. The thought that he felt it too, that she had the power to do this to someone else…to Hunter…

The image that had been tantalising her, of touching his warm skin, became a need as urgent as breathing. She dragged his shirt from his buckskins and with a moan of relief spread her hands as far up his back as his clothes allowed. His skin was heated silk over muscles that bunched and shifted as she caressed him.

She needed to feel him. Soon it would be over, he would leave and she had to remember what it felt like to explore, to remember this freedom and this sense of control. She could even feel his breathing, shallow and unsteady as he started drawing back. The thought that he might stop made her slide one hand around his nape, grasping his silky dark hair in her fist and anchoring him as she pressed her mouth back to his. She wasn't done yet, not even close.

There were limits. No one could expect him to be in control when her body was all but glued to his, one hand like a burning brand on his bare back and her lips drinking him in, coaxing his soul out with sweetness and fire.

He never should have marched her out of the stables like a troglodyte dragging his woman off to a cave. But right now that was precisely what he felt like, reduced to a pulsing mass of need without brain or common sense.

Oh, how he wanted her. She was becoming a compulsion. How he was going to stop himself from stripping her, touching her, tasting her everywhere… It was beyond him.

He cradled her face in his hands and gave all his attention to that lush, delicious lower lip, mapping it, caressing it with lips and tongue, following it inward, outlining its corners where her smile bloomed. She stilled under his exploration. He could feel her arms shaking slightly but otherwise she remained motionless as he took possession of her mouth. He would make it utterly his; no one had ever known it as he did, made it tremble like this, made her shake with need like a racehorse at the gate, ready to surge when the restraints were dropped. He wanted to feel that leap against him, but he held her there, tense and needy and waiting for him, as if holding her at bay would keep him safe, keep them both safe.

She would make the most incandescent of mistresses if only she wasn't a damn innocent. It felt as though it would kill him at the moment to stop kissing her, to put away her long elegant body when all he wanted to do was drag her down onto the grass between the trees and leave her as bare as nature and pay the same attention to every inch of skin, visible and hidden, as he was to her mouth.

He had never entered an embrace wondering if he would be able to stop, knowing there was a point he was fast approaching that would challenge his control. He had told her she was testing his sanity, but it was worse than that. She kept encroaching on boundaries he had erected before he had even understood what the word meant. He had loved his family, but he had never needed them. It had been his job to be needed and that was fine with him. It was power, being the centre of the universe. He didn't *need* anyone; that was anathema to who he was. He had had more women than he felt was quite fair to remember and he had enjoyed them mightily, but he had never once mistook lust for need. He gave, he took, he didn't need.

This wasn't need either, he told himself. This was just lust, glorious and painful though it was and unfulfilled as it was likely to remain. On her part as well. She didn't need him any more than he needed her. This was sheer want, take.

His mind insisted and his body categorically ignored the lecture.

'Nell. Kiss me back, now. Please.'

Was he reduced to begging? But he got what he wanted. His words released her from her passive acceptance of his exploration. Her hand twisted back in his hair, her other hand just skimming his cheek, and her lips parted against his in an assault that rocked him backwards and made his arms tighten around her as if she could keep him from falling. She wasn't gentle. She tugged his lower lip between hers, tasting it with her tongue, catching it with her teeth and letting it go only to sink into him, her tongue searching for and finding his, her breath filling him with her whimpers of pleasure and impatience.

This was the girl who galloped as though she owned

the universe, who would ride him into heaven if she was his.

He couldn't help meeting her assault, leading and following as she grew bolder. Her hands slid under his shirt again, but this time they skimmed the line above his buckskins, and the heat became unbearable. He could feel the surface of his skin, prickling with perspiration and raw nerve ends, adding to the clamour of every part of his body that wanted to be touched by her, kissed by her, with precisely that total abandon.

'Hunter, tell me what to do to make this stop,' she moaned against his mouth, her hands biting into his waist as she pulled herself against him.

'I don't want it to stop,' he all but growled at her. Ever. Not until I'm lost in it, erased. Not until I surrender.

That thought, clear and sharp as splintering ice, finally woke him. If he had needed an answer to the question would he be willing to throw himself off a cliff to bed her, he had it. It was—pretty damn close, but not quite.

'I don't want to, but we have to stop. Now.' He managed to quiet his voice even if his body was screaming at him. She froze, too. Her fingers trembled against his back, sending darts straight into his groin, and he closed his eyes tightly, praying she not take the surge in his already painful erection as an invitation to continue. But when she pulled away he gritted his teeth even at the brush of her arm against his side.

They stood silently for a moment, both staring off into the woods, as if waiting for someone else to arrive.

'You should return to the house. Meecham will be waiting for me with Courage.' He couldn't help how curt he sounded, but when she turned to leave he reached out to tuck a wisp of hair as light and airy as a down feather behind her ear and cursed himself for his pathetic inconsistency. He took another step back, putting her out of easy reach.

'You should go rest before the fête this evening.'

She nodded and headed towards the house.

'Will you save a dance for me?' The question was out before he could censor it and she turned and he thought he could read both surprise and relief in her eyes before she nodded with something approaching her usual smile.

'From what I remember, what takes place on the village green is nothing quite as orderly as dancing. More like a cross between wrestling and a mad game of croquet.'

'We'll wrestle, then.' He firmly resisted the now-reflexive rise of his hands towards her. Finally she was gone and he returned to the stable where Hidgins was standing with Meecham and inspecting Courage. He had told her horses couldn't solve all ills, but he hoped they would help him reclaim his equilibrium because he needed to think about what he was going to do about her and right now that question only had one answer.

Chapter Twelve

The grounds of Welbeck Manor were so obviously constructed to accommodate equine matters that the modest ornamental gardens where Hunter had taken her the first night at Welbeck were of scant interest to anyone but Lady Welbeck during daylight hours, which was precisely why Nell made her way to them. She needed to calm down. She needed to think. She needed to understand what on earth was happening to her. She needed…

She hugged her arms around her as she turned down the yew-hedged path. She was unravelling, just like her hair; every time she managed to pull herself back on course some other part of her took flight. She might want to blame Hunter's seductive skill, or her treacherous body, but it felt larger than that. It wasn't just her body that was waking and rushing beyond her control. Just a week ago she had thought she had known herself rather well, her strengths and her many weaknesses. She had felt quite content with the life she had built and the only thing she had felt was missing was love and she had actually been proud of the constancy of her adoration for Charles. She had thought it proved she possessed that precious gift the poets eulogised—true love for a perfect man.

She shivered, though she wasn't in the least chilly. No wonder Hunter had been so scornful. She had sat there lecturing him about love when she had had no idea what she was talking about. She deserved his scorn. Within mere days he had unintentionally undercut her foolish fantasies and worse—he had planted another more damaging fantasy in their stead.

She leaned against the wooden frame of the bower. A few late autumn buds were still trying to push forth and their sweet scent lingered as she rubbed their soft cream petals, just tinged pink at the edges. She wanted to go home. Back to Mrs Petheridge and safety. She didn't want to even think what had happened to her. If she did it might make it real, inescapable. No, she needed some space to think. Perhaps this upheaval was just the product of fear? Perhaps it was a reaction to the transition from the fantasy to the reality of Charles? He was a nice man and perhaps it was even a good thing he wasn't unsettling like Hunter.

Unsettling. She closed her eyes as her body was swamped by the sensations he had evoked. Unsettling wasn't quite the right word. Dangerously cataclysmic was closer to the mark. She wanted to go back and stop him from stopping; she so wanted to find out where this was taking her. She felt like Odysseus's sailors, about to cast herself onto the reefs for the price of a siren's song.

He wants you in his bed, not his life, Nell. He entered this engagement under the influence of grief and guilt and very misplaced chivalry. He doesn't really want *you.* Why would he when he has his experienced Lady

Felton? If you hadn't all but thrown yourself at him, he probably wouldn't have even touched you.

She wished Anna was there; someone to tell her to be sensible. Odysseus had tied himself to the mast so he couldn't follow his sailors to their destruction. Perhaps she should tie herself to sweet, pleasant Charles and eventually she would forget siren songs even exist. Or perhaps Charles's kisses would excite her just as much. It was possible, though it didn't feel very probable.

You are a fool, Nell Tilney.

She was so deep in her confusion and misery it took her a moment to react when a couple entered the garden. Charles didn't see her, his attention wholly on his companion, but Lady Melkinson's eyes met hers for a moment before Nell instinctively moved deeper into the bower.

The fading leaves weren't much of a barrier and she watched as the beauty raised her hand to stroke the fair-haired hero's cheek, as she drew his head down to hers, as her eyes met Nell's the moment before the kiss.

Surely she should feel something? This was Charles, the man she had been in love with for as long as she could remember. How could she feel nothing but embarrassment at witnessing their embrace? Perhaps she, like Hunter, was only capable of physical passion? Perhaps her dreams of something deeper were just mawkish fictions as Hunter had said. Perhaps there was no answer to this deep loneliness, this need to share her life with someone…

'You can come out now, little girl. I've sent him back to the house.'

The contempt in the other woman's voice on top of her confusion was like a blow to the stomach. She didn't want to face that perfect, petite beauty who had taken part in the shattering of her dreams from the day she had arrived. She wanted to be spirited away until she could recover her balance.

'I hope you learned something useful spying; if you mean to deal with men like Hunter you need to acquire some skills, my dear. Oh, I forgot. You're in love with Charles. Such a pity his interest lies elsewhere. Still, he knows he cannot marry me, so he might make do with you. All that money and adoration make you quite tempting, you know...'

Nell wanted more than anything to move away, but she wouldn't run. She had come too far, hadn't she? But holding her ground in the face of the avid enjoyment on Lady Melkinson's perfect features was costing her. She had seen that look before. For years and years and years. Like the yellow-eyed focus of a wolf, intent and predatory.

'I do admire you, my dear Miss Tilney. The undeniable charm of your oh-so-tempting inheritance wasn't enough for you, was it? You had to get them all hot and bothered, playing them off against each other. I started the week ready to applaud the masterly performance Hunter was giving of actually being attracted to a beanpole like you, but I must admit you rival him in bravura. Even Charles has started eyeing those long legs of yours. But do you think Hunter or Charles would even look at you without your acres and gold? I know what makes these men tick, believe me. I've learned the hard way. I've had to earn every privilege, every dress on my back, every ribbon, using the one gift God gave me. You're as bad as any of the men who think they can buy me for the price of a necklace. You make me sick, you pathetic little girl. You're no rival to me. You're nothing but a scrawny, spoilt…'

Somehow Nell started moving, but Lady Melkinson followed and the words kept coming, soft spoken and vicious, hardly above a whisper, making everything fade but the poison. Even her face shifted, the bloom of anger in her cheeks and the perfect teeth giving way to another face, older, uglier, leaning towards her just like that, spewing just like that. Nell's own cheeks were icy, her hands sagged limp like two flaccid sacks filling with ground glass, and though she kept moving, her legs were beginning to shake. There was still a voice shouting inside her to fight back, to do something, but she had no defence. She had already realised the truth of Lady Melkinson's accusations. Her childish dreams had no more substance to them than she had ever had in standing up to her aunt or father. She was no one and no one wanted her, not really.

Her blood pulsed thickly in her head and whatever part of her searched desperately for a way to stop this assault was fumbling in the dark for a weapon that didn't seem to exist. The words came like a litany, again and again. She was no one and no one wanted her. She was a child again, alone, abandoned without explanation, and now without even the comforting fantasy of her knight in shining armour.

'What's wrong? Nell?'

She hardly noticed when Hunter approached. He said something to Lady Melkinson, but all Nell heard was the hammer blows of blood in her ears, like waves striking again and again. She was hiding inside her treacherous body, but it was no sanctuary, just a familiar prison. She had so wanted to believe these attacks were far behind her, that she had managed to become strong enough never to fall back like this, and yet here she was, no better than a kicked, cowering dog. Lady Melkinson was right; she was pathetic.

His hands pressed into her arms and she could feel her muscles shaking against them. She didn't want him here. She didn't want anyone. She just wanted to be left utterly alone. Because that was the truth.

'Nell.'

His voice was gentle and she squeezed her eyes shut harder, like a child, as if that would prevent him from seeing just how weak she was. His arms went around her and the will went out of her, every inch of her body begging to lean into his warmth, his strength. Oh, she was spineless, useless. Pathetic.

'No.' She dragged enough strength to push away from him, but he still held her.

'Phyllida said you saw her and Charles embracing.'

Shame finally penetrated the fog.

'She *told* you that?'

Nell used a word she rarely even heard in the stables, but somehow had stowed away in a corner of her mind. She clung to the coat-tails of her rising fury as she would to a rope being tossed to her as she sank into a bog, the words exploding out of her.

'I hate and loathe her!'

'She isn't really worth hating, Nell. A woman like Phyllida is all about her beauty and for the next forty years she will have to watch her very essence fade. It's not an enviable fate. She has nothing to do with the fact that you're not really in love with Welbeck. You're not twelve and he isn't a fairy-tale prince. Grow up.'

The stain of anger that entered his voice did what his

gentleness didn't. The scrape and thud of her nerves and the flagellating anger of self-loathing gave way to anger at him. This was all his fault anyway.

'I don't need your lectures! As you said, I'm not twelve. My feelings for Charles aren't so puerile!'

'Aren't they? Do you still think you're in love with him?'

It was humiliating to admit that for ten years now she had built her future around an emotion that didn't exist. That in this, too, she was pathetic, weak.

'He was all I had! Oh, damn you!'

She squeezed her forehead with both hands.

'I needed someone to love. He meant something to me. You don't understand…'

She laughed at the childish words, a strangled sound. That was just what her schoolgirls would say. *You don't understand.*

'I needed him.'

That at least was true. He had always been there for her. His sweet teasing smile had guided her through many dark hours at Tilney.

'Well, it isn't him. You had no idea who he was and now you do. So tell me—do you still think you are in love with Charles Welbeck?' It was a challenge, not a question.

Her arms and legs were tingling now. She had no idea whether he had done this on purpose any more than she had known if he had four years ago, but he had somehow dragged her out of her little hell. Not that she felt very grateful at the moment. She was still shaky and, even more than that, ashamed, and she didn't appreciate being pushed.

He surprised her again, his hands cupping her face,

very gentle, tilting it up. His thumbs brushed lightly over her cheekbones, his palms warm against her still-clammy skin.

'You don't need Charles any more, Nell. Not the one in your mind and definitely not the real one.'

'I don't need anyone.'

His fingers stilled. There was such calm conviction in her words she was surprised by the truth in them. He had told her before that she didn't need rescuing and he had been right. If she had really cared for Charles, she would be in pain. The after-effects of her attack were still there in the faint tingle in her hands, the over-awareness of her skin, but the thought of Charles was already fading, like mist clearing, revealing a very different landscape. Not a prettier one. It was still lonely and bare like the view across the tarn far above Keswick and now without that mystical promise of a rainbow to tempt her forward.

Perhaps Hunter had been right all along. She was a naïve fool to be hankering after something beyond physical passion or companionable affection. It would be beyond foolish to transfer her fantasy of love from Charles to Hunter, wouldn't it? But standing there, feeling utterly hollowed out and exhausted, she felt that question had already been answered and to her disadvantage. She shook her head. It felt stuffed with wool and she needed to think.

'What I need is to pack.'

He drew his hands away and, because she wanted to move towards him, she stepped away. It would be so easy to take his comfort, to sink into the drugging warmth of the physical excitement he offered, but Lady Melkinson's words kept ringing in her ears. This man was clever and passionate, but he didn't love her any more than Charles and, unlike him, she needed that. She might have been utterly wrong about Charles, about herself, but she wasn't wrong about that.

'I think it is best I leave tomorrow as well. My father can find me at Bascombe.'

She looked at him as she spoke. He hadn't moved and she couldn't read his face. He looked very much as he had that night in London, cold and watchful. What was he thinking? Was he worried that she might not hold to her side of the bargain now that she was turning her back on Charles?

Why can't you love me?

The words were so loud inside her, for one panicked moment she thought she had spoken them aloud. But he still hadn't moved and so she did, hurrying towards the house, wishing she could leave her treacherous thoughts behind. This time she went straight to her room and locked the door.

Chapter Thirteen

A band of musicians was beginning to play on a small dais by the inn, their sound just barely rising over the happy pandemonium of the fête. It was chilly, but the air was fuzzy with smoke and the scents of apple and clove and roast pork mixed with charcoal and pine. The excitement of the music and the crowd that filled the village green was infectious and she was glad she had decided to attend the fête with the other guests rather than hide in her room until her departure tomorrow. Not just her departure, Hunter's as well.

Once again the thought struck her hard, starting from her stomach and spreading out in a sick ache. Tomorrow she would be leaving—not Welbeck, but Hunter. She turned instinctively towards where Hunter stood next to Lord Welbeck and Lord Meecham, his mouth held tight and his gaze on the shifting raucous crowd of dancers. She looked down at the tips of her sandals under the dress and shivered, rubbing the rise of goosebumps along her arms.

'Are you cold?'

Her head jerked up. How had he moved so quickly?

She shook her head, but changed it to a nod. It was better than the truth. Even if she had been cold, just having him standing so close was warming her from within and without.

'A little.'

He picked up the lapel of her cloak, fingering the pale fabric with absent concentration.

'I'm not surprised—this isn't very substantial. You should have worn your other cloak.'

It was such a prosaic thing to say an edge of her tension relaxed. At least he didn't appear angry with her any more. She didn't want the last exchange between them to be acrimonious. She didn't want there to be a last exchange between them. She searched desperately for something to say, but already he was turning away.

'Wait here.'

She watched as he disappeared into the crowd, resisting the urge to follow him, trying to shake off the tension that refused to release her from its grip. How was she going to do this?

'Here, this will keep you warm.'

She turned. Hunter had come behind her and was holding out a glass of cider, its coil of milky steam carrying all those smells upwards, as if he had somehow encompassed all the joys of the fête in a single receptacle. Most potently the joy that welled up in her just at seeing him. It was ridiculous to feel so happy just at another person's presence, but she did. For a moment all the agony of unrequited love and impending loss fell away under the weight of the joy of the moment. For right now Hunter was with her, a smile beginning to form in his eyes as he looked down at her. She took the glass, breathing in the scent of the cider, and sighed.

'It's just cider,' he said with a laugh, his expression losing the remainder of its uncharacteristic grimness. 'You look like I am offering you the elixir of the gods.'

She shook her head and tasted it. In all her years attending the fête with her father she had never been permitted to taste this hedonistic brew and it had achieved mythical proportions in her mind. It didn't disappoint. It slid down her throat, evoking a thoroughly sensual response like stepping into a warm spring swirling amber and amethyst and gold. She closed her eyes to let the taste spark the colours and surround her, fading away at the end, leaving just the fundaments of apple and cinnamon and a hint of clove. She opened her eyes with another sigh, letting it go.

'That was my first time.'

As the silence stretched and with the glow of the bonfires lighting the same colours in his eyes, she might have believed she had conjured Hunter from the same pagan spring in her mind. It took her a moment to even realise her words might be grossly misconstrued.

'My first cup of Wilton cider,' she explained.

'You have an interesting way with firsts, Nell,' he remarked and the spirits in the cider, which had been tumbling through her quite leisurely, chose that moment to expand in a rush of heat that spread through her like the birth of a sun.

She turned to watch the dancing, waiting for the heat to fade, and when Hunter plucked the glass from her hand and took her arm, leading her towards the green, she protested.

'I'm not finished yet.'

'You're already swaying like a willow in a stream.'

'I was moving to the music.'

'There's more room for that here.'

She glanced around the rowdy, swirling dancers. He was drawing her deeper and deeper into the mayhem, holding her close against the buffeting. She clung to his hand, raising her voice to be heard.

'I don't even know the steps.'

'Neither do I. Can you waltz?'

'Yes, but this isn't...'

Apparently there was more than one way to waltz. Nothing that would pass muster at Almack's, but much, much more enjoyable. They were on the other side of the green, far from the Welbeck crowd. There was too much chaos around them to move more than a couple of feet in either direction and Hunter's arm around her was as much a guard against the merry jostling as a guide for the rhythm.

'This most certainly isn't a waltz.' Nell laughed as he swung her out of the way of a portly couple who were clearly interpreting the music as a reel.

Her laugh collapsed into a gasp as her attempt to avoid stepping on his boot brought her sharply against him and somehow his leg slid between hers, straining her skirts against her thighs in a manner that definitely didn't happen in a waltz.

'I never said it was. No, don't pull back yet. Trust me.' His voice was as warm as the cider still tumbling through her and she didn't even manage to scoff at this outrageous demand, too stunned by the sensation of being held there in the middle of the chaos, just swaying gently against his thigh, his head bent next to hers.

She had ridden astride more times than she could count; she knew what it felt to have something firm and muscular between her thighs, the pull of fabric over that sensitive inner flesh. But not this. They continued to move, with no regard to the rhythm, his leg shifting between hers, hard and muscled, scraping and pressing in a way that should have been thoroughly uncomfortable and it was, it was, just not in any way that she wanted to stop. It made her skin heat and tingle and begin to shake, and for one mad moment, still misted in the fumes of the cider, she thought it might be the return of that horrible fear, but that thought passed immediately. It wasn't that kind of shaking. It was… She was coming apart and re-forming around a completely new heat at her centre. That burst of sun had sunk from her chest and stomach and settled between her legs, insistent and aggravating and in a dialogue with his body she could barely follow.

There were other things occurring, his arms around her, still masquerading as shields against the crowd except that his hand was moving so softly up and down the small of her back she wondered if it had somehow worked its way under her gown, she could feel his fingers so distinctly on her flesh.

He bent his head, his mouth beside her ear as if talking to her, and perhaps he was, if talking was that gentle slide of breath over the curve of her ear and every now and then his lips brushed its tip and the heat between her legs would gather in and prepare to shoot up through her to capture that caress and out into the heavens.

It never occurred to her to do anything but to hang on and survive this multiple-fronted assault as she would have clung to a bolting horse, focusing on keeping herself safe until the horse wore itself out and could be checked. But soon hanging on wasn't enough.

The kiss by the paddock had been a revelation, a ripping back of curtains on a part of the world she had only known at the level of gossip or myth. That heat and pleasure had been sensuous and unnerving and made her yearn for something more. The kisses in the linen closet and the copse had confirmed her suspicions that she was probably a thorough wanton. Now she was being dragged higher or deeper and once again all she could think was that there must be more to these amazing sensations—everything he was doing told her so, was an invitation to proceed and discover what she was capable of. She. *She* was capable of this, not just him. She knew it.

Her hands had just been clasped on his coat and she loosened them and let them slide around him, her body sinking against his as it had yesterday. As her breasts pressed against his chest she realised they had wanted this. Every part of her body, which she had always thought of as a rather necessary unit for getting about the world, was now a clashing collection of needs and demands. Right now quite a few of them were making utterly new demands of her and of Hunter and rewarding her with wonderful but also thoroughly frustrating sensations like a band of musicians engaged in a cacophony begging to be drawn into a single tune.

'Hunter.' She turned her head to breathe against his neck, and his scent, his essence, warm and spicy and inexplicably vivid, flowed through her like the cider, twisting through to every one of those elements of her body taking part in the uprising. It did something to him, too, because he wrapped around her with a sudden shiver, pulling her against him painfully, breaking the rhythm. Then they were separate again. The only point of contact was his hand on her arm as he led her out through the crowd back towards the relative calm of the stalls. She kept her eyes on her pale slippers darting in and out from under her skirts as they threaded through the chaos and did a little tripping stumble as Hunter stopped abruptly.

'May I have this dance, Nell?' Charles asked over the noise and she looked up. He had stopped directly in front of her and the light from the torches and fires that turned his hair into a blazing sunset was also in his eyes and for a moment she stood mute and breathless before the embodiment of a dream. She had actually daydreamed of this precise moment. That in the midst of the fête this man, his hand held out to her, would single her out. It had been with her for so long, clung to during her aunt's vicious scolds or during the quiet hours before sleep at school. She would sail away in his arms dancing in this very clearing, with the world fading away around them as he looked into her eyes. It wouldn't be like the chaos of sensations and heat of dancing with Hunter that left her confused and frustrated. It would be as light as gossamer and would empty her of doubts and fears because Charles wanted her.

He stood, hand outstretched, with the boyish smile she had revered, and she had an urge to slap him. She couldn't blame him for his affair with Phyllida, but she could for this shameless attempt to take advantage of an infatuated young woman. She held firmly to her smile, but it felt like a grimace.

'Of course,' she answered and held out her hand.

'You look lovely, Nell,' he said once they began dancing at the edge of the green.

'Thank you, Charles.'

'I mean it. You're so lovely I wish…'

'Please don't insult me by feigning emotions that

don't exist, Charles. I am betrothed and I know you
and Lady Melkinson are lovers.'

He stumbled, but didn't let go of her hand.

'Nell! Really! Someone might hear you!'

'Is that what concerns you? What a hypocrite you are.'

He looked both shocked and rather desperate.

'Lady Melkinson and I are merely acquaintances.
You are the only woman who has touched my heart.'

'Do you often kiss your mere acquaintances in the
garden? Oh, don't bother explaining. I thought I cared,
but I must be as shallow as you because I don't. Please
don't say anything else, Charles. Let's enjoy the dance
and part friends. Please.'

She could feel him struggling, but thankfully he complied with her request and they completed the dance
in silence. As the music slowed she stepped back and
smiled.

'Goodnight, Charles.'

She turned and searched the crowd lining the green
and her eyes met Hunter's. She moved towards him
without thinking and he took her arm and they walked
through the stalls of roasting, sizzling and bubbling fare.
She didn't particularly care where they were going, just
that he was with her, his hand securing hers on his arm
and the press of people forcing her often against his side.
There were jugglers and a man with dogs who danced on
their hind feet and a man tossing lighted torches into the
air. People gasped as sparks burst upwards like comet
tails. One torch fell to the ground by her feet and Hunter
pulled her back, his arm about her waist.

'It's dangerous to play with fire,' his voice murmured
close to her ear. She turned her head towards him without thinking and his mouth grazed her cheek. Around

them the crowd kept moving from one spectacle to another, a pulsing, noisy current around their stillness. Not that she felt still. The heat that had been suspended restarted the inner drumming, feeding off every point of contact with his body. It made no sense that never during her dreams of Charles had she imagined him kissing her. Now all it took was for her to stumble into Hunter, for his hand to brush against her, for him to speak...

She wanted to cry out in anguish. Hunter had ruined everything! She had been within sight of land after years adrift and he had pushed her back into the treacherous current that would eventually leave her becalmed and alone again.

But she didn't stop him when he finally moved, guiding her out of the crowd and towards the tree-lined path towards Welbeck. Not even when he stopped and turned her to him, pulling the hood of her cloak over her hair.

'It's getting chilly,' he explained as he tucked back a tress of hair that must have fallen free during the dance, but it slid free again and he stood with it draped over his palm for a moment before raising it.

'Baked apples, with cinnamon.'

'What?'

'Your hair smells of baked apples and cinnamon.'

The very earthy statement eased her rising tension slightly. She tried to gather her hair, but only succeeded in dislodging Betsy's carefully positioned pins and a hunk of hair tumbled down her other shoulder.

'You're just making it worse. Here, let me.'

Hunter pushed back her hood, inspecting the damage, and Nell felt the return of the familiar embarrassment at her unfashionably straight-as-sticks hair.

'It's hopeless. It just won't curl.'

'Thank goodness for that; why on earth would you want to torture something so beautiful into curls is beyond me.'

'That's because you're a man.'

'You noticed. I have clearly done something right, then.'

He picked up another tress that had slipped free and ran it between his fingers, watching her.

'This one is cider and cloves.'

She presented him with another felled tress.

'The whole fair smells of cider, so that is nothing extraordinary. What about this?'

With his eyes on hers Hunter brushed it just gently with his lips and all conscious thought faded like the last gasp of a sunset.

'This is Nell.'

How did he make his voice do that, reverberate through her like a musical instrument? It made her body dance, but it was still an intrusion and a warning.

His words were like the cider, warm and drugging, and like the cider she wanted more of them. He wasn't looking hard and grim any more. The fire that was pulsing away inside her was in his eyes as well and she wanted it so much it terrified her. He wasn't hers to keep, but how could she let him go? The thought was so terrifying she withdrew, trying to find the stable ground of the laughing, sophisticated flirtation he had taught her.

'That sounds rather unappealing after all those delicious scents. Try another one. We need some more substantial fare than baked apples and cider.'

He shook his head, dismissing her weak attempt to bring them back to the mundane.

'You're wrong. This...' He ran the lock of hair between his fingers, just an inch, but enough for a shower of tingling heat to cascade from her scalp downwards. 'This is the most exquisite scent of them all. If I could describe it, all your poets would have to bow before me.'

Far behind them she could hear the roar of the crowd, but it was all just a rumble of sound around the reality of a man holding her hair and turning her body, turning her, into the rest of the universe.

Her mind and senses were raw, but enough of her remained to be scared she might never regain her footing. If she stepped into the void now, how would she return? There was no one she could really trust to guide her back to safety. No one. So it made no sense to let him secure the hood of her cloak again and take her hand and lead her up the path towards Welbeck knowing that it wasn't over. As they walked down the dim and silent corridor towards her room she was conscious of a growing elation that something was going to happen. Tomorrow she would have to go back to her old life, but right now she could take this. Him.

Outside her door she turned, straightening, preparing herself to do something she never would have imagined was within the realm of the possible just a week ago. With one hand already turning the knob, she held out her hand to Hunter. He took it and held it against his lips for the space of two breaths.

'Goodnight, Nell.'

No!

She grabbed his coat and pulled him in and either she took him by surprise or he didn't offer much resistance, only stopping once he was inside the room.

'This isn't a good idea. It's the cider and the dancing. I took advantage of your inexperience, Nell, but I have my limits.'

He spoke very slowly, enunciating each word as if she were dim-witted. She knew the moment would come when he would push her away, bring down the curtain on their little play. A more experienced woman might take this dismissal with a laugh and a teasing comment, but she couldn't. The best she could do was to try not to show him how much this hurt. She raised her chin.

'Goodnight, then. I'm going back to the fête.'

She pushed past him, opening the door, but he shut it again, hard, his hand flat against it.

'No. You're not.'

'I most certainly am!'

'Nell, listen to me.'

'No. You will say something clever and convince me whatever you want is for my own good and I don't want to hear it. Let me go.'

'Nell, it's precisely because what I want is far from your own good that I am trying to be sensible. You don't even know what you want!'

'Oh, and you do?'

'I do, which is why I am trying very hard not to accept your offer. But there is no possible way I am letting you go back down to the fête alone.'

'I wouldn't be alone. I am certain Charles would be only too happy for another dance.'

As a threat it was rather weak. He knew very well she wasn't in love with Charles and that Charles was only interested in her inheritance, but it was all she had in this uneven struggle. She didn't expect him to react so fiercely.

'You're not going,' he said, his hands tangling in her hair. 'I won't let you.'

She raised her mouth to feel the words against her lips, leaning into him as she had in the dance, and his arm came around her again, not so smoothly now, dragging her against him.

'Nell, tell me you won't go.' The certainty was gone; there was just entreaty and something else that made her want to wrap her arms around him. She slid one hand into his warm hair and it felt like a sigh between her fingers. It might be playing with fire, but this was *right*. Now her body was coming back to her, gathering, defined by every point of contact between them. This time she must have been the one to start the kiss because for a moment he still held back and then with a half-groan his hands shifted, positioned her, and she lost all control of the situation.

She was no longer playing with fire. She was fire, he was living flame and he was devouring her. She gave him everything he demanded, opening herself, helping when his hands untied her cloak, unfastened her dress, slipped down the sleeves of her gown. He paid homage to every inch of skin he uncovered with his hands and mouth, bringing it to tingling life, finding places she had never realised could make her writhe merely with a breath and flick of his tongue, like the dip below her collarbone, and further, where the skin of her breasts began to rise… She tried to tug down her chemise and stays because they were in the way. Then they weren't and the cool air gathered around her breasts and her breath shook in relief and agony.

Do something.

For a moment his hands just held her arms and his

gaze mapped her. Then he reached out and did the same with one finger, very lightly, first over the delicate swells, dipping between them to gather and release the pearl at the end of her necklace before following the curve under her breast. Then his hand cupped it and she watched, transfixed, as he bent towards her.

'Nell.' His breath was torture enough on her exposed nipple, but when he touched his lips to it, the lightest feather touch, she gave a little cry, digging her fingers into his hair, not knowing whether to stop him before something terrible happened or to press herself to him, to be consumed utterly, demolished utterly.

She moaned and gave up all thought as he took the hardened bud into his mouth and the pleasure echoed in the thudding heat between her legs. Every touch and lick on her breast was answered by a pulse of pleasure, a damp heat that was gathering.

She didn't resist as he nudged her legs apart with his knee, and when he pulled up her skirts she helped him. She didn't even have enough shame to stop him from releasing the string of her drawers and then caressing the heated, shaking skin above her garters. Quite the opposite. She wriggled her undergarments to the ground and when he raised his head to kiss her again she anchored her hand in his hair and kissed him with all the confused need bursting inside her.

She was lost. Her body was acting without her because she would never have dreamed of taking his hand and pressing it against her aching breast. And when his other hand skimmed up her thighs, between her legs, she had no idea how but she moved towards it so that it pressed his large hot palm against the fire at the juncture of her thighs. Her legs tightened instinctively, locking him there, and the hard texture of his fingers pressing against the most intimate part of her condensed the fireball into molten lead that was begging to spill free.

'Hunter...' His name was one long plea for the pleasure she knew awaited her. But just in case she wasn't being clear enough, she added, 'Please...'

It was an eternity, but finally he moved again, and though she should be shocked or ashamed, all she could do was move to the rhythm of his fingers in total wonder that this was even possible. She had thought the kisses were magical, bringing extraordinary revelation about her body, but this... Where had this been all her life? How could this completely ignored and negligible part of her have transformed into the whole universe and Hunter's hands and body and lips become the very essence of the laws that governed her new reality?

She heard his voice against her mouth, a deep growl that made her legs tighten about him again.

'I want to taste you there...kiss you and take you until you unravel.'

She was unravelling already. His fingers circled and skimmed and tugged and then the chaos became a new rhythm. She was riding his fingers, back and forth, clinging to him, saying things she couldn't even understand until everything faded into a litany of 'yes, yes...' and then that gave way as the ground fell out from under her. She was being torn apart by waves of pleasure so intense there was even a moment of fear that she might never escape this, and then with a long moan it all gave way to warmth, like sliding into a steamy, viscous bath, sliding into a new body.

Her mind came out of its cave and noticed that he was holding her tightly against him, but rigidly. Her body tingled all over, very aware of the cold air against her damp skin, of his hand still pressed against her, but not moving, just holding her. She could feel her pulse there against his fingers, hard thumping beats that slowed as she waked.

Then came embarrassment and she squirmed away from his hand and he let her, but his other hand was still tangled in her hair. Her skirts slid back down her legs and he leaned his forehead against hers and drew in a shaking breath, before stepping back and pulling up her sleeves.

She shuddered and his hands rose towards her again, but fell back, fisting.

'Are you all right?' His voice was rough and strained.

'Yes. I was afraid for a moment.' Her voice was just as rough and she cleared her throat, adjusting her bodice. His dark brows drew together.

'I'm sorry, Nell. I swear I didn't mean to frighten you.'

'No, I didn't mean that. There was a moment I didn't know if I would be able to get back. That I might lose myself.'

He didn't answer right away, but then he took her hands in his. She could feel how stiffly he was holding himself, but she didn't know what it meant or what to do.

'You are a humbling experience, Nell. I was trying to find a way to apologise for taking advantage of you, but I don't think I will. That would be to sully something amazing. You are amazing. Now I am going to thoroughly amaze myself and leave.'

When he reached the door she stepped forward impulsively.

'Hunter, may I ask you something?'

He paused at the door and took another long breath, as if preparing to plunge into a lake. Then he nodded warily.

'Why didn't you…? I don't think I would have stopped you just then, before. I mean you could have. Didn't you want to…?'

'Are you trying to kill me? I am barely clinging to the tatters of honour here which at the moment are so threadbare they are practically transparent. Now, I'm going to my room and you are staying here and I am giving you fair warning that the next time you…we… Goodnight! And lock this door!'

Nell stared at the closed door. Her laugh startled her and she looked guiltily about her room. It didn't look any different, but it was. She was.

Hunter closed the door to his room and leaned his forehead against it, debating whether to lock it just to make the point very clear that on no account was he to head back down the hallway and take advantage of his impossibly seductive betrothed.

Except that he was in absolute agony. If someone had told him a week ago that he would be standing with his hand on the doorknob of his room, desperately trying to prevent himself from going to complete the seduction of an inexperienced virgin, he would have drunk a toast to their fertile imagination.

Inexperienced. Not the most experienced of his mistresses had ever reduced him to such a state of quivering need and it certainly wasn't her innocence that was doing the trick. She had given herself over to pleasure with a hedonistic abandon and her release was the most beautiful surrender he had ever seen. Her eyes, warmed to melting, had fixed on his, giving him more than he was giving her, locking him into her joy, promising him the same if he would just let her.

The girl was a natural wanton. He should have known that was so even years ago from the way she had ridden Petra. She had been freedom and joy incarnate, just waiting to slip the leash that life and her brutal aunt and apathetic father had cinched around her. Well, she was slipping it now and he was just slipping.

'Oh, hell.' He groaned, shoving his forehead harder against the door. This was pathetic. Every single one of his stratagems was coming back to bite him. But what he couldn't do, no matter how much he needed to, was take further advantage of her state of arousal and confusion. Maybe he should. Just go bed her and have done with it. Then the choice would be taken away. Maybe it already had. He might not have taken her maidenhead, but he had done something worse. He had seen her joy and right now he felt he would kill before he let another man see her as he had. It would also finally put to rest whatever idiotic girlish fantasies she might still harbour about Welbeck, because if that man touched her just one more time, he would... He had been so entangled in the moment he had been completely unprepared when Welbeck had waylaid them as they left the green. He had just watched dumbly as she had taken the man's hand and followed him back towards the chaos of dancers as if she hadn't all but melted against him a moment earlier. She hadn't even looked back once, just smiled at Welbeck and placed her hand in his like this was the one moment she had been waiting for.

Could she still, even after what she had witnessed, be caught in her childish fantasy? He had really begun to believe she no longer cared for Welbeck, but perhaps that was just wishful thinking. He had barely held himself back from following them, pulling her hand from Welbeck's and staking his claim like the cave dweller he was deteriorating into. But if that was what Nell had been waiting for—her dance with her prince—to ruin that, to do anything at that point, would be cruelty incarnate. He couldn't do that to her, whatever it cost him to stand there and suffer the spears of hell as she looked up at Welbeck, her lips parted and a ribbon of pale gold hair loosening down her back...

He was becoming well acquainted with all forms of agony these past few days. He might have years of experience having pugilists pummel him, but these kinds of levellers were new to him and that scared him.

For the first time in his life he wanted someone to see him as he was.

Heat and clammy cold spread through him in waves, just like they did when he woke from the nightmare, as if the admission itself was a virulent disease. He had never needed anyone. People needed him, not the other way around. His mother, his brother, his aunts, his mistresses. Just as it should be. Not one of them had ever taken him by the hand and tried to soothe him and he had never wanted them to, until now. This girl had reduced him to a fool barely worthy of a lending-library novel. The worst was that some no longer hidden corner of himself was enjoying it and looking forward to more of the same.

He had to clear his mind and think.

Even if he succeeded in seducing her into marrying him, playing on her pain and disappointment with Charles, what did he think was going to happen? Nell would not be easily stowed away at Hunter Hall while he went about his business. Sooner or later he would slip up and she would discover his weakness and then what? In fact, it had been getting progressively worse this week. At least until recently the nightmare, horrific though it was, had been a kind of fixed constant. She had forced her way into his horror, making it a thousand times worse as he was helplessly forced to witness her destruction. How could he cope with watching himself fail her every night? What if one night he actually acted on that terror and hurt her? Biggs and Hidgins knew better than to approach him at night and at Hunter Hall his own wing was far from the servants, but what would happen if she became curious? How could he protect her from himself?

He gritted his teeth, trying to force a way through the physical and mental confusion. He wanted to go to her room and just tell her what she had done to him. What he needed from her. Then he would slide the remaining pins from her hair and finally do something about this raging fire that was surely damaging his higher faculties.

The only stable points in his seething mind were the need to go to her and the determination not to. He groaned and locked the door. The way he felt right now, he doubted he would manage to sleep, but right now he would even welcome the nightmares if they gave him some respite from this aching need.

Chapter Fourteen

Nell stopped in the doorway of Lady Welbeck's parlour and the mid-morning sun bounced brightly off Charles's curls as he turned towards her.

'I was told your mother was here.'

He glanced around the room, looking flustered.

'I was looking for her as well. I dare say she'll return soon. But I'm glad you are here, Nell. I want to speak with you…'

She took a step back, shaking her head. 'I really must pack. I just wanted to thank her.'

'You're leaving?'

'Yes. If my father does arrive, please inform him I will be at Bascombe. Thank you for your hospitality, Charles.'

He grasped her hand, stopping her.

'Wait, Nell. Please don't leave. We were just becoming reacquainted. I realise you saw me and…well…but it doesn't mean anything!'

'Please don't deny your relation with Lady Melkinson, Charles. I really don't care.'

His hands tightened on hers.

'I don't know what Phyllida told you, but I promise there is nothing serious between us.'

She tugged her hands away.

'Your affairs are of no interest to me. This is not only unnecessary but improper, Charles. I am engaged.'

For the first time she saw anger and frustration mar his pretty face.

'Are you? You didn't really discourage me this week, betrothed or not. So what if I had another interest? Everyone has them. I promise you that once I'm married I'll be faithful, which is more than your fiancé is likely to offer. Together we can turn the Welbeck stables into the finest in England. Think of it, Nell...'

His voice and face softened again, lighting with the smile that had been the staple of her dreams for years.

'What do you say, Nell? Tell Hunter you've found what you want right here. You'll make me the happiest man on earth...darling,' he murmured, his arms sliding down her back.

His mouth settled on hers, soft and coaxing. She had been searching for certainty in the chaos of feelings and revelations this past week and now she had it, just not the kind she had expected. She felt the scrape of her lips over her teeth as he pressed his mouth to hers and his taste was all wrong. She twisted away.

'Charles, stop. I don't want you to kiss me.'

'Yes, you do. You've been begging for this since the day you showed up. Don't play coy now, Nell. You're a passionate woman now. Let me show you, darling.'

She pulled away sharply as his head descended again and they both stumbled backwards, his foot catching the flounce of her dress with an ominous ripping sound. She tried to grab at a small table, but it just came with them and the garish figurine of a courting shepherd and shepherdess bounced and somersaulted onto the wooden floor, sending porcelain lovers and sheep in all directions as they landed on the floor, her shoulder making painful contact with his cheekbone.

'Blast! Now look what you've done!' Charles accused, rubbing his reddened cheek.

'What *I've* done? I told you not to kiss me!'

'You wanted me to!'

'I did not!' she snapped, scrambling to her knees and gathering pieces of the shattered statuette. When he didn't respond to her juvenile denial she glanced up and realised they were no longer alone. Standing just inside the doorway were Lord and Lady Welbeck, Hunter and her father.

'Nell!' her father bellowed.

'What on earth is going on here? Oh, my shepherdess!' said Lady Welbeck, hurrying towards the debris.

Nell remained where she was, vaguely wondering where her father had sprung from, but her attention was on Hunter as he strode towards her. She took his outstretched hand, shaking a beheaded sheep from her skirts. Charles also moved towards her, but stopped as Hunter turned, the look on his face as palpable as a blow. Without thinking, Nell tightened her grip on Hunter's hand and they stood suspended. Then the moment of near violence passed as Lord Welbeck went to right the table.

'What has happened in this room?' Lady Welbeck demanded.

'Yes, do tell us what precisely happened to your face, Welbeck,' Hunter added. 'And to Miss Tilney's dress as well.'

'I fell,' Nell said quickly.

'I...uh, tripped,' Charles said at precisely the same time. Hunter bared his teeth.

'I suggest you practise to be less clumsy in future, Welbeck,' he said, pulling Nell past her father's immobile and frowning figure. 'Or if you must trip, do so as far from my betrothed as possible.'

Nell didn't particularly like being all but dragged along like a child, but the truth was that she was glad to be extracted from that room. At her door Hunter merely opened it and walked in.

'You can't come in here!'

'It's a bit late for prudery, isn't it? I've been here twice already. Besides, in light of your tryst with Welbeck, protestations of delicacy are out of place right now.'

'We didn't... It wasn't a tryst.'

'I see. You merely fell. Oh, sorry, it was Welbeck who "tripped". You should co-ordinate your stories ahead of time when next you plan to "fall" or "trip".'

'I was merely looking for Lady Welbeck to tell her I was leaving, but Charles was there and...he proposed to me.'

She went and sat on the side of the bed, feeling a little ill. Her father was here and now she would have to gather the strength to follow through on her agreement with Hunter. He would receive his water rights and she would receive her freedom... She was shaking inside, not like an attack, just with loneliness and the anticipation of pain. What would Hunter do if she asked him to sit down by her and just hold her hand? Maybe even ask him if he would reconsider his offer?

Silly fool.

'So the little girl gets her prince.' Hunter spoke at last, his words harsh and mocking. 'Phyllida had the

right of it after all. You played us all finely, didn't you?
A bit melodramatic for my taste since it was clear from
the moment we arrived Welbeck was more than willing.
Flirting quite that outrageously with me was a bit of a
risk, though, don't you think? Or were you having too
much fun playing all fronts by then to care? You probably expect me to congratulate you, too.'

'I don't expect anything.' Her words were as muted
and dull as she felt. There was no point. He had begun
his acquaintance with her feeling pity and now it would
end with him feeling contempt. She must have been mad
to think there was something she could offer him.

She hardly even noticed the knock until Hunter spoke.

'Get rid of whoever it is,' he snarled under his breath,
moving in the direction of the dressing room.

Nell walked over and cracked open the door.

'My dear, dear Nell, may I come in?'

'Lady Welbeck! What? No! I mean, is something
wrong?' Nell remained lodged firmly behind the door
and Lady Welbeck glimpsed worriedly up and down the
empty corridor before hurrying into speech.

'My dear, how can you ask me that? I am quite dis-
traught at my failure as a chaperon and hostess. Lord
Welbeck and Charles are with your father now, trying
to explain… What will Sir Henry think of us? You must
believe it is only because my poor Charles is so very
passionately attached to you that he has allowed his
emotions to overcome his judgement. He is quite, quite
broken-hearted, my dear. I know you have always loved
him and surely such deeply rooted tender feelings cannot be dislodged merely by a momentary lapse in dear
Charles's restraint. Men, my dear, are often swayed by

urges us women know little of and it behoves us to show patience if—'

'Lady Welbeck,' Nell interrupted this flow as firmly as possible, 'there is no possibility of an alliance between Charles and I.'

'None?' asked Lady Welbeck wistfully.

'None, Lady Welbeck. Thank you for your hospitality, but I really must pack.'

Gently but firmly she closed the door.

'You refused Welbeck's offer? Why didn't you say so?'

Hunter had himself under control now, and though his eyes were still intent and darker than usual, the anger that had pressed at her was, if not gone, at least well hidden. Was he worried now she had abandoned her plans to marry Charles he might have to marry her after all?

'When during your tantrum was I supposed to do that?'

'My tantrum… Did you refuse him because of Phyllida?'

'No, not because of your precious Phyllida. Now if you have nothing useful to say, would you please leave? I must send for Betsy so I can pack.'

'She's not mine, thank heavens, and we're not done yet.'

'If you won't leave I shall start packing anyway.'

She marched over to the dresser and ceremoniously extracted a carefully folded stack of chemises, placing them on her bed. If she had expected to embarrass Hunter into leaving she had clearly miscalculated, for he just leaned back against the wall and watched. She wavered, realising she had chosen a very inappropriate threat, and though she might have come a long way from the inexperienced girl of a week ago, she still wasn't comfortable standing in front of a man with a stack of undergarments in her arms.

She was saved from backing down by another knock on the door. Hunter shifted against the wall, but otherwise didn't speak as she laid the stack on the bed and went to open the door a crack. When she saw who it was, it took all her determination not to slam the door shut again.

'Father!'

'Let me in, Nell. I want a word with you.'

His voice boomed down the corridor, but she put her foot firmly against the door.

'Whatever you have to say you can say from there, Father. I'm already undressing,' she lied.

'You insolent girl! I can see that what I have just heard from the Welbecks about your conduct this past week is only too true. You had no business coming to Wilton without my express permission and making a fool of yourself over young Welbeck. You are an engaged woman, not a fanciful child, and I wouldn't be surprised if your antics have given Lord Hunter a disgust of you. Hester was right that you would ruin matters if given half a chance. I should never have agreed to his demand that you remain in that Petheridge woman's care. We will leave for Tilney Hall in the morning and meanwhile I will speak with Lord Hunter and see if I can yet salvage this debacle.'

Nell felt her cheeks were as red as her father's. She didn't know what she had expected of this man after four years. Had she secretly been hoping he would be glad to see her? Might even say he had missed her? His whole handling of the engagement should have re-

minded her of her father's limitations. It was ridiculous
to be so hurt, to feel the dampness of her palm against
the metal knob and the skittering of nerves gathering in
preparation for the rising storm. She had a sudden urge
to lean her head against the door and cry. No—to slam
the door in his face. Several times. Hard. Until it splin-
tered into smithereens.

'No, Father. I will not go to Tilney Hall. Have you
forgotten? I am of age and you are no longer even my
trustee. I can go where I wish, with whomever I wish,
and if I wished to marry Charles I would and there is
nothing you could do about it. What are you worried
about? That the Bascombe money might make the Welbeck stables more successful than yours? Are you so
petty? Now excuse me because I really must pack.' She
started closing the door in his stunned face, but stopped.
'Oh, though I might consider inviting you to Bascombe
if you could ever bring yourself to apologise to me, you
can tell Aunt Hester she will never, ever be welcome in
my home. She is a mean, vicious, pathetic b—witch and
you can tell her I said so. Goodbye, Father.'

She locked the door before he could respond and
leaned her forehead on the door frame, waiting for the
shaking to stop. She didn't move even when Hunter's
hand settled on her shoulder or when there was a tentative knock on the door. She must have scared her father
quite seriously for him to knock like that.

'I meant it! Leave me alone!' She gritted her teeth
and tried to shake off Hunter's hand.

'Nell?'

'Charles?'

Hunter's hand fell away, flattening against the door

by the side of her head. She could feel the heat of his body behind her, anger emanating off him like waves.

'I must speak with you. May I come in?' Charles's voice was muffled by the wood as if he, too, was leaning against the door.

'You most certainly may not. What do you want? I am packing.'

'I wish you wouldn't. Leave, I mean. Please give me another chance. I love you.'

'No, you don't.' Nell was burningly aware of Hunter behind her.

'Yes, I do. I always liked you and I think you'll be an excellent horse-breeder's wife and—'

'Oh, for…! You don't love me, you are enamoured of my inheritance, and I wish, I really wish, Grandmama had succeeded in convincing Grandpapa not to will Bascombe to me because if ever there was a poisoned chalice this is it. Goodbye, Charles.'

'Nell…'

This time she didn't answer and eventually she heard his footsteps recede.

'Do you think Lord Welbeck might also be coming to throw his hat into the ring, or is that the lot?' Hunter asked behind her.

Nell felt a sob expand in her throat and she covered her eyes, leaning her forehead on the door.

'Nell, I'm sorry… I didn't mean…'

She hadn't cried for years. Not even when she had ridden out of Tilney for the last time, furious and scared and tentatively triumphant. The last time she remembered really crying had been a month after her mother's death and her arrival at Mrs Petheridge's. Then Mrs Pether-

idge had sat and hugged her on a sagging brocade sofa,
her plump arms surprisingly strong.

The strong arms that drew her onto his lap as he sat
on the side of the bed were certainly not plump, but Nell
leaned into their embrace with the same weary abandon
as the long-ago girl had leaned against her headmistress's pillowy bosom. Mrs Petheridge had patted her
back, but Hunter was stroking her hair, which was unravelling again, and his hand was steadier than his voice.

'Nell, Nell, I'm so sorry. Oh, don't cry like that,
sweetheart. You're tearing me apart.'

She shook her head and cried harder. Her eyes burned
and stung and her shoulders and throat ached. It was
splitting her from the inside. She was lost again, and
alone again, but this alone was a thousand times worse
than before because loving Charles had never ached. It
had been wistful and hopeful and embarrassed and a
host of other timid things. But loving Hunter when he
didn't love her in return felt like being thrown from a
horse, both the moment of shocked protest at having the
world snatched out from under her and the jarring, biting pain of impact. It wasn't her bones that were shattering, but an inner structure that held up who she was,
an entity she was only beginning to recognise as herself.

'Sweetheart, Nell...' His voice was husky and plead-
ing.

He was probably desperate for this to be over so he
could escape and she couldn't even walk away because
her face probably looked as blotchy as if she had been
ill for days. She grabbed one of the chemises from the
bed and shoved her face into it and tried to stop the way
her breath kept catching as the sobs finally subsided.

She resisted when he tried to pull the cloth away,

but not when he folded her back against him, his breath on her temple as his lips gently brushed her hair. Trust Hunter to use seduction to stop a sobbing fit, she thought, but she still didn't move away. Soon it would be over and right now...right now she needed this. Him.

She was drained hollow and so weary she just wanted to stay right there, held just like that. Today he would leave and she might never see him again but as a neighbour and she couldn't bear it. The agony of that thought shivered through her and his arms tightened, pulling her more securely against him, cocooning her.

'It's all right...' he murmured into her hair, and though it was a ridiculous thing to say when it was clear nothing was all right, it comforted her. She rested against him, thawing into softness, just breathing, the world evening out and slipping away. She no longer felt weary, just tired, very tired, and very safe...

She jerked awake at the sound and it took her a moment to recover her bearings.

She was lying on her bed, fully dressed, and she wasn't alone. She opened her eyes. Hunter's arm was draped over her breasts, holding her against his length, and her foot was pressed between his legs. By the small clock on the dresser it was just past midday, which meant they must have slept less than an hour, but she was marvellously rested. The events of the past days and her sleepless night must have exhausted her more than she had realised but she never would have imagined she would just fall asleep like that... It was so embarrassing! And why hadn't he just left her? He had also looked exhausted. Perhaps he also had trouble sleeping, or perhaps he had been otherwise occupied that night... She shut her eyes against the snake of jealousy uncurling inside her. It would be better just to soak in the warmth of the moment, how peaceful it felt, how right...

Hunter shifted and she opened her eyes, realising what had woken her. He was dreaming.

'No! Stop!'

His voice was muffled against her hair and his body twitched, his hand jerking against her, and she picked it up gently, pressing it between hers. He had been relaxed a moment before, but she could feel tension gathering through his body, his fingers splaying, and she frowned. The next move when it came was so abrupt she was completely unprepared. He pulled away from her, his hands fisting on the sheets, anchoring himself to the bed, his mouth moving, but she could make no sense of the hoarse mutterings. He looked so tortured she raised herself on her elbow and reached out instinctively, but she had hardly run her hand down his cheek when he suddenly grabbed it, pulling her towards him so that she fell across him, his chin striking her forehead. She cried out more in surprise than pain, but it was enough and suddenly she was thrust away from him and he was out of the bed, staring down at her in horror.

'Nell! I hurt you! What have I done?'

She scrambled to her knees, holding out her hands.

'You didn't hurt me. I'm fine!'

But he had covered his face with his hands and she could see he was shaking. She moved towards him, but he stepped away, turning his back on her.

'I can't believe I fell asleep. I just didn't want to wake you, you were so tired, but I never should have...'

He sounded so agonised she shook her head, trying

to understand. His reaction was completely out of step with what had happened.

'Gabriel…'

'No! I never should have let this happen…'

'Hunter, calm down…'

He rounded on her, his eyes so fierce she took a step back this time.

'Calm down? Calm down? I almost… I might have… Just who do you think I am? Do you think you can just use me to play your little seduction games on that pretty boy and then when you find out he has feet of clay you can come cry on my shoulder and expect me to play the comforting protector? Is that my role now? Haven't you figured it out yet? I am no one's protector. I can't even protect you from myself!'

'I don't expect anything of you…'

'Good! At least you learned something useful from me even if it's only to lower your expectations. Now, get dressed. As for this betrothal, there is no reason we can't co-ordinate the denouement by means of the post. I think it is preferable if we don't see each other until this is all over. Goodbye.'

Nell stared at the door that snapped shut behind him, her hand still outstretched towards him and her mind still reeling.

Chapter Fifteen

If Hunter had hoped that escaping back to the familiar territory of London would relieve some of his confusion and pain, he had not taken into account being balked by his own servants. They had not taken kindly to being told, in graphic terms, that their questions about why Miss Nell was staying at Welbeck while he departed precipitately were strictly unwelcome.

Not that they said anything aloud. Their commentary was passive, but very clear. They went about their duties as usual, but the act of being shaved by Biggs had taken on such a menacing cast that Hunter had decided to forgo the experience altogether. Hidgins, for his part, had discovered his ancestors' Gaelic gloom and on the one time since his return that Hunter had forced himself to take Valiant out to try to gallop out his depression, the only words Hidgins had deigned to address to him had been a very non-subservient 'You're a fool' and, adding insult to injury, 'My lord'.

Hunter hadn't even been tempted to land him a facer. He had swung onto Valiant's back and said nothing because there was nothing to say. He had considered pointing out to the two of them that their punishment was superfluous because he was already sufficiently deep in hell. There were two versions to that hell—it hadn't taken as far as Potters Bar to realise he wanted to turn back. That the thought of leaving her, even if it was the right thing to do, was…frightening. Instead of turning back he had forced his poor horses to the edge of their ability and probably broken the Wild Hunt Club's record on the road to London.

Back in London the nightmare had shifted once again—even here she had completely taken over. For the first time neither Tim nor his mother were present, just Nell; there was no blood, no disintegrating bodies, just the inexorable rise of fear as Nell headed towards the cliff, and though he ran as fast as he could, she receded into the distance and then he had woken, not in his bed, but in a casket, the sound of earth striking above, and he realised they were burying him instead of Tim. He had finally woken in earnest, but not before scoring his wrist with bloody scratches as he tried to escape. He had lain there, frozen and panting and ashamed.

There was even relief in having Biggs and Hidgins angry at him. It was certainly more palatable than the solicitous or pitying looks that the truth would likely elicit. He also would have happily avoided his friends, but the evening after his return Biggs knocked once on the library door and announced to the ether, 'Lord Ravenscar. My lord.'

Ravenscar strode in without waiting to be invited.

'What has bit Biggs?'

'What do you want, Ravenscar?'

'That's a fine welcome from master and man.' Ravenscar went over and poured himself a brandy. When Hunter didn't answer Ravenscar poured him a glass as well.

'So, how fares your engagement?'

'It's over.'

Ravenscar raised a brow.

'I don't know whether to offer condolences or congratulations.'

'You can offer me the sight of your backside as you leave. I'm in no mood for company.'

The knocker sounded again and Hunter surged to his feet to tell Biggs not to let anyone else in. But Biggs was already taking Lord Stanton's hat and cane.

'Et tu?' Hunter said, resigned. 'Biggs, do me a favour and tell everyone else I've gone to the country or to hell or something.'

'To hell? Most assuredly. My lord.'

Stanton stared in surprise at Biggs's receding back.

'What's wrong with Biggs?'

Hunter shrugged. He was raw and restless, but the thought of being left with his own thoughts was almost worse. No, it *was* worse. He still hadn't got thoroughly drunk because he hadn't taken that path in years. Since Tim's suicide. But with each passing hour the temptation of revisiting that oblivion grew. He downed the brandy Ravenscar had poured him and walked over to the sideboard to pour a more substantial glass.

Ravenscar answered Stanton's question.

'Biggs is sulking and our friend here is in a foul mood. Makes one wonder what happened at the horse fair. Didn't know losing those water rights would have such an effect on you.'

'I didn't. She's selling me part of the riverfront.'

'Is she? That's very generous. So what's the problem?

You don't actually need the estate itself. By all accounts you should be celebrating.'

Hunter smiled down at the brandy and raised his glass.

'I am. I got what I wanted. To have my cake and eat it, too. Clever me.'

He drained his glass and Stanton moved towards the fireplace, frowning.

'Are you guilty about the girl? If you manage it carefully, you might be able to avoid too much scandal, and quite frankly with her inheritance she won't have a problem finding a husband, so…'

'I'm well aware of that!' Hunter snapped. 'She already had the offer she wanted from her childhood hero, Charles Welbeck.'

Ravenscar's brows rose, but there was a considering look in his eyes now.

'That was quick! My hat off to the girl.'

'That's enough, Raven,' Stanton said quietly and Hunter poured himself another measure of brandy. He had been right—solicitude was worse than anger. It was clear they saw through him. What was the point?

'I can't stand it.'

There was a moment's silence. Then Stanton came and poured himself a glass as well. Ravenscar went over to the fireplace and crouched down to shove twists of paper between the logs. Hunter forced himself to break the silence.

'Never mind. It's for the best.'

Ravenscar lit the fire and stood up, brushing his hands. 'As little as I want to see you hitched, man, I think you're an idiot. Why the devil did you just leave the field if you actually wanted her?'

'What the devil can I offer her? I can't promise I could even keep her safe from myself, let alone from life. She deserves better.'

'Damn, I take offence on your account. She won't find anyone better. If you care for her, go do something about it. Might be a little uncomfortable for you if she marries someone else and settles into Bascombe Hall and you have to watch her crooning over little ones that might have been yours, but you'll recover eventually.'

'Very helpful, Raven,' Stanton said curtly as he watched Hunter.

Hunter took his glass to the armchair by the fire and sat down. His mind had dubbed it 'her armchair' since every time he saw it he remembered that first night she had appeared on his doorstep. The thought of going through life at Hunter Hall, just a few miles from her, watching her married, having children, a life… He sank his head into his hands. It hurt. Physically. He never would have believed that. Even his grief over Tim had been more internal and it had been easier to turn it into rage at the world, and into that wilful self-destruction that his friends and their joint commitment to help men damaged by war had finally put an end to. But this—this locked him down, it filled his body with lead and sank him.

She's better off without you. Remember what you did to her? No wonder she had looked so appalled. If that hadn't happened he might have even succeeded in convincing himself he could keep her safe. It hadn't even been night time! He hadn't even noticed he had fallen asleep. That just showed how dangerous she was. No, how dangerous *he* was. He hadn't hurt her badly this time, but what would happen next time? If he ever really hurt her… It was unthinkable. She deserved better.

She was probably still at Welbeck and the shining prince was hard at work wearing down her defences. She had been shattered by his betrayal. He had noticed only too well she hadn't denied outright that she still loved him. Perhaps in the end she would…

He had been outsmarted, outmanoeuvred and felled by a twenty-one-year-old Saxon witch. And she…she deserved someone honest and serious and who would cherish her…love her…

Every time his mind presented this commendable resolution his heart fought back with a less articulate but much more visceral protest. *I* would cherish her. With every breath in my body. I would love her. Lust for her, love her, live for her, whatever it took. The words, childish and insistent, kept beating at him from inside. *I need her.* For the first time in his life he needed someone. He didn't even understand what she did to him, but something had just begun to happen to him. He wanted desperately to be selfish and take that risk. It wasn't right that she hold his hand and offer to let him rest, then leave him to writhe alone.

He should never have played God in her life, but this punishment was just unfair.

In his mind he conjured her into the study and sank to his knees and knelt against her, which was as pathetic as anything he could imagine, but there it was. He should have known from the beginning… He had known. There had been enough signs. Even trivial gestures like lacing his fingers through hers after finding her in the paddock with Daisy. He hadn't done anything that mawkish since he was a child being taken for a walk—no, not even then.

With her it had been so natural he hadn't even noticed the incongruity. He didn't just want her. He wanted her with him. In whatever ditch he next found himself in life, he needed her with him.

Everything was narrowing down to one need—to be with her. None of the arguments he had carefully formulated had put the slightest dent in that conviction. It was as futile as trying to explain to a three-year-old that there weren't really monsters in the dark. He needed her.

He stood abruptly and the way the room tilted and the level of amber liquid in the decanter made it clear he was well on his way to achieving his ambition to get drunk. He ignored his friends and tugged on the bell pull. When Biggs appeared he moved towards the door as steadily as he could.

'Pack a bag for me. Tell Hidgins to bring round the curricle.'

'Bring…now, my lord?'

'Now.'

Biggs lost his stiffness, his eyes darting to Ravenscar and Stanton, but they both shrugged helplessly.

'It's almost nine in the evening, sir, and you're drunk. In the morning we…'

'Biggs. Pack a bag and send for Hidgins or I'll do it myself.'

'All right, I'll find him, but he will drive. You're in no fit state…'

'Fine. You find him, I'll pack.'

'You most certainly will not…'

'Then I'll find him, you pack.'

Biggs planted himself firmly in front of Hunter, feet apart, chin up.

'My lord, you will sit down and I will bring some

bread and cheese because you haven't eaten all day and then I will speak to Hidgins and I will pack, and if once you have eaten you still wish to drive your precious horses through the night in a state of inebriation, you may do so. Otherwise I shall instruct Hidgins to lock the stables and swallow the key.'

'I can pick locks, you know.'

'I do know. I taught you. Lord Ravenscar, Lord Stanton, do make him sit down and talk some sense into him.'

Biggs disappeared and Hunter went and sat and a wave of dizziness and despair washed over him. He sank his head into his hands. Even his hair ached.

'I can't stand this,' he mumbled. 'I need to return there. Now.'

Stanton spoke, his voice gentle.

'We'll take you there if you want, but Biggs is right—you can't go like this. The only place you will end up in this state is a ditch.'

Hunter squeezed his head. They were right, he knew he was in no state to drive, but even the thought of waiting until morning was unbearable. Now that he had admitted his weakness, it was impossible to wait. He needed to see her now.

The knocker sounded and for one mad moment Hunter thought he had, by sheer force of will, conjured her up on his doorstep. He groaned.

'Whoever it is, tell them to go to hell.'

Chapter Sixteen

Nell looked up at the door. There was a light in the same room as a week ago and she prayed that meant he was at home. Alone. She remembered he had said he didn't entertain women here, but the thought of encountering Lady Felton was painful even in the realm of pure possibility. She took a deep breath and marched up the stairs. This time she not only succeeded in knocking, but it seemed a long wait for the door to open. Biggs's expression when he saw her shifted from haughty dismissal to shock.

'Miss Nell!'

'Is his lordship in, Biggs? And alone?'

'No, miss. I mean, yes, miss. I mean his lordship is in, but he isn't alone. Come in.'

She took a step back, trying not to let the burning turn to tears.

'Never mind, Biggs. Just inform Lord Hunter...'

Biggs moved down the stairs towards her.

'Lord Ravenscar and Lord Stanton are with him, miss. They are his closest friends and utterly trustworthy. But you must come in, please. You cannot be alone in the streets at this hour. I will make you some tea. And sandwiches.'

She gave a watery laugh and followed him into a room as he hurriedly lit a couple of candles from the taper he held.

'I am going to inform Lord Hunter you are here. Will you promise not to leave?'

The door closed behind him and she tugged her cloak more tightly about her. She heard another door open and before she could even move towards the unlit fireplace Hunter entered the room.

He was never very fastidious about his dress, but he looked almost as unkempt as he had after his brawl with Hidgins. He wore no coat or cravat and his shirt hung loose, and his hair looked as if she had definitely interrupted a tryst, so she wondered if Biggs had lied to her.

'I'm sorry. I didn't mean to interrupt your evening.'

'It's no bother. We were just leaving,' said a voice from the doorway and she turned to see two exceedingly handsome men, one dark and one fair, inspecting her.

'Go away,' Hunter said without turning to them. The fair one smiled at her and bowed out of the doorway, but the dark one lingered for a moment with an assessing smile on his face before the fair one tugged him away.

'Are you all right? Has something happened?' Hunter asked as the door closed and Nell shook her head.

She had meant to launch into her prepared speech, but the words that came out were an expression of all the wonder and confusion she felt.

'I was here just a week ago.'

Surely it was impossible to be so transformed in a matter of days? What would have happened if he had not come to Tilney four years ago? If eventually her infatuation and dowry had enticed Charles into offering for her? She might never have realised that she wasn't even very fond of him and that Charles hardly knew her and didn't really want to, not as she was, flawed and thirsting for life. How could she have known she needed a man who could make her laugh, and burn, and make her worry about him and want to hold him?

It had taken all her resolution to navigate these past couple of days—her father's anger and Charles's repeated attempts to make her stay at Welbeck had been difficult, but nothing like the disappointment when she had gone in search of Hunter only to find he had left immediately after their confrontation. Her tentative knock on his door had been answered by Biggs and she had stared past him at the open trunk and the pile of clothes on the bed. She didn't know what she had expected, but to hear that Hunter had already left had held her frozen. It was only the obvious compassion on Biggs's face that had set her moving again and she had retreated to lick her wounds in the privacy of her room.

It wasn't possible to force Hunter to care for her, not the way she needed, but it made no sense that she wouldn't see him again. It just wasn't possible. This was Hunter—of course she had to see him again. That single-minded thought clung to her, warping everything else around her.

In the end it was Betsy who helped tip the scales—her sniffling and red eyes as she had dressed Nell for dinner had distracted Nell from her own misery enough to realise that she was not the only sufferer from Hunter and Hidgins's disappearance. But if Betsy had no power to control her fate, Nell did—she was a wealthy woman and had to answer to no one. If she could not marry the man she loved, she could at least love him in the only way open to her. It might be outrageous and scandalous, but she would deal with the repercussions later. She didn't doubt that he wanted to bed her, and if all he could manage at this point was a mistress, she was determined to be that mistress. Later she would do her best to find her way through his defences to the generous heart she knew was there. She might fail, but she had to try.

Betsy had been only too happy to help her arrange for the hire of a post-chaise and to give her notice at Welbeck to become Nell's maid. Together they had collected Mrs Calvert from her sister's at Stoke Newington and continued to London. She had no idea what Mrs Calvert and Betsy thought of her actions when they reached London but they were quite content to trust her, probably more than she trusted herself.

She had fully expected to find that Hunter was out, or busy, and she still expected him to try to send her packing—but that at least she was determined to resist.

'You shouldn't have come here,' he said into the silence, confirming her thoughts. 'It isn't fair.'

She must have shivered because he took her hand and she followed him into the other room where the fire was still high. She sat down in her chair gratefully and he picked up a half-full glass and stood watching her. There was more light here and she saw he hadn't shaved and there was that bruising beneath his eyes that reminded her of how he had looked four years ago. He had moved deep inside himself and was watching from the battlements.

There was a knock on the door and they both started.

'Tea, sir, and something to eat for Miss Nell.'

Biggs set down the tray.

'Shall I send word to Miss Amelia?' he asked the silence.

'There is no need, thank you, Biggs,' Nell answered as she took the cup of tea he offered. 'Betsy and Mrs Calvert are waiting for me at the Red Lion. Or rather for Mrs Jones, widow.'

For a moment Hunter's eyes warmed with laughter before closing down again and that and the tea started thawing her out.

'It's nice to see you follow at least some of my advice, however dubious. But you still shouldn't be here.'

Nell sipped her tea.

'Am I keeping you from something?' she asked politely once Biggs had withdrawn.

He just shook his head, his eyes fixed on her so intently he seemed to be looking through her. She put down her tea.

'Good. I was worried Lady Felton might be here. Even though you said she doesn't come here, I still wondered if you might be with her. But I dare say you saw her yesterday, didn't you?'

He shook his head.

'Today?'

'No, and I won't be seeing her tomorrow either. Whatever relationship we once had was effectively over before I left London. I am apparently more honourable than I had once thought.'

He put down his glass. Some of the amber liquid sloshed onto the table and he stared at it and rubbed his forehead. 'You shouldn't be here.'

'You said that before. Twice.'

'It's still true. Why are you here?' His voice was less assured now.

'I have a proposition to make.'

'A proposition?'

Even though the fire had warmed her, she was shaky and cold inside. Now she would have to find the strength to tell him what she had come for and the strength not to tell him what she was really here for because that would undoubtedly drive him away, back past those battlements that kept him safe and separate. She needed some of that cider to give her courage again. She needed him to touch her instead of just watching her like that. Even if he didn't love her, even if it was just the kind of lust he obviously took so lightly as to dismiss his latest mistress without a backward glance, he could still hold her until this aching became bearable.

She fumbled at the strings of her cloak. She had come as a prospective mistress and so it was best to begin somewhere.

'What the devil?'

Nell flushed as she removed her cloak to reveal the low-cut Parisian evening gown Anna had convinced her to commission, but which she had been convinced she would never have the nerve to wear. She had made Betsy cinch her stays to the point where her breasts balanced precariously against the silvery lace and embroidery of the bodice, making it a miracle they hadn't yet decided to escape. She had come ready to compete with the Lady Feltons of the world, well aware she was in a losing position and needing whatever added inducement available to her. But his shocked response shook her confidence.

'Don't you like it?'

'Are you trying to kill me?' His knuckles stood out sharply as his hand closed on the back of the armchair opposite.

That was better.

'So you *do* like it?' she asked, lowering her voice.

'Nell...you can't do this to me. Come here. Like this. I warned you.'

His eyes rose to hers and she read hunger in there and leashed desperation. Her heart surged ahead and her lungs strained at her tight stays. Perhaps she shouldn't have had Betsy cinch her quite so well. It was time for the next stage in her battle and she needed to breathe to do that.

'I know you did. You still haven't answered my question. Do you like it?'

'Like is not the word that comes to mind. In fact, very little is coming to mind at the moment. It's all going elsewhere, which is why you need to put your cloak back on. Now.'

'I'll take the dress off if you don't like it,' she offered, shrugging the delicate lace sleeve just an inch off her shoulder.

Hunter groaned and shoved the armchair aside, pulling her to her feet and sinking his face into her hair.

'Nell, I'm in agony, I'm half-drunk and I have no willpower left. If you don't leave now, I'm going to strip off that impossible dress before it disintegrates and take everything on offer and not Beelzebub himself will be able to stop me from ravishing you. So—leave. Now!'

His stubble scraped against her cheek as she turned his face to hers, her mouth seeking his. The most beautiful mouth in the world, she thought, her whole body flooding with desire as she tasted him. She started with his lower lip first, because it was tense and needed extra attention. Slowly, lovingly, tracing it and drawing it in between hers very gently. His body vibrated against hers and his hands were fisted in her dress. It would probably be ruined, but it would be well worth it if only she could be ruined alongside it. Ruined and rebuilt. This amazing man was all about ruin and rebuilding and whether he knew it yet or not he was hers. Not just his body, but all of him. No matter how long it took or how many mistresses she had to circumvent to win him.

She gave his lower lip one last lingering caress with her tongue and leaned back against his arms. His eyes had turned pagan again. Apparently Beelzebub wasn't going to interfere with his minion after all.

'More?' she asked. 'Or shall I stop?'

The hard ridge of his arousal was pressing under her stomach, a hot, thudding presence that was in dialogue with its twin soul between her thighs, and she wanted nothing better than to shift so that they could carry on a much more intimate conversation. As the silence stretched she turned, reaching for the hooks at her waist.

'Could you help undo my laces? Betsy tied them dreadfully tight and I'm afraid I might swoon if we carry on like this. I won't be needing them again tonight, will I? I told Betsy I probably wouldn't return tonight and I am very glad you were here and there wasn't anyone with you. Anyone female, I mean. Well, are you going to help? Oh, never mind. I'll do it.'

He shoved her hands away, his own fumbling with the laces.

'You're killing me, Nell. I'm done playing fair. Do you hear me?'

The relief as the stays were released made her sigh with pleasure and she leaned against him, kissing and licking at the hot skin of his throat, tasting him with avid joy as he peeled away all the unnecessary layers, giving herself utterly into his care.

It was still a shock when his hand very gently cupped her breast, hot and hard against her though he didn't move, just held her, his hand warm and peculiarly gentle against her sensitised skin. She rested her mouth on the galloping pulse on the side of his neck, feeling its mirror under her own skin where he held her, feeling the gathering of her flesh, tightening, hardening until the bud of her nipple pressed against his palm. The moment of contact coursed through her body and his, a shared shudder that set him in motion, and her dress, her flimsy petticoat and drawers were sheared away, disintegrating as he had threatened.

He touched her everywhere, her back, her buttocks, dipping between her thighs, receding, finding her breast again, more insistent, his palm and thumb caressing the sensitive nipple, sending spears of fire through her, weaving a web of fire around and through her body, everything gathering towards the new centre of her universe.

It was everything she had wanted, but still not enough. Her stockings, his shirt and pantaloons were all in the way. She wanted *him*.

She dragged up his shirt, sighing as her hands skimmed over his back. Later she would explore this beautiful surface, inch by inch…and his waist. No blows below the waist, that was very clever. She didn't want anything to harm Hunter anywhere and especially not where that heat was pressed against her and she wanted so desperately to touch.

'I want to touch you again. There,' she said against his mouth, or tried to say because her voice would hardly form, so she made her point by pressing her hips even more insistently to his.

Once again he stopped and his arms closed around her, freezing them for a moment.

'Not a good idea right now.' He sounded underwater. 'This is your last chance to draw back.'

She tightened her arms around his neck, rising on tiptoe to say the words against his mouth.

'You will have to forcibly remove me from this house if you want me to leave. You should probably dress me first, but don't expect any help from me.'

He grunted and swung her into his arms and turned towards the door and for a shocked moment she wondered if he would carry through on his threat and put her out as she was, but then his long strides took them up the stairs and she leaned back against him, smiling in relief.

'I'm awfully heavy,' she said apologetically as they made it to the top.

His arms tightened on her.

'You're perfect.'

'You must be drunk.' She laughed and he nudged open a door and slid her down his body, his hands shaping her, curving and lingering over her buttocks, and her legs tried to separate, to make room for something.

'Not any more. Not on brandy. Wait here. I'll light a fire.'

She grabbed at him as he started to move away.

'I don't need a fire. I'm already on fire. I need you to do something about it.'

He cupped her face in his hands and rested his forehead on hers for a moment.

'Very well. There are other ways to keep you warm.'

Not warm. Ablaze. That was what it felt like when

her breasts finally were pressed against his chest. How on earth would she ever be able to move away again? He was as hard as a sculpture, but silky smooth and hot, and the hair on his chest teased her breasts, making it impossible not to move against him, rub herself over him like a cat begging for a caress. His growl did sound like some species of the larger of the feline family as his hand obliged her, gathering her against him again. With his other he released the fall of his pantaloons to strip them off, but before she could even register the long hard heat of his arousal pressed against her she found herself on her back on a bed that must have been one of the biggest she had ever seen.

She lay there, absorbing this new state of affairs, one of her legs bent on the bed, the other dangling over its side, her hair scattered everywhere. She was naked except for her stockings while a very tall, very large, very naked and very aroused man stood over her with a look that gave credence to all his talk about marauding. Then he smiled, a very marauding smile. His gaze moved over her, slowly, his expression shifting with each curve and dip travelled, heating her as he went. It was an invasion and a branding and when he reached her abdomen her legs drew together protectively, but he leaned his knee on the bed between them so that they clamped against him. He traced her cheek with his knuckles, so softly she had to turn her head into the caress to feel him.

'Don't hide from me. You're beautiful. All of you.'

She could feel her body shake and she sank her teeth into her lip to hold back the words. It was too soon, too much. She said the words loudly inside her head so that they wouldn't escape.

Mine. Hunter. My love.

* * *

Hunter watched her teeth sink into the plump rise of flesh and his own lips were singed with heat. He wanted her to sink her teeth into him, into any part of him. The need to see her lips part, open for him, just as he wanted her legs to open for him, felt like a compulsion. He was still sane enough to know he was falling off a cliff, but there was nothing to grasp to slow him down. He needed to be closer; he needed to feel her pliant, lithe body under him, over him. He needed her scent, her heat. It felt as though he needed to be inside her more than he needed to breathe.

He was still not clear how his erotic dreams of Nell had become a reality. How he had gone from black despair to this wanton display of long sleek limbs and impossibly silky hair on his bed, but it didn't matter. He would deal with the challenges somehow. Nothing mattered but that she was here, with him, his. She was his and would soon be irrevocably so. He was done being sensible.

He lay down beside her, sliding one leg over hers to anchor the warmth of her thighs in case she had any ideas about moving as he worked his hand upwards from her hip. When his fingers reached the shadowed curve below her breast her chest expanded on a panting breath and her lip finally slipped out, moist and reddened, and it was all he could do not to just haul himself on top of her, spread her legs, thrust into her, disappear into her damp heat until he erased himself completely.

His erection was as hard as a rock against the bite of her hip bone, but he stayed where he was, just cupping her beautiful cream and rose breast, his thumb brushing just below the nipple, watching it harden, gather, as it had downstairs, until her neck arched back in a cry she wouldn't release. He bent and tasted that arch, salty sweet and filled with her wildflower scent. He breathed it in, trying to capture it, like the last breath of air before sinking to the bottom of an unrelenting sea.

'You're mine. Mine...' he whispered against her skin, tasting her, kissing her, grating his lips and teeth and tongue over her skin until she began to squirm against him, her panting breath raising her body against his, her legs trying to part under the weight of his. One of her arms had anchored around his shoulder and her fingers bit into his flesh, sending sharp spears of pain and pleasure through him.

'Hunter,' she moaned. 'Stop, please, do something!'

'Do you want me to stop?' he murmured against her breast, his lips drawing in her nipple, tracing it with his tongue, rough and soft. He slid his fingers through the silky curls at the juncture of her thighs. She was so damp and hot his own hips surged against his will.

'No, oh, don't stop. Please...' She twisted and he shifted, letting her spread her legs to his fingers, her own leg sliding between his, seeking his tension, his weight. It pressed against his erection and he breathed in, concentrating only on the music of her body. He wanted... he needed to pleasure her, to watch that golden moment of joy and light once again.

'Just relax,' he whispered against her lips, coaxing and sliding. 'Trust me. Open your legs for me, sweetheart.'

A shudder ran through her and she sighed, lying supine as he stroked away the tension from her body, until she shuddered again, half-rising on her side to press against his body, her legs parting, and he slid his hand between her thighs, finding the silky skin, so hot and damp he couldn't control his own shudder of desire. But he concentrated on the slow torture of teasing her towards ecstasy with his fingers and body and mouth, using every skill he had and every ounce of self-control that remained to focus purely on her. Her body rose against his hand, finding her rhythm, now guiding him, her hands moving to touch him as he touched her, testing his control to its limits.

Almost as devastating as her hands were her little moans as she began to writhe under him, telling him she was so close. He wanted desperately to taste her, drink her in, but he held back. There would be time enough for that, for everything. She was his.

'Hunter, don't stop, please, I need to feel you.' Her voice was sapping his concentration and his resolve and when she pulled him to her he didn't offer much resistance. She moaned as his weight pressed her back onto the bed, her legs spreading for him, rising against his erection and burning through whatever part of his mind was still conscious and in control.

'I don't want to hurt you,' he managed to gasp out as her legs anchored around him, pulling him closer, sliding against his arousal and his fingers.

'I want this,' she whispered, her gaze holding his as she traced her fingertips down his chest. 'Even the pain.'

Her hands ran down his back, sliding over his buttocks as she raised her hips slightly. He groaned at the friction.

'If it hurts too much, stop me. I'll stop, I swear.'

Her hair gleamed gold as she shook her head.

'I want you.'

His last coherent thought as she began following and

matching the motion of his body was that he hoped she would still feel the same when she eventually realised what he was. Then he was only sensation, the rising build of beautiful tension he could feel in her body until her head arched back as she climaxed, calling out his name, and he abandoned scruples and control and sank into her, pushing past the resistance of her maidenhead, a confusion of contrition and joyous possession and physical exultation.

She froze for a moment, her nails digging into his shoulders, but then her body shifted, taking him in, and he heard his voice call her name again and again as he moved, the waves of pleasure crashing over him, reducing him to a single point of joy. Just her name, but inside the vastness of his body as it rose to break into a million shards of pleasure was a deeper cry.

I love you. My Nell. I need you.
Just don't let me fall asleep.

He was crushing her, he realised sleepily, forcing himself to shift his weight and pulling her on top of him as he groped for the blanket. He wasn't in the least cold himself, not with the blood flowing tangibly through his veins and her long body was stretched the length of him and her breath against his neck and her beautiful breasts…

Nell. Here, in his bed. His. If this was a dream, it more than compensated for his years of nightmares.

He opened his eyes in the dark. He didn't want to, but he couldn't afford to go to sleep.

'I'll light a fire.'

She murmured something and reached for him, then

snuggled deeper under the blanket, and he fought the urge to climb back into bed with her and just…

He took his dressing gown and went to bring a candle from the hall, stopping as Biggs climbed the last stair with a neatly folded pile of very feminine clothes in his arms.

'Here are Miss Nell's clothes, my lord. Will you be needing anything else?'

'I…' Oh, what was the harm? 'Yes. Some hot water and linen.'

'Shall I send word to Hidgins you will be needing him to drive Miss Nell to the Red Lion afterwards, sir?'

Hunter grimaced at the unspoken rebuke, but nodded. He didn't want to let her go, but considerations of propriety aside, he couldn't allow her to stay the night. He didn't yet know how he would keep her and still manage to keep her safe from him. There had to be a way, but right now his brain was too contented to think clearly. She was here. She was his. He would deal with reality later.

Back inside the room he crouched down to light the fire and then with a deep breath he went to sit down on the side of the bed, gently stroking her thigh through the sheet, enjoying the very feeling of having her here in his bed. He was glad no woman had ever been in this bed before. This was Nell's place now. When she was in London he would have to find somewhere else to sleep, perhaps fit one of the rooms on the empty floor above. Even if he wasn't sleeping in it, he wanted to know she was in his bed.

The nascent flames struck her eyes with silver and her hair with gold where it spread over his pillows. Then her eyelids fluttered down and in an instant he was submerged in scalding heat again, as if his release had merely been a prelude. He bent towards her, but drew back at the soft scratching on the door, and she disappeared under the blanket with a faint squeak. Hunter suppressed a groan and drew back. He should have sent for cold water instead.

'You can come in, Biggs.'

Biggs entered, his eyes firmly on the broad tray he carried, but his voice was suspiciously shaky.

'Hot water, linen towels and a spare dressing gown. Anything else, sir?'

Once Biggs left, Hunter rose resolutely and took the dressing gown from the pile. Nell sat up, clutching the blanket to her, and he draped the dressing gown gently over her shoulders. It swallowed her up, drooping over her arms, and he remembered how she had looked in his jacket in the Welbeck gardens just a few days ago, a whole existence ago. She looked up and he saw the memory mirrored in her eyes and he kissed her quickly and moved back.

'Later I will have Biggs prepare a bath and join you in it, but for the moment we will make do with this. Are you very sore?'

She shook her head, but her flush was so extreme he could tell she probably wouldn't tell him if she was. He really should leave her, give her some privacy to deal with this herself, but he didn't want to, not yet. The ritual wasn't complete. It would be like leaving a wedding before the vows were spoken.

'Don't worry,' he said gently as he dipped the linen into the water. 'Just relax.'

'You said that before,' she answered, her voice hitching on the end as he moved towards her.

'So I did. I'm consistent. Just open your legs… And don't tell me I said that before as well.'

Her hand shot out and grasped his arm, stopping him. Then she let go.

'You did.'

'I told you; I'm consistent.'

When he was done she looked up suddenly and smiled. He turned away, battling another wave of pain, this time in his chest. He should feel calmer now that she was unequivocally his, but he didn't. In fact, a peculiar fear was taking hold of him and he fell back on the safety of practicality.

'When you are dressed I will see you back to the Red Lion and tomorrow I will go to Doctors' Commons to procure a special licence so we can make an honest woman of you.'

She sat down on the side of the bed, holding her clothes to her chest.

'No, Hunter. I didn't come here to entrap you into marrying me.' She was pale, but her voice was very clear and he felt his nerves stretch further.

'I know that. There is no question of entrapping. We are far beyond that. We have other matters to discuss.'

'Such as?'

Her eyes narrowed into her stubborn look and he hesitated.

'How we are going to proceed. I didn't want you… anyone to know about…my difficulty sleeping. But I can't very well push that under the rug now, can I? I will just have to make sure you aren't…exposed to any risk.'

Her eyes narrowed.

'Putting aside the question of marriage for the moment, how precisely would you propose to do that?'

'Well, you will be at Hunter Hall most of the time and I will arrange for a bedroom in the East Wing which is closer to the servants and where you won't be...disturbed.'

'I see. And here in London?'

'You will probably spend less time here and when you are here I will sleep in a bedroom on the next floor. The house is big enough.'

She crossed her arms.

'No.'

'What, no?' he asked, wary of her expression. That determined look typically boded ill for him.

'I told you, I didn't come here to force you to do something you so obviously find onerous. I came here knowing that I wanted to be part of your life, even as a mistress, and I am willing to pay the price for that choice. But I am not willing to marry you because you think it is the right thing to do. If you ever do wish to marry me...I mean *really* wish to marry me because you want to be with me, I will consider it, but I will not agree to a cold-blooded arrangement based on your arbitrary conditions.'

'Damn it, they aren't arbitrary conditions. They are measures. For your safety.'

'No, they're for *your* safety!'

'Nell, don't you understand how serious this is? I cannot allow myself to fall asleep with you and if you are here...all the time... Damn it, you must see why there has to be some distance between us. I had to fight to stay awake just now! If I start relaxing my guard... I have to protect you...'

He was begging again, but she didn't look in the

least understanding. She looked adamant. She stood and picked up her clothes.

'You loved Tim and you felt responsible for him and frustrated with him and it all mixes up to feeling responsible for his life and his death, and however much I don't think you have any grounds for guilt, I can understand that in a way it is inevitable. But this is different, Hunter. I do not need to be protected from myself or from you and I won't allow you to dictate my life based on considerations of safety. I am willing to risk my heart with you. I am not willing to be put in a box because you are scared of risking yours. Now, I really should return to the Red Lion. When you are willing to talk sensibly, we can discuss this further.'

'You *are* mad! There is nothing to discuss. We have already anticipated the wedding night. Now there is only a very simple "Yes, I will"!'

She shrugged her dress over her chemise.

'No, I won't.'

He turned away and grabbed his own clothes and began dressing, trying to ignore the eager rush of heat that had burst in him at her melodramatic nonsense about risking hearts. He might have revised his own assessment about whether or not love was a fantasy, but he couldn't forget that a week ago this girl had thought herself head over heels in love with another man. Now simply because she had fallen out of love with Welbeck and into sexual excitement with him, she fancied herself in love again. Well, however much he might want it to be true, he wasn't so gullible. Besides, none of that changed the fact that the issue wasn't even in question— of course she was going to marry him.

'You don't have the prerogative of saying no, not after

last night. Has it escaped your notice that you might even now be carrying the next Lord Hunter?'

Her hand rose towards her abdomen and he was shocked by the possessive heat that swept through him at the thought of her holding his child, a little girl with her eyes. A boy. She would be an amazing mother. Oh, God, if only she wasn't trying to destroy him. Because if he hurt her, it would. He wouldn't be able to find his way back from that. Ever. That would be the end.

Her whole body had tightened at the mention of a child, gathering herself to shield that hypothetical being. He looked so tortured and guilty that Nell's resolution faltered. He was offering her so much already; so much more than she had dreamed possible just a few hours ago. She had come here because the thought of not having him in her life, in whatever guise, had been unbearable. But she could see that her actions had pushed him into a corner—he was not really a rake worthy of the name. If she refused to marry him, their association would end—he had only succumbed to temptation on the assumption that they would marry. But if she agreed, on his terms…

She flexed her hands. She didn't know how to fix this, but at the very least she owed him some honesty.

'Perhaps I never should have put you in this position, Gabriel. I should have realised you would find it hard to accept me as a mistress, but I wasn't strong enough to just let you walk away. I know you don't love me as I love you, but that is all the more reason for me to insist not to be put into a neat little drawer and kept separate like everything else in your life. If you do choose to marry me one day, it will have to be on the understanding that I will not respect those boundaries.'

Her voice began to shake and she tried to rally herself.

'If you will only let me be there with you...'

She gave up and reached for the stocking that had wrapped around the bedpost. He hadn't moved and when he spoke his voice was unlike him, cold and derisive.

'I thought I told you it was unwise to confuse sexual pleasure with love. Until a few days ago you thought yourself in love with Welbeck, or have you forgotten?'

She deserved that, but she wouldn't back down.

'You were right that I didn't understand what it meant then.'

'Oh, and now you think you do?' he mocked.

'Yes.'

His mouth closed tightly, but she waited, watching as he grabbed a cravat from the back of a chair and began winding it around his neck.

'Is that all it takes with you? A few days and some fun in bed? At that rate you'll find someone else to fantasise about in a week.'

She was surprised how little his contemptuous comment hurt. It was so unlike him that it rang utterly false and contrarily it fed the determination that had brought her to London. He was mangling his already crumpled cravat and he looked so defiant, so determined to keep her at arm's length, so...young.

'I love you, Gabriel.'

'You should be a stickler for accuracy, schoolmistress—"I lust for you" is the proper term. What the devil is so amusing?'

She couldn't prevent her smile from widening at his outrage.

'I was just remembering that I called you a dandy a week ago. Your poor cravat.'

He dropped his hands from the abused linen.

'Nell…!'

'I love you, Gabriel. If I do agree to marry you, you will have to accept that I intend to share your bed, your nights and your nightmares. I'm not scared of you. You may think keeping apart from people makes you safer, but it doesn't; it just makes you scared.'

'Nell…'

'You should be grateful that my conditions don't include a demand that you love me in return, but I will stand firm on the others.'

He covered his face with his hands.

'But that is the only demand I *can* comply with. What the devil do you think this is all about? I love you. I had no idea this was even possible until I was in the middle of it; it felt like it was killing me to leave you there. Can't you see that is precisely why I can't let you too close? If I ever hurt you…it would destroy me, Nell. I'm not strong enough to survive hurting you.'

She stood up slowly. She wanted to believe him so very badly.

'I am not so easily broken, Gabriel. I am asking you to trust me.'

'You're asking too much.'

She nodded. Perhaps she was asking too much, too soon. For now perhaps his admission was enough. She, of all people, should know how powerful fear was and that rushing her fences wasn't wise.

She went to him and gently pulled down his hands, clasping them in hers. It was amazing how expressive his face could be when he wasn't on guard. She smiled at him. He was so beautiful and he was hers. She was sure of it now. How clever of her to be brave and come to him.

'Very well. For now we will go ahead with the marriage. We can discuss terms later.'

He looked down at her, his mouth tight. His hands rose to clasp her face, tense, pressing.

'You have no intention of conceding an inch, do you?'

'How can I? I love you and you are asking me to let you suffer alone. I could never promise that.'

He dropped his hands.

'You're not really in love with me. Nothing that will survive the reality of what I am and how little I have to offer.'

'Now who is being insulting? I know you think I am weak, but I don't think I am, not when it really matters; I'm much stronger than you think. I will go to Bascombe tomorrow and...'

He pulled her against him, pressing her face into his shoulder, his own voice unsteady above her.

'I don't want you to go.'

She pushed away, reaching up to brush back his tumbled hair.

'I'm just going to Bascombe, not the Antipodes. Or you could try to convince me to stay. I would like that.'

He wavered, his eyes turning into tawny fire, but she could see the fear was there in the way his gaze flicked to the bed behind her.

'If you do fall asleep and make a nuisance of yourself I'll push you out of bed,' she offered, tracing a line from his cheekbone down the groove by his mouth to his jaw. It was going to be very tiresome, making it clear to all those women he wasn't available any longer. It was almost a pity he was so very handsome. 'Perhaps we should put a mattress on the floor so you don't hurt yourself when I shove you off.'

'This isn't amusing, Nell.' She didn't know if he sounded more annoyed or desperate.

'I will never force you to do anything you don't want to do,' she replied, tracing the line of his lower lip now. 'If you can't bear living with me, then you won't. But we both know this is more than a fear of falling asleep with me.'

He dragged her against him again, his mouth pressing into her hair.

'This is torture. I don't know what to do.'

She managed to turn her head enough to kiss the side of his neck. She loved the velvet-smooth skin under his ear, the cooler softness of his earlobe. She loved the way his breathing caught as she tasted him there.

'That's a good sign,' she murmured. 'Until now you've known precisely what to do and you've been completely wrong. If I had been foolish enough to listen to you, I wouldn't have come here. Why don't you try listening to me for a change?'

His arms didn't release their near stranglehold on her, but a reluctant laugh shook through him. 'You don't pull your punches, do you, schoolmistress? What makes you think you know better?'

She put enough distance between them to take his face in her hands again.

'I don't. But the thought of not being with you is worse than any alternative. I would rather brave a thousand terrors than lose you. Can't we try? Even if we fail? I am quite certain you don't *want* to hurt me...'

'I would rather kill myself than hurt you!'

'Well, I would rather pursue a third option instead.

I'm beginning to see that having horses with such melo-dramatic names as Valiant and Courage might not be purely coincidental.'

As she had hoped he laughed, brushing his mouth over her ear, slipping over its curves until she started to quiver under him.

'I think I've had enough insults from you for a life-time, love. How the devil do you always make them sound so reasonable?'

'I'm clever like that,' she murmured, turning her head to give him better access to the sweep of her throat.

'My clever, brave love…' He kissed the hollow be-neath her ear, drawing her skin gently into his mouth, and a shudder ran through her, arcing her body against him, her legs parting invitingly, and he slid his leg be-tween them. 'We'd better lock the door before Biggs comes demanding I deliver Mrs Jones, widow, safely back to the Red Lion for the night.'

'Does that mean I can stay?'

'It means I can't let you go, heaven help us. But one more insult and I'll…'

'You'll what?'

'Once I regain my sanity I'll think of something.'

'I look forward to it. Meanwhile, kiss me, please…'

* * * * *

COMING NEXT MONTH FROM

♦ HARLEQUIN®

ℋISTORICAL

Available November 21, 2017

All available in print and ebook via Reader Service and online

THE RANCHER'S INCONVENIENT BRIDE (Western)
by Carol Arens
William English rescues Agatha Magee from being shot out of a cannon, and the potential scandal means they must get married! Can Agatha make this more than a marriage in name only?

A SECRET CONSEQUENCE FOR THE VISCOUNT (Regency)
The Society of Wicked Gentlemen • by Sophia James
Viscount Bromley returns to London with no memory of his one night with Lady Eleanor and no knowledge of the daughter he fathered. But now, as he regains his lost memories, there's no hiding from the past!

SCANDAL AT THE CHRISTMAS BALL (Regency)
by Marguerite Kaye and Bronwyn Scott
Join *the* Christmas party of the Season in these two closely linked stories of forbidden Regency romance. Will Lord and Lady Brockmore's guests find true love when they embark on a scandalous affair to remember?

BESIEGED AND BETROTHED (Medieval)
by Jenni Fletcher
A marriage bargain is brokered to bring peace between two enemies: warrior Lothar the Frank and Lady Juliana Danville. But is blissful wedded life possible with a dangerous secret hidden within the castle walls?

AN UNLIKELY DEBUTANTE (Regency)
by Laura Martin
To win a wager, Lord Alexander Whitemore is to take Lina Lock from gypsy dancer to perfect debutante. As Lina takes Alex up on his offer, she learns she must curb her rebellious instincts *and* the unexpected passion he awakens in her...

RESCUED BY THE FORBIDDEN RAKE (Regency)
by Mary Brendan
When Faye Shawcross's younger sister goes missing, alluring viscount Ryan Kavanagh comes to her rescue. He will fix her impending family scandal for a price: he wants Faye as his mistress...

If you are receiving 4 books per month and would like to receive all 6, please call Customer Service at 1-800-873-8635.

YOU CAN FIND MORE INFORMATION ON UPCOMING HARLEQUIN® TITLES,
FREE EXCERPTS AND MORE AT WWW.HARLEQUIN.COM.

HHCNM1117

Get 2 Free Books,

Plus 2 Free Gifts—

just for trying the Reader Service!

HARLEQUIN® Western Romance

Get 2 Free Books,
Plus 2 Free Gifts—
just for trying the Reader Service!